He pushed the doo...
fully open before st....... ...
woman stood beside the sofa. She
looked up. She looked at him.

All the breath left his lungs. It was her. It was Olivia.

Even if he hadn't recognized her, he would have known the scent of her. The taste of her. He would have known because he could hear her heart pounding as loudly as his own.

Olivia. Beautiful and strong and bold as he remembered. His Olivia. His wife. Thirty years had passed and he still didn't know if he wanted to kiss her or kick her to the street. She obviously hadn't forgiven him. He could live with that. He hadn't forgiven her either.

"Hello, Liv," he said. "Happy anniversary."

Kathryn Smith

Let the Night Begin

BROTHERHOOD OF THE BLOOD

AVON

An Imprint of HarperCollins*Publishers*

AVON BOOKS
An Imprint of HarperCollins*Publishers*
10 East 53rd Street
New York, New York 10022-5299

Copyright © 2008 by Kathryn Smith
Excerpt from *Before I Wake* copyright © 2008 by Kathryn Smith
ISBN 978-0-06-124503-9
www.avonromance.com

First Avon Books paperback printing: July 2008

Avon Trademark Reg. U.S. Pat. Off. and in Other Countries, Marca Registrada, Hecho en U.S.A.
HarperCollins® is a registered trademark of HarperCollins Publishers.

Printed in the U.S.A.

10 9 8 7 6 5 4 3 2

This book is dedicated to my sister, Lynda, who says I'm one of her favorite authors—despite being her baby sister. And who insisted that she should have a vampire for her own. Love you, Lynnie.

Also, to Jenna Petersen, my cosmic twin, who was kind enough to read this book in its infancy and still be my friend when she was done.

And finally to Steve, who may be mentioned last, but always ranks 1st with me.

Let the Night Begin

Chapter 1

England, 1899

Olivia Gavin was a bit of a curiosity to the people of Clovelly.

She lived in a whitewashed cottage high up the cliff, overlooking the harbor. *Alone.* She had servants of course, and everyone knew that servants didn't count as family, or even friends. For such a comely woman, her face unaffected by the sometimes cruel wind that blew across the water, she had decidedly little male company. In fact, she had little company at all.

She was obviously a woman of some means because she did not have to resort to any kind of labor, although she would sometimes make jewelry and small trinkets, which were sold in Henrietta Jewel's little dress shop. She was very generous with loosening her pocketbook strings whenever funds were being raised, or help was needed. Despite this, she had very few servants— a housekeeper, a maid, and a man of all work.

This struck most of the townsfolk as being far too practical for someone of the upper class, so they assumed that Mrs. Gavin was most likely a wealthy tradesman's widow.

People about town liked her, though they rarely saw her. Rumor was that she kept city hours, staying up most of the night working on her baubles and gewgaws and sleeping away the day. There were those that scoffed at such fancy habits. There were also those who distrusted a woman who hid her face from the bright light of day. To support this theory, they argued that Olivia Gavin never went to church on Sunday morning.

If Vicar Hathaway were within earshot of these busybodies, he informed them straight away that, "Mrs. Gavin is no stranger to God's house." And with that question answered for the time being, the speculation then fell upon *Mr.* Gavin. There were some who thought he didn't exist, and others who thought maybe his lovely wife had put him to rest in an early grave. Some made her the heroine of a gothic novel, the victim of a twisted and abusive marriage that she had fled in the dark of night, and Clovelly was her refuge. Most rejected these theories, and said that gossip was the Devil's fishing net—nothing it dredged up could ever come to any good.

And of course, there were those who wished the private Mrs. Gavin would give them something more to gossip about.

But despite her strange hours and seemingly obsessive desire for privacy, no one in Clovelly had a bad word to say about Olivia Gavin. And on those infrequent occasions when a young man from the village would wake up in someone's stables or in the back room of the Horse and Hare Tavern, pale and claiming to have no idea of how he got there, no one ever suspected that Mrs. Gavin might know the answer. And a good thing that was as well.

Because Olivia tried very hard to conceal the fact that she was a vampire from her fellow townsfolk.

That was one lesson Reign had taught her that she actually appreciated. Never reveal what you are—unless you have to. Of course, he hadn't told her just how difficult it would be to conceal what she was on occasion. To be fair, she supposed she hadn't given him time to teach her much else, and if he had tried she certainly would not have listened.

People tended to notice when a woman only went out at night, or if she was unnaturally strong, Olivia reflected as she tossed a bale of hay that weighed roughly the same as she did into the loft high above her head. It was an effortless task for her, and it saved Charles, her man of all work, from having to do it. Of course, she lied to him and told him she hired a couple of boys from the village to do it.

Charles knew what she was, but that didn't stop him from thinking ladies shouldn't toss hay—vampires or not. "It just ain't right," he argued, and then he would watch with a grimace as Olivia did the work he would have done were he thirty years younger—work he wished he could still do.

Wiping her hands on the thighs of her split skirt, Olivia took the lantern from its hook, patted each of her horses on the muzzle as she passed, and left the barn. It was after midnight and she was hungry.

The lantern lit the path a few feet ahead of her—not that she needed the light to see. Her feet were sure and steady as she made her way along the worn, broken stones, but anyone stumbling upon her would expect her to have a lantern—anyone human would, on a night this dark. And since she was seen as a bit of a mystery by the townsfolk, it wasn't unusual for a small group of boys, made brave by their determination to not be seen as cowards, to try peeking in her windows for a glimpse of something scandalous.

The moon might be absent, but the tar-black of the sky was littered with stars, glinting like diamonds carelessly tossed on black velvet. A warm wind rolled off the turbulent tide, pushing at her clothing and bringing the scent of salt, sea, and fish to her sensitive nostrils. The tide was turning, and unless she was mistaken, it was going to bring a storm back with it. Those boats listing like bored schoolboys would soon each be lifted and tossed about like a rag doll caught between snarling dogs.

Olivia sniffed the air. The scent of rain hung heavy on that increasing wind. It was going to be a beautiful stormy night that she could enjoy from the balcony of her bedroom, and then escape to the warm haven of her bed just as dawn broke the horizon.

Hers was a good life.

She hadn't always felt that way, and sometimes she still cursed the immortality that kept her unchanging—kept her moving from one town to another before people realized she hadn't aged. Mostly, when she felt that way, she cursed the man who had made her this way.

Reign.

She hadn't thought of him in quite some time. The spaces of quiet were growing longer for her now, but every once in a while the memory of him snuck up on her and ravaged her for days. Were it not for him she would look like a woman of sixty now—her true age—perhaps with grandchildren and a plump lap to sit them on. Her face would be lined, and not just with the faint cobwebs that hovered perpetually around her eyes. She might even have gray hair. And a sweet husband with gray hair as well—a husband who thought she was beautiful no matter what her age.

Instead she was a woman of sixty who, despite all that she had seen and experienced, still looked like a woman of thirty, and she always would. There would be no fat lap, no bouncing grandchildren. Perhaps if she had stayed, she might have had a husband to tell her she was beautiful, but he would not be sweet. Never sweet.

"There's a messenger here for you, ma'am," Agnes, her housekeeper, informed her from the door of the cottage when Olivia reached the house. She'd been so preoccupied with her own thoughts she hadn't heard the door open. But if she couldn't let down her guard on her own property, where could she?

A messenger? For her? How positively antiquated. So many people used the telephone these days—or the older telegraph system. But to send a messenger? Well, that notion was older than she was. Antique that she was, even she had a telephone at her cottage, just in case her nephew James needed to get in touch with her while he caroused in London with his mates.

On the cottage's front step Olivia removed the boots she wore to do her chores and slid her feet into her slippers. As she crossed the threshold into her snug little home, it occurred to her that it was a very strange time for a messenger to come banging on the door. It was the equivalent of midday for her, but for most humans it was the middle of the night. A messenger by those standards usually meant bad news.

Or the message was from someone who knew she would be up.

She pushed that suspicion away as she passed quickly through the warm, lemon-and-beeswax-scented foyer into the little parlor on the right. She hadn't always had a suspicious nature, but her husband had changed all that. The thought of him brought a frown to her brow. There was something niggling in the back of her mind. Something she should remember but couldn't quite wrap her head around.

She was still frowning when she entered the parlor, and the young man sitting on the little peach sofa looked at her with some concern as he rose to his feet.

"Mrs. Gavin?" he asked, fiddling with the battered leather hat he held in his hands.

Why had she never changed her name? To be sure it was convenient to be thought a widow, but for thirty years she'd been reminded of her husband—her second one; she scarcely thought, when formally addressed, of the first anymore.

"Yes. And you are?"

"Hillyard, ma'am." He held out an envelope to her. "My commission is to see this delivered into your hands."

Brow knitting, Olivia took it. She didn't recognize the seal on the back—a simple chalice in bright red wax.

"Now that I've done my duty, I'll be off."

She lifted her head—quicker than she ought, for she startled the young man with the movement. "You're not to wait for a reply?"

He watched her carefully, like a cat watches a dog, ready to bolt at the first sign of trouble. "No, ma'am. I was told to deliver the letter and that was it."

Curious. "Then I won't keep you." She gave him what she hoped was a serene smile. "See the housekeeper, she'll give you a little something for your trouble." Whoever had sent the missive had no doubt already paid—that was the way things were done these days, but Olivia was from an era when post was paid for by the receiver, and some habits were harder to break than others.

Plus, it was good form to offer a gratuity. The messenger would be less likely to remember that she had spooked him if she gave him a generous bonus.

"Thank you, Mrs. Gavin." He gave her a short bow, then placed the worn hat upon his russet curls and took his leave. Olivia waited until she heard him speaking to Agnes before popping the seal on the envelope. The note inside had been written on a typewriting machine.

To one Olivia Winscott Gavin:

Olivia frowned. How could they know her maiden name? Only a handful of people knew her maiden name, and none would refer to her as such so formally.

It is not without some regret that I inform you that your nephew, Mr. James Burnley has been taken into my custody. The reasons for his abduction—

Abduction! Olivia's heart clenched tight in her chest. Why would anyone abduct James? The answer seemed fairly obvious. Because she was James's guardian, and whoever had him knew that she would move heaven and earth to see him safe. Perhaps given the status of some of James's friends, they might think him from a wealthier family than he was. Any money he had came from a trust set up by his grandfather, not from Olivia.

They might even know what she was, as difficult as that was to entertain.

—may seem obvious to you, but I urge you not to jump to any hasty conclusions. There are two people who can see that James is safely returned to you, Mrs. Gavin. One of those people is you. I know it could not have been easy for you, playing mother to the boy given your . . . proclivities— Oh God, they did know what she was—*but you have raised him well. Now it is time for you to do one last thing for him. All I ask is that you bring your husband—the second person to whom young James will owe his freedom—to Scotland and deliver him into my keeping. I will leave instructions for you at the Wolf, Ram and Hart Inn in Edinburgh one week from the day you receive this letter. Do this and James will go free.*

Fail to acquiesce and the next time you see your nephew will. be to bury him. Do not disappoint me, Olivia.

It was unsigned. The coward hadn't the courage to give her his name so she would know whom to kill. Instead, she was at his mercy.

Or perhaps not.

She didn't bother with shoes or a wrap. Her only thought was James—the young man who was more her son than nephew. She hadn't been able to save James's mother, her sister Rosemary, but she'd be damned if she let anyone take James from her.

And she'd be damned if she'd go within ten miles of her husband.

The door banged against the side of the house as she threw it open. Two running strides were all she took before vaulting herself into the night sky. There was only one road leading to and away from her home and she could see a good distance in either direction from above the trees.

The messenger was heading east, as she expected. That was the road that led toward London, where James had been when last they spoke. Now he was in Scotland? Held against his will, and for what? Why would they want her husband in exchange? If they knew what she was, they had to know what he was—and he was infinitely more dangerous than she. Who in their right minds would tangle with that kind of power? Only someone stupid or more powerful.

Sweet God, the idea of James being held by such people . . .

From high above, Olivia flew over the messenger, her acute vision trained on him as the moonlight lit his path. She passed him and then swooped downward, the wind rushing through her hair, pulling it from its pins as she rushed toward the ground. Pivoting her body, she landed on her feet in the middle of the smoothly packed road, the ground cool beneath her stocking feet. She stood there, shoulders back and heaving with barely restrained rage, the crumpled letter in her fist, waiting for the messenger to appear.

She saw him before he saw her. His mount saw her before he did as well, and the gelding sensed her aggression. Glossy chestnut forelegs glinted as they pawed the air. A high-pitched whinny cut through the stillness of the night. The messenger struggled to maintain his seat.

And Olivia approached.

Reaching up, she caught the bridle in her fingers, guiding the horse's front half downward. She gave the beast a gentle pat, letting it know that she meant it no harm.

The messenger stared at her, the whites of his eyes full and bright. "Mrs. Gavin."

Olivia's other hand seized the boy by his belt. One yank had him on his arse on the ground, gaping at her with a mixture of confusion and horror. His horse sidestepped, and Olivia let it go.

"Who sent you?" she demanded, holding up the fist that held the ransom note. "Give me a name."

The messenger shook his head. "I don't know, ma'am. I was given your name and direction by my employer. I don't know who sent it."

She grabbed him by the front of the coat, lifting him up until he hovered above her like an overgrown child, his feet dangling around her shins. He looked around, understandably amazed that anyone, let alone a woman, could hold him off the ground with one hand.

"What of your employer?" she demanded. "Would he know? Or is he as useless as you?"

"T . . . the letter was dropped off at the office with payment and instructions attached. The boy who brought it said he had been hired by a gentleman."

Damn. Whoever they were, they knew enough to be careful. They knew enough about her to be even more cautious. She gave her captive a little shake. "If you're lying—"

"Don't hurt me," he squeaked, covering his head with his arms.

The sight of him cowering from her permeated Olivia's furor. He wasn't lying, the poor child. God help her, she was on the cusp of doing something stupid. It had been a long time since her instincts lorded over her logic, driving her to act like a predator rather than a human. She would not allow those instincts to win now.

Slowly, and with great control, she lowered the boy to the ground. He wasn't so afraid that he had lost control of his bladder, but he was trembling all the same. She made certain his legs would support him before she released him.

"Forgive me," she murmured as she turned to walk away. She didn't look back, but after a few moments—a few strides—she heard him mount his horse and gallop away as though the hounds of hell were after him.

Once she was certain he was gone, Olivia leaped into the sky once more. Her guilt for terrorizing a poor boy overshadowed her own fear. She didn't have much time. There were but a few hours left before dawn and there was still so much she had to do.

She had to pack. She had to prepare. She would leave for London as soon as possible. The kidnapper's time constraints would not give her time to get to the city and search for the boy who originally delivered the note to the agency. For all she knew, James was on his way to Scotland—if not already there—as she soared toward her home.

No, there was no time to waste. No matter how much she despised having to ask for his help, she was going to London to strike a deal with the devil himself. Her husband. That gorgeous black-haired, blue-eyed bastard who had made her a vampire. The man she had no qualms about handing over as ransom.

Reign.

* * *

"Are you in need of diversion, sir?"

Reign blinked. What? Out of the corner of his eye he saw the woman standing beside him and he turned to face her. Where the devil had he been that he hadn't sensed her approach? Even in a house full of people he should have smelled her, heard her when she got so close. He simply hadn't sensed a threat—and a social maven such as his hostess was always a threat to a man seen as fair game on the Marriage Mart. Never mind that he had made his opinions on marriage clear. All these years of civilized behavior had dulled his edge.

"Diversion?" he repeated, flattering his hostess with a flirtatious smile. "My dear Mrs. Willet, whatever do you have in mind?"

Mrs. Willet smiled, her youthful face lighting up. She was a lovely woman in her forties with graying blond hair and pale blue eyes. Her full figure was draped in a gold evening gown encrusted with beads and crystals that sparkled under the chandeliers. Even still the gown could not match the brightness of her eyes, or the glowing goodness in her countenance. "Saucy. That's what you are, Mr. Gavin."

"I prefer incorrigible, my dear."

She tilted her head. There were crystals in her hair as well. "One of the things I like about you, sir is your ability to make me feel younger than you, even though I know full well I must be at least ten years your senior."

More like fifteen if one went by physical age, as Reign had been almost thirty years when he became immortal. However, that had been more than six hundred years ago, so he was more Mrs. Willet's senior than she could possibly imagine.

He pulled his brow in a mock frown. "But that would make me a mere lad of seventeen, would it not?"

She tapped him on the arm with her closed fan as she chuckled. "Incorrigible indeed. Will you dance this evening, good sir?"

"Trying to toss me to the virgins are you?"

She laughed—a bold and raucous sound that brought a smile to Reign's lips. "It is not the Season, Mr. Gavin. You are in safe company tonight."

No, the Season was over, thank God. Company was thin, but a number of families kept permanent residence in London, especially those who were not of the peerage. Reign could have had a title, centuries ago, but people paid far too much attention to heirs and titles. That kind of scrutiny was something he didn't desire any more than he desired the numerous virginal misses tossed in his direction every time he resided in London for those few months. He may not have a title, but he had a fortune that was just as envied. Occasionally an elderly matron would tell him she had fancied—or been afraid of—a man who looked rather like him decades earlier. His grandfather perhaps? And Reign always had to be careful not to say anything that might give himself away. It was deuced difficult, and sometimes downright painful, especially when it was someone he had known and thought well of in that "other" lifetime.

It had only been thirty years since the last time he was "out" in society. His would be a dangerous game if anyone recognized him, but he had moved in different circles then, in a different part of the country. It was unlikely that he would meet anyone from Hertford in London during this time of year.

"Are you quite all right, Mr. Gavin? You look very strange."

Jerking back to the present, Reign smiled apologetically at his hostess. "My apologies, Mrs. Willet. A memory struck me. Nothing more." The memory of Hertford and how he had been the happiest of his long life there.

"I hope it's nothing too dreadful?" Of course she wouldn't expect him to admit if it was something dreadful, but her concern was genuine all the same.

"Nothing at all."

And nothing was the sum of his life. Nothing in the years that followed had come close to touching that happiness. Or the emptiness. Yes, he needed a diversion. This time of year he needed to be diverted in the worst way.

He offered the lady his arm. "Shall we dance, madam?"

She smiled prettily, placing her hand on his sleeve. "I thought you would never ask."

As they danced, whirling and prancing in a figure that hadn't changed in a hundred years, Reign let his mind wander, speaking only when spoken to. He shouldn't be in society tonight. He was too distracted. Too out of sorts. He should have gone to Maison Rouge and visited with Madeline and the girls. He could have drunk, maybe fed and gotten a little slap and tickle. There was that strong, buxom brunette he'd had his eye on the other night.

But then Madeline had told him that Chapel had been by and Reign forgot about the girl. Chapel had been to the brothel? The same Chapel who had spent the last five centuries playing whipping boy to the Church? What the hell? And why hadn't the bastard come to see him? They might no longer be the friends they once were, but they were still brothers, united by the cursed blood that took them from simple soldiers to immortal beings.

But if Madeline's account of that night was true—and he had no reason to think otherwise, even though he could tell she left out many of the sordid details—Chapel had glutted himself at Maison Rouge. No one had been hurt, but every girl in the house, with the exception of Maddie's daughter, Ivy, had given her blood to Chapel. Not sex. Just blood.

That meant that his old friend had a woman. It was about damn time.

As the music ended, Reign escorted Mrs. Willet off the floor. "Thank you for gracing me with your favor, ma'am."

Snapping open her delicate silk fan, the woman cooled herself with lazy strokes. "You are so courtly, Mr. Gavin. I find it so refreshing. Most young men these days don't give a thought to manners."

Reign smiled in response. Young men hadn't been so keen on manners in his youth either, but it seemed to him that ever since Walter Scott published *Ivanhoe,* society in large had taken to romanticizing knights, bloody fights, and big swords. The human race was too enthralled by the past. Even he couldn't seem to focus on the present, much less look to the future.

The butler approached. "Beg your pardon, Mr. Gavin? I'm sorry to disturb you, sir, but there is a lady asking for you at the door."

"For me?" His first thought was that something had happened to Madeline or Maison Rouge. "Did she give her name?"

The man's stoic countenance never wavered. "Mrs. Gavin, sir. She says she is your wife."

Reign's heart—damn it—flipped in his chest. "My wife?" Could it really be Olivia?

Mrs. Willet looked positively indignant. "What nerve! Send her away, Postman."

"No." Both the butler and hostess looked alarmed by the force of his tone. "I would very much like to speak to her." He turned to Mrs. Willet. "That is, if you do not mind granting me use of a parlor, ma'am?"

"Of course not," she replied with a frown. "If you are certain you wish to address this person?"

"I am." He couldn't be any more certain.

"Then show her to the peach parlor, Postman."

The butler bowed and took his leave. Reign prepared to do the same.

"This is not quite the diversion I had in mind," Mrs. Willet informed him with a wry smile.

"Is it not?" Reign grinned crookedly. "It is exactly how I hoped to end the evening."

His hostess bade him farewell and left to attend to her other guests. Reign straightened to his full height of six feet and forced himself to leave the ballroom at a leisurely pace. If Mrs. Willet was as discreet as he believed then no one would be watching him, but if she had a tongue for gossip . . . well, he wasn't about to add any more fuel to that fire than necessary.

His heart pounding, his muscles coiled tight like an overwound clock, Reign walked down the corridor, mindless of the paintings and the pretty wallpaper. His gaze was fixed on the door at the end, the one Postman just exited.

He didn't pause to check his appearance or draw a deep breath. If it was Olivia, she would know what he had done and she would congratulate herself for it. As it was she who would no doubt hear the clamorous beating of his heart.

The last time he saw her she had looked at him with a wounded gaze—a gaze that accused him of things he didn't want to entertain even three decades after the fact. He had made himself a monster in her eyes. Was he still? When he thought of that night—their wedding night—it was with a mixture of regret, guilt, and anger. Mostly regret.

He pushed the door, letting it swing fully open before stepping inside. A woman of good height and strong build stood beside the sofa. She looked up. She looked at him.

All the breath left his lungs. It was she. It was Olivia, the woman he had loved like no other before her. There had been no one since that could make him feel so vulnerable—so oddly human.

He liked that feeling.

Even if he hadn't recognized her richly hued hair—strands of faun and gold and sable, even if he hadn't remembered those big almond-shaped brandy-colored eyes, sharp nose or wide lips, he would have known the scent of her. The taste of her on the air. He would have known her because he could hear her heart pounding as loudly as his own.

Olivia. Beautiful and strong and bold as he remembered. His Olivia. His wife. And she was staring at him with a resentment he found relieving. It was so much kinder than the hatred he had last seen on her face when she discovered what he had done. Thirty years had passed and he still didn't know if he wanted to kiss her or kick her arse to the street. She obviously hadn't forgiven him. He could live with that. He hadn't forgiven her either.

But she had balls, to show up on this, of all nights, knowing what it was.

"Hello, Liv," he said, taking as much control of the situation as he could. "Happy anniversary."

Chapter 2

Olivia couldn't speak. Damn him for looking marvelous. Damn herself for wanting to throw herself on him and kiss him until dawn. She shouldn't be so happy to see him and want to kill him at the same time.

And damn him for remembering that it was their wedding anniversary—that was the little something that had been niggling at the back of her mind before leaving for London. She had almost made herself forget the significance of this date. And then it came rushing back when she woke just after sunset, along with a host of other memories she wished she could just throw away. She remembered how his fingers had trembled when he slid the wedding ring onto hers. She remembered believing that he loved her. Worse, she remembered loving him.

She had dressed and primped and hired a hack to take her to Reign's house in Belgrave Square only to find out he was out for the evening. He'd always been a bit of a social animal, telling her once that spending time with humans helped him remember his own humanity.

It also made feeding easy, Olivia told herself snidely.

Fortunately for her, Reign's valet had stumbled upon her as the butler attempted to shut the door in her face, and recognized her. Clarke had been but a boy of James's age the last time Olivia saw him, now he was a man of fifty. He didn't trust her, but he knew it had to be important for her to come looking for Reign and told her where he was. She could have waited at the house for Reign to return, but she hadn't the patience or the inclination. And she hadn't been welcome. She wanted this over with, before she lost her resolve.

It wasn't right, exchanging Reign for James, but she would do it. Obviously she wouldn't be able to confide in Reign. He had proven himself untrustworthy in the worst way in the past, and there was no guarantee he would go along with the kidnappers for the sake of a boy he didn't know.

No, it was better to let him think she was in his debt. Better for him to think he was the one in control. She refused to wonder what the villains had planned for him other than to tell herself he was neigh on indestructible. Probably he had betrayed them in some way in the past as well. These thoughts stoked her anger. James would be safe if not for Reign. All she had to do was remember that. James would be safe again once Reign was delivered as ransom.

She hated coming to him. Hated putting on a fine gown and rouge. Hated putting her hair up so elaborately. The only thing she liked about the ensemble was her earrings, and she had made those herself. Those hadn't been chosen with this evening in mind. With Reign in mind. She had even worn plum, a color he always liked her in. The fine fabric felt sticky in the summer heat.

They stood watching each other, as all opponents did, taking the other's full measure. He looked older. That was impossible, of course, but true all the same. His eyes, once so bright and crystalline looked faded and gray. His mouth, thin but well shaped seemed less generous, more unforgiving. He had changed his hair according to fashion. It was longer than she remembered, the thick inky locks curling ever so slightly over his forehead. It was a good style for him, softening the lines of his blunt cheekbones, strong jaw, and a nose that had to have been broken more than once, and hundreds of years earlier.

Emotion changed his face so easily. She remembered how devastatingly handsome he could be when he smiled, how heartbreaking he looked when grieved. Oh, and frightening. He could look so frightening when he wanted.

Obviously he wanted to tonight, because he stared at her with a mixture of desire and antagonism that both scared and thrilled her, but mostly it fueled her own anger. How dare he look at her as though she was the one who ruined their marriage. He had betrayed her. All she had done was leave.

It was that conviction in the rightness of her actions that allowed her to finally find her voice. How long had they been standing there in terse silence? "Hello, Reign."

He didn't move, didn't even blink. "What are you doing here?" The low rumble of his voice still sent a shiver down her spine. She remembered it, lying on the sofa with her head on his thigh as he read to her from a book, or the newspaper.

He never sounded so cold back then. That he did now only eased what little guilt she felt at deceiving him. She felt many things at that moment—anger, a little fear. But not remorse. Not after what he had done to her.

"I need your help."

A bark of derisive laughter burst from his throat. The look he shot her was incredulous at best. "After thirty years of nothing, you come *expecting* me to help you?"

She didn't expect anything, not when it came to him. "It's not as though you made any effort to see me during those years either." Why did saying that out loud make her feel queasy? It wasn't as though she wanted him to come looking for her.

"You tried to kill me," he reminded her bluntly. "I had no desire to repeat the experience."

Like a wound, the old hurt opened—raw and festering. "How convenient that your memory has made it all my fault." She wouldn't be here now—James wouldn't be in trouble—if not for Reign.

If she hadn't left him.

"You ran."

"You betrayed me." Her voice shook in that maddening way that sounded more like tears than rage.

"You promised me forever." The low pitch of his voice never changed. They were having a conversation, nothing more. Yet there was a hardness to his gaze. "I thought you knew what that meant."

She might have gasped at that barb, so deep it stung, were it not for the indignation that flooded her veins. "You never asked." It had happened so long ago and the bitterness still choked her. "You never asked, and I wasn't prepared."

Some of the harshness drained from his features. "Liv . . ."

"You took all my choices away." Why did she have to cry when she was angry? That was his fault too, somehow. "You son of a bitch."

If Reign saw the blow coming he didn't try to block it. The impact would break the jaw of a mortal man, perhaps even shatter his skull. Reign didn't even stagger backward. His head snapped back as the sound of their flesh connecting echoed throughout the room. Olivia's knuckles tingled from the impact, as did the length of her arm.

There was blood in the corner of his mouth as he faced her once more. His eyes glittered like perfectly cut diamonds as he licked the crimson away. "One," he warned her, low and cold. "You get one of those. Next time, I hit back."

Why did the promise of violence excite her? How much satisfaction could she possibly glean from pounding on him with her fists? She had learned to fight over the years, obviously—and much she had learned on her own—but there was no doubt that she was no match for a six-century-old vampire. Still, drawing blood gave her some pleasure.

Maybe violence would finally end whatever lingered between them. Maybe, if he didn't kill her, she would be able to go on with her life and never think of him again.

It was stupid of her, but she went for him again, even though she knew the punch would never meet its mark. This time he was ready and he grabbed her, pulling her against him, holding her arms tight at her sides.

Good God he was aroused. She could feel the hard ridge of him through her skirts, though not as bluntly as if there were fewer layers. She was ready as well, damn it. She could climb him right now, take him inside her even as she fought to rip him apart. Physical attraction had never been a weakness of their relationship, though it might certainly prove to be one now. She had bedded him long before discovering what he was. Bedded him the night she met him.

She'd been a widow just out of her weeds at her first party since her husband's demise. Her first husband, Allan, had died of a fever. Theirs had been a marriage of economics rather than emotion and Olivia wasn't ashamed of not missing her husband as a more devoted wife might. She had never thought of herself as the type to be swept away by passion, but then someone introduced her to Reign Gavin, the most magnificent man she had ever laid eyes on. They flirted and talked and drank. They laughed and danced. Reign had murmured low against her ear, likening her to a plum, dark and sweet with juices, begging to be plucked. God, how he had plucked her.

The thought almost made her smile, brought a slow heat churning between her thighs. Reign's nostrils flared as his eyelashes shuddered, but didn't close. Olivia could smell her own desire and knew he could as well. As easy as it would be to kill him right now, it would be just as easy to forget the last thirty years and try again.

Lifting up on her toes, she brought her face closer to his. Her mouth closer to his.

And licked a drop of blood from the edge of his lips.

His blood. Blood that ruined everything, but was so sweet and salty on her tongue. Blood that ran in her veins and called to her even now, even though she'd rather slit her own throat than admit it out loud.

After all this time, he could still make her want it. Make her want him.

Reign shivered against her. It was a slight movement, but enough to let her know the effect she had on him. "Witch," he murmured. And then his mouth was on hers and he was kissing her, tasting her, driving her back, her slippers grasping for purchase on the carpet until she hit a piece of furniture—a table or a desk. The poor thing groaned under the force of their passion, its legs inching across the floor as Reign's tongue rubbed against hers.

The sound of splintering wood froze them both. Reign lifted his head. His lips were flushed, his eyes bright. This was the Reign she remembered— at least a shadow of him. The man who seemed to find her as intoxicating and irresistible as she had found him. "I could bend you over this desk right now and fuck you."

Bend her over so he didn't have to look at her. Olivia met his gaze and smiled coolly. So much for the man she remembered. "You can fuck me if you want, but you'll have to look me in the eye while you do it. I want you to see what you've made."

Perhaps it was the bitterness in her tone, hearing his own crudeness echoed back at him, or perhaps he merely came to his own senses, but Reign released her then and stepped back. Her arms felt bruised and her body chilled, but Olivia refused to let it show. As she pushed away from the desk, it wobbled a little. Hopefully their host wouldn't realize they had broken it.

"I didn't think you'd agree," she taunted. It shouldn't hurt. She shouldn't be surprised. And damn it, she should *not* be disappointed.

"You didn't come here for my help. You don't want *my* help." He wasn't the least bit affected by her words as he eyed her with a mixture of amusement and suspicion. Damn him. Any desire he had felt seemed to have evaporated into the night, while her thighs were still trembling. "What's going on, Liv?"

An image of James's boyish face flashed in her mind and she knew she had to be careful. The kidnappers wanted Reign, and she would never convince him to trust her, or offer his help if she didn't keep her nephew at the forefront of her thoughts. And he would never willingly offer himself in exchange if she told him the truth. James was nothing to him. She was nothing to him. No, it was better to appeal to him and let him think he had power over her. And it was better for her if she didn't think about the fact that he truly did have power over her. If he refused James could be seriously hurt. Or worse.

"I think they know what I am." That much of the truth she could give him. The rest would have to follow.

Her admission startled him and he seemingly made no effort to hide it. He glanced toward the door, as though he suspected someone might be listening. "This is not the place to discuss this."

She was almost amused. He would fuck her in a stranger's home, but not talk to her candidly? How delightfully male. How very him. But then, he always had been a master at getting his own way. And she usually gave it to him. Let him think this time was no different. "Where then? When?"

"Belgrave Square," he replied. He was going to make her return to the house that should have been hers. She had been so excited about picking out new draperies and furniture. So excited about her new life with the man she loved so much. "Go, and I'll make excuses to the lady of the house."

A mocking smile twisted her lips. "Yes, wouldn't want to have to introduce me, would you?"

He didn't flinch. Didn't even blink. In fact, he looked bored, both with her and their situation. "You are more than welcome to accompany me if you wish to waste time with introductions and explanations as to why the wife no one knew I had has suddenly appeared."

"You are right," she conceded, hating him all the more for it. "I will wait for you at your home." She couldn't bring herself to call it theirs, even though by rights it was.

Of course he never spoke of her. Why would he? But if she'd harbored any hopes that he still might feel some tenderness for her, some emotion other than lust, she now had her answer.

It would make betraying him all the easier.

He couldn't trust her. That went without saying. And that was the only thing Reign knew for certain as his carriage pulled up in front of his home in Belgrave Square. He lived on the eastern side of the highly fashionable property, having taken a lease fifty-two years earlier. As with all of his property, the lease had already passed on to his "heir" once and would again in a reasonable amount of time.

That was the one hardship of being immortal, he reflected as he climbed the shallow steps of the freshly whitewashed town house. He could never settle in one place for an indefinite amount of time. He always had to move on. He didn't mind the travel so much, and wouldn't mind relocating at all if he had someone to share it with.

The only person he had ever found that he could entertain spending eternity with had shoved a dagger into his chest thirty years ago. She might be in London to finish the job for all he knew. Maybe he deserved it, but he had no regrets save that he had handled it poorly. Olivia had left and he had let her, foolishly thinking that she would be back once her temper settled.

If the facer she'd given him earlier was any indication, her temper had yet to settle at all.

Which begged the question, just what the hell was she doing in London? And claiming to need his help? He had never met a woman more capable than Olivia. She didn't need his help.

But she wanted him, he thought with a smile as he gave his butler his outerwear. Just as much as he wanted her. He hadn't ruined that, and it was something he could use to his advantage. Because unlike his absent wife, he had meant his promises. As far as he was concerned, Olivia was his until one of them ceased to exist, and even then he wasn't certain he'd be prepared to give her up.

Clarke came toward him as Reign walked down the hall. Olivia was there. He could smell the amber scent of her perfume on the air. It would linger for days, damn it. Just like the memory of the fire in her eyes when she told him he could fuck her if he wanted to, but only face-to-face.

He had been so tempted to do just that. And not with anger or with violence, but with regret and thirty years of bitterness and longing. For the first decade he'd been so certain that he had been the victim of their wedding night, but then uncertainty set in, and with it came guilt. He would not feel guilty now.

"Where is she?" he asked before the other man could speak.

"Drawing room," Clarke replied, running a hand over his graying brown hair. "Reign, what's going on?"

Since Olivia could hear them if she so chose—
and Reign had no doubts that she would eavesdrop
if she thought she might learn something to her
advantage—he merely smiled and said, "I have no
idea." But he handed his friend a note he had scrib-
bled in the carriage on the drive home.

Frowning, Clarke opened the missive. Thankfully he'd been Reign's employee long enough to
know not to read aloud. *Find out what you can
about her.*

Clarke looked up, his dark gaze locking with
Reign's. He looked grim, almost sympathetic, and
Reign shook his head in response. He didn't want
sympathy. He had no illusions where Olivia was
concerned. He had wanted her back for thirty
years and he wanted her still, in his bed and by
his side, but he wasn't going to let that cloud his
judgment.

Women did not forgive without a gesture of
atonement. Since he hadn't made one—hadn't the
chance to—then it stood to reason that Olivia had
yet to forgive him. And he'd be damned if he'd
make any offer to her now when she might take
the opportunity to slit his throat.

So, if she felt so strongly still, why come asking
for the aid of a man she despised? Either she was
in deep trouble, or she was looking to exact a little
revenge. Perhaps both.

If he wished to get any closer to the truth before
the sun rose in a few hours and burnt him to a

crisp as he stood, a baffled idiot, in his front hall, he should attend to his wife.

He straightened his cuffs and cravat before entering the drawing room. Olivia was at one of the windows, the dark green curtains drawn wide to allow the golden rays of streetlights outside to kiss her raised face. Her eyes were closed, the dark curve of her lashes resting against the soft, honey-hued flesh of her cheek. He loved that every inch of her was shades of gold and bronze with subtle hints of pink. Loved her thick hair, even though she wore it up in a tight bun. Loved her nearly aquiline nose and the faint lines that fanned outward from her eyes. Loved how the tight bodice of her rich plum gown accentuated her waist and round breasts.

He loved her. Or at least, he had once upon a time.

"Praying?" he inquired with more hauteur than intended.

Her shoulders stiffened. Slowly, her eyes opened and she turned to face him. Gone was the mature, irresistible woman he had fallen in love with and married, replaced by the hardened creature she had become. That he might have contributed to the change shamed him.

"You never did approve of me praying," she remarked in her low, rich voice. At least that remained as he remembered.

"He's not listening, so why waste your time?"

"He listens," she replied with the blind certainty of one with more faith than sense. "He listens and he answers—if you let yourself hear it."

Reign snorted. Horseshit. If that were true, Olivia would have returned to him years ago. She never would have left.

But she was here now. He wasn't naive enough to think his prayers had been answered. If anything, she'd been sent to him as punishment for his sins.

It was awkward, both of them standing so stiffly, so he went to the glossy mahogany cabinet to his left and withdrew a snifter. "Drink?"

"Please."

He liked that about her. Olivia liked to imbibe now and again even before she turned vampire and discovered she could drink more than the average human before feeling the effects. They met at a party. She had a glass of whiskey in her hand— her third if he remembered correctly. God, they'd had fun that night. They talked and laughed until three, and then she invited him to go home with her. He could have been a gentleman and refused, but he knew it must have taken courage for her to ask, and he knew how long she had been alone. He had been flattered that out of all the men attending the party she had picked him, and so he went to her house and to her bed, and he ended up spending most of his time in Hertford glued to her side. During the day they played by the rules—she had a reputation to consider—but at night . . . At night she made him feel more alive than if he was truly mortal.

He poured two snifters and carried them to the small japanned table between two comfortable dark green wingbacks. She watched him, hesitating for but a moment before joining him as he sat.

"You need to tell me why you are here, Liv. You said 'they' know who you are. Who are 'they'?"

"I don't know." She sighed, but didn't make him wait any longer. As he remembered, she'd always get straight to the point. "Two nights ago a messenger came to my door with an unsigned letter telling me that my nephew James had been kidnapped."

There was no denying the anger and fear in her voice and manner. "James?" He didn't remember any child by that name.

"Rosemary's boy." She spoke absently, expecting him to know of whom she spoke—that is, assuming her own family was important enough for him to remember.

Reign nodded. He did indeed remember Olivia's younger sister, Rosemary. She had stood with Olivia at their wedding. It had been to her Olivia had run when she left. Rosemary had been killed eighteen years ago in a carriage accident. He had sent flowers to the funeral. He hadn't known she had a son or he would have set up a trust for the boy. How come he never heard of Olivia raising him? He had people check on her periodically over the years and none had ever mentioned the boy.

"You and he are close?"

"I raised him." She smiled a little as she met his gaze, almost as though she expected him to express disbelief. But then her smile faded, replaced by naked anguish. "She died because of me, you know. If I had been able to travel during the day . . ."

"You cannot blame yourself."

"Who else is there to shoulder the responsibility?" She gestured toward him with her drink, bleak honesty in her eyes. "I blamed you for the longest time."

That hardly came as a surprise, nor was it a burden he couldn't bear if it meant giving her peace of mind over something she could not have controlled. "Then blame me again, but you cannot hold yourself responsible for the circumstances surrounding your sister's death."

Olivia shrugged, obviously unimpressed with words or the generosity they attempted to express. "It hardly matters now. Rosemary is gone, and so may James be if I do not adhere to his abductor's demands."

Ah yes, this was what he had been waiting for. "Which are?"

"I'm to go to Edinburgh within the week to await further instructions."

"Edinburgh? They took him to Edinburgh?"

She glanced away, seemingly embarrassed, for what reason he couldn't fathom. "I didn't know it, but James had apparently gone to Scotland with friends."

Ah. James was as headstrong as his aunt it seemed. Still, the youngster should have enough respect to let her know when he left the country. "Have you talked to the families of the friends?"

"Yes. Apparently it had been planned by the boys and the father of one of them for some time." The flush in her cheeks darkened. "Obviously James forgot that he hadn't told me."

Obviously James was a spoiled, inconsiderate brat, but since Olivia was obviously hurt by her nephew's neglect he wouldn't comment any further. Instead he moved to more important matters. "Why do you believe they know what you are?"

"They made reference to my 'proclivities.'"

Reign almost laughed. "Proclivities? That could be anything from unnatural sexual urges to an unusual liking for ice cream."

Olivia gave him "the look." The one all wives give their husbands when said husband makes a joke that no one but him could possibly find amusing—at least in the wife's estimation. "They said they understood how difficult it must have been for me to be a mother to James, given my proclivities.

Really, Reign, what else could they have meant? I lead a perfectly normal life—or as normal as I can given the circumstances."

She was right, of course, but it disturbed him to no end that someone might have determined her vampire nature so easily. He could berate her for not being more careful, or he could suspect James of having offered up the information—either freely or under duress. He chose the latter. "Did the note state what they want?"

She looked away. And that's when he knew there was more to the story than she was telling. "No. Only that I'm to go to Scotland to await further instructions, but I don't think they're going to just hand James over. I think they're going to want something from me."

Of course they would. That was what kidnapping was all about—having the upper hand and forcing someone to give you what you wanted. "What part do I play in this?"

"I can't find James and free him by myself. They'll expect me to try something."

"But they won't expect me?" How gullible did she think he was?

"I haven't been with you since before James was born. How could they? I need your help. Whoever took James must have seemed like a friend, someone of good society. You have social ties in Edinburgh, do you not?"

"I do, yes." He had just been there earlier in the

spring, and the fact that she'd thought of that eased some of his suspicion, but not by much.

"We can ask questions of the right people, find out who James was spending all his time with before he was taken. You can get me into parties and soirees where his friends will be—events I couldn't get into on my own."

In other words, he would be useful. He knew she merely wanted to exploit him, so why this pricked feeling in his chest? "Do you think James told them you were a vampire?"

The look on her face gave away her surprise. Obviously the thought hadn't occurred to her as it had to him. "He would never do that."

Under the right circumstances people would do just about anything, but he wasn't going to tell her that. She was already worried enough about the boy without him announcing that James was either being tortured or had willingly betrayed her to his captors. Neither would be a huge surprise, given what he knew humans to be capable of.

"Somehow," she continued, "someone has discovered what I am, and that someone has taken James and is using him to get to me. I am not going to allow them to get away with that."

What she said made sense, but there was something not quite right with all of this.

"What aren't you telling me?" He almost laughed. What did he expect, that suddenly she'd confess all?

"Nothing." She was lying. She met his gaze too determinedly to be doing anything but. He had no idea why, but he did know one thing—her desperation was not false. Whatever her motives, it was very important to her that he accompany her to Scotland. As much as he didn't trust her, he could not let her down. And he couldn't let her go alone and risk her own safety. Not when she was the only woman he had ever truly loved in all his long, long life.

"I will help you," he told her, watching the relief soften her strong features. "But on one condition."

Her brandied gaze met his, hope replaced by suspicion. "And that is?"

"If we are to appear as husband and wife in public, then we will act as husband and wife in private."

She arched a brow, but her expression remained composed, with just a hint of mockery—just enough to emasculate a lesser man. "You want me to fetch your slippers?"

She was playing coy and he knew it. "No. I want you in my bed."

There was a slight pause, but not enough for him to gloat over. "And where will you be?"

He loved how she always made him spell it out. She would have made a damn fine barrister were women allowed such an occupation. She would ask those questions while making love, and he enthusiastically responded, telling her everything he wanted to do to her in exquisite detail. "In you."

Her throat constricted as she swallowed, but he smelled the change in her body. She was not loath to the prospect of bedding him again, not in the least. Christ, they were a fine pair. Perverse, both of them.

"You will help me find James in exchange for the use of my body?"

Put like that, it sounded so cold, but it was far from that. He burned for her, and if she planned to leave him again—or dispose of him in some other way—when he had served his purpose, then he would take of her what he could. "Whenever I want, yes."

She thought about it for a moment, no doubt searching out some way to use his base desires to her own advantage. "If I say no, will you force me?"

That her opinion of him was so low shouldn't surprise him—didn't surprise him—but it angered him all the same. "I'm not a rapist, madam."

She wasn't so certain, damn her. Did she truly think him so loathsome? "Answer me." She straightened her shoulders, as though bracing for an attack. "If I say no, will you stop?"

Apparently she thought even less of him than he suspected. "Of course." Pride made him add. "But you won't ask me to stop and we both know it." This was as much true for him as for her. She wasn't afraid of him, not really. She couldn't be.

Her eyes narrowed. "You haven't lost any of your arrogance when it comes to your prowess."

He shrugged, not about to rise to the bait and ask whether or not she'd had better over the years. "Do we have an agreement?"

She met his gaze with one the color of steeped tea—but without any of the warmth. "We do."

Chapter 3

God help her, she was playing a dangerous game.

Olivia's fingers shook as she lifted the brandy to her lips. Reign was watching her, much like a hawk watching a snake—with a mixture of predatory interest and obvious suspicion.

She should not have come to this house. She should have made him come to her hotel where the balance of power would have been tipped more favorably for her. This room was too much *him* for her to think clearly. The rich fabrics and dark colors made him stand out all the more. His scent filled the air. His mere presence enveloped her, made her cagey and eager to escape before she did something rash and confessed everything.

"You agreed very readily." Was it just her guilt, or was there accusation in his tone? What, no satisfaction?

She met his cool gaze and forced herself to hold it. All she had to do was remember what he had done to her. How it had felt. "You would have preferred I rail against you a bit longer?"

He shrugged—a careless lift of broad shoulders. "I thought you might."

"To what end? I want you to help me. You want to have sex with me in exchange for that help. If I'd said no then you would have refused to help me and I cannot afford to play games where James's safety is concerned."

Any satisfaction she took from the flash of contrition in his eyes was short-lived when he said, "I cannot decide if you are the most honorable woman I have ever known, or the most manipulative."

"Pick whichever you find the least attractive." That would be safer. This . . . *situation* did not need to be made any more complicated. For the two of them, sex had never been something easily dismissed. Their emotions ran too high, were too easily engaged when their bodies were joined. It was a terrible gamble for both of them to enter into this idiotic bargain. If she could keep as much emotional distance between them as possible, she just might survive sharing his bed, and get back her son.

Nephew. James wasn't hers.

Reign laughed, but there was little humor in it. "I've missed your bluntness, Olivia."

"I haven't missed you at all."

Arrogance curved his lips. "You're a liar as well."

That was too close to the truth for comfort, and his smug expression rubbed her nerves raw. She rose to her feet. "It is time that I took my leave."

"So soon?" Mockery added bite to the amusement in his tone.

"Not soon enough, I fear."

For a moment, Olivia thought he might try to persuade her to stay, bully her into his bed, but he didn't. He just watched her with far too keen pale eyes.

"I will need two nights to put my affairs in order."

"So long?" She couldn't keep the irritation from her tone. Had she not explained the severity of the situation adequately enough? Did he not understand that she needed to get to Scotland?

"Not nearly long enough, but it will do. We will leave Wednesday evening. That will put us in Edinburgh by Thursday. Meanwhile, I'll send word of my arrival so some of my acquaintances will extend invitations to any events. Will that do?"

She nodded, unable to speak she was so surprised by his sudden sincerity. The kidnappers would not be leaving word for her until Sunday, and as much as she'd like to be there sooner, there would be very little they could do before that. Not to mention that leaving now would only put her in Reign's company for more time than she was comfortable with. In the meantime, James would be fine. She had to believe that. "Yes."

She blinked and he was suddenly there in front of her. She hadn't seen, hadn't heard him move—a sobering reminder of his superior abilities. Humans were no match for her, but this man—this vampire —might prove to be too much for her to withstand. Olivia stiffened, prepared for whatever strike he might make.

The lines in Reign's tanned brow deepened. "I'm not going to hurt you, Liv."

As though that meant anything. "You've told me that before."

His expression darkened, making his eyes all the more unnerving. That couldn't be pain in his gaze; Reign didn't know the meaning of regret. "I lost control."

"Oh yes, I know." It was almost painful to hold his gaze, but she did anyway. "I was the one you lost control on." In her mind came the memories of how it felt, the burning as he tore into her. The pain. The fear.

"You were the last person I ever wanted to hurt."

He looked so sincere she could slap him. How dare he apologize now after all this time? If he hadn't wanted to hurt her he wouldn't have, and if he had regretted doing so he would have come after her—regardless that she had tried to kill him. "I'm sorry to hear that, because you did. We can't ever go back, Reign. Please don't assume for a moment that my coming to you means more than it does."

"I wouldn't be stupid enough to assume anything where you are concerned," he replied gruffly. "I'll have my carriage take you to your lodgings."

"I'll fly."

"You'll risk being seen."

But then at least he wouldn't have the address of her hotel and know exactly where to find her. "I'll be careful."

"Take my carriage. I don't want to risk anyone seeing you fly from my home."

"And you want to know where to find me."

"I could follow you by air as well, Liv. Take the carriage."

He was right, of course. And she had no other excuse. "Fine. But only because it's not worth arguing with you."

"I find that amazing," he drawled. "Wednesday evening. Be here at precisely six."

"Or what?" she asked with a hint of a smile. "You'll leave without me?"

The look he shot her could have frozen a house fire. She swore there were shards of ice in the smoky depths of his gaze. "I'll consider our arrangement null and void."

He meant it. Olivia felt the chill of his words right down to her toes. "I'll be here." With the arrangements finalized, there was no reason for her to linger any longer.

"Reign?" She said as she stopped at the threshold, turning her head to look at him over her shoulder.

"What?"

Somehow she managed a smile, even though a tendril of guilt wrapped itself around her stomach. "Thank you."

She was being followed.

Olivia peered out the back window of Reign's luxurious carriage, her sharp gaze purposefully studying every shape, every vehicle and silhouette underneath the murky streetlights. That hack, had it been with her since Belgrave Square? And what of that man on horseback? Was that Reign, or just her imagination? Trying to scent him out would do no good amongst all the odors of London. Their kiss earlier insured that his smell clung to her like an expensive perfume, confusing her senses and pulling at her heart. She would have to bathe once she returned to the hotel.

And scrub herself raw. Perhaps she'd burn her clothes. Grinding her teeth, Olivia drew a deep breath. She would not become a hysterical fool just because a man's scent threatened to choke her.

Regardless of the fact that she could smell him, why would Reign follow her when his man would easily divulge her destination? Perhaps her husband thought her a murderess now and feared for his driver's safety.

Or perhaps he feared for hers.

That was a romantic thought she had no business entertaining. Reign was no more in love with her than she was with him. Too much had happened between them, too much bitter time had passed. Regardless of anything she might still feel for him, or feel for him again, there was nothing that could change the fact that it wasn't going to last. This time she was going to betray him, and anything that might be left between them would never survive it.

Turning around, she leaned back against the padded velvet seat and closed her eyes. What matter did it make if someone was following her? They wouldn't be for long. And unless it was another vampire, or a small army of men, there was little anyone could do to harm her.

Indeed, her strength and agility were two great perks of vampirism. Never again would she know the fear of a lone female walking at night. She would not fear sickness or injury. She wasn't physically intimidated by man or nature. Never again would a human man, or several of them, inspire her to quicken her pace as her heart pounded in her chest. Only one man incited such a reaction in her and he wasn't human.

How could she react so strongly to him given all he had stolen from her? Had their short time together been that amazing that her body could forget so easily? Had the pleasure outweighed the pain? Even now, that same thing that had hurt her so badly came to her veiled in erotic images of their bodies entwined, yielding and clinging to each other like sea to sand.

Their first night together was as sharp and clear in her mind as her own hand—perhaps more so. The memory of his touch brought a flush to her skin, a tremor to her spine. She had never experienced anything like it. And Reign had held her in his arms afterward and confessed the same.

"Pathetic." Saying it aloud made it all the more real. It was sexual attraction and nothing more. It had been too long since she'd wanted a man and too long since she'd had one. She had always thought Reign to be a physically perfect specimen of maleness, so it only made sense that her body would react to that.

In fact, there was no reason why she shouldn't enjoy herself since she'd already made the devil's bargain by agreeing to sleep with him while they were in Scotland. It was a small price to pay for James's return, and if it made Reign malleable, then all the better. Sometimes sex was the most powerful weapon a woman could have, aside from her intellect.

What did the kidnappers want with him anyway? She didn't want to know. She had to stay cold, stay removed. James was her first priority. Reign could take care of himself. All that mattered was getting her boy back.

Nothing but trouble. That's all James had ever been, she thought with a smile. How many times had she gone up to his school to collect him after some matter of mischief? Curiosity, it seemed, was the root of all his trouble. Impulsiveness too. Hadn't he at the age of twelve—after learning Olivia's secret—decided that he wanted to be a vampire as well when he grew up? Eternity seemed a grand adventure at that age, and what boy wouldn't want to be stronger and faster than his peers? James never thought any decision all the way through.

And he always knew his aunt Olivia would save him. That was why he hadn't told her about Scotland. He considered himself old enough that he didn't need permission, and unfortunately that was closer to the truth than not. He hadn't seen a reason to inform her because he knew if he needed her, she'd come.

"Oh, Jamie," Olivia whispered in the darkness of the carriage. "What have you gotten yourself into this time?"

She was saved the burden of speculating when the carriage rolled to a stop in front of her lodgings. She had chosen the newly rebuilt Claridge's Hotel for a number of reasons. Located on Brook Street, it was in a fashionable part of town and close to almost any place she would desire to visit. Its red brick façade was pleasing to the eye and inside it was outfitted with every modern convenience including lifts, electricity and en suite bathrooms.

Olivia liked traveling in luxury—it made traveling so much more enjoyable. Plus, the drapes in the windows were heavy enough that when paired with the black velvet she always brought with her, they kept the murderous sun from creeping in and killing her while she slept.

Most importantly, the staff at Claridge's respected the privacy of their guests, and no one seemed the least bit concerned that she stayed in her suite all day, not leaving until the sun went down.

The footman opened the carriage door for her and lowered the step. Olivia accepted his hand as she exited, taking a brief moment to gaze around for any suspicious characters. She saw many and none. Anyone could be an enemy, but no one person stood out or made the hairs on the back of her neck stand on end.

The man on horseback was nowhere to be seen, and yet the sensation of being watched lingered. She glanced around, but her vision, despite its enhanced keenness, saw nothing. If it was Reign, he wouldn't allow himself to be seen so easily.

Olivia didn't dally outside. She thanked the driver and hurried into the sanctuary of the hotel lobby. There was a small crowd inside, their warmth and scent immediately overwhelming her senses. It happened this way sometimes, when she wasn't prepared. The smell of blood, the gentle thumping of all those hearts . . . it hit her with a shudder of pleasure. It wasn't unlike the feeling she would have as a child when cook would make breakfast on Sunday morning or bake cookies on a fall afternoon.

But just as she was in danger of exposing her fangs to the entire lobby she caught a whiff of sharp sweat and her hunger died a quick death. It was like walking into a bakery and smelling fish. She gagged and looked around for the source of the stink, but couldn't narrow it down. No one there looked dirty, they just smelled it.

Did this offensive odor belong to the ghost who seemed to be following her? She couldn't see him, but she could certainly feel and smell his presence. Or maybe she was trying to solve a puzzle that didn't exist. Perhaps there were simply people amongst the upper classes who clung to the archaic belief that regular bathing was dangerous or, at the very least, unnecessary.

The lift opened and Olivia ran into it, eager to escape the suspicions and sensations making her edgy. An older couple joined her. They smiled at her before chatting to each other in German as the gate slid shut. The lift operator watched her out of the corner of his eye. He was a handsome young man with dark hair and light eyes. He reminded her of Reign, and the clean scent of his skin, coupled with his obvious physical interest in her whet her appetite. He was fortunate then that they were not alone, else she might have given in to her hunger and taken him right there. And he would let her. They always let her.

She was trembling by the time she stepped onto her floor. After her quiet life on the shore, London was too much for her. It was the city that was to blame for this antsy, dangerous feeling. Yes, the city.

She hurried down the elegant, well-lit corridor. The thick carpet muffled the staccato fall of her feet as she ran away from an invisible foe, real or imagined.

The second she entered her suite much of the tension left her. The scent of lemon and clean sheets welcomed her. Here the sounds of the outside world were muted. There was no one watching her. No boys tempting her. No vampire with pale gray eyes to set her very nerves on edge.

Sagging against the door, she pressed her shoulders into the wood and drew several calming breaths. She was made of stronger stuff than this. She had to pull herself together. She couldn't hide in her room. She wouldn't.

She stayed in the suite long enough to regain her equilibrium and splash some water on her face. Then, she went to the French doors and lifted the latch, letting the night inside.

Her suite was on the back side of the hotel on the sixth floor. The balcony—if it could be called such—was a delicate wrought iron affair that was little more than a place to step. It was all she needed.

After ascertaining that there was no one around, no one watching, she closed the doors behind her and pushed herself into the sky.

Let someone try to follow her *now*.

The force of her own body soaring through the night tugged the pins from her hair and made her eyes water, but she pushed onward regardless. There was only one place that she would find peace this night, and she was determined to go there.

The steeple for St. Martin-in-the-Fields rose in the distance. Arms at her sides, Olivia sped toward it like a pebble propelled from a child's slingshot as her skirts flapped around her ankles.

She touched ground just behind the church and stepped out of the shadows while trying to restore the wind-loosened locks of her hair.

The massive building dwarfed her as she climbed the steps. Grecian columns rose high on the portico, supporting a roof that deepened the shadows night cast across the smooth stone. Were it any other building in any other place, it would have seemed daunting, perhaps even sinister, but here there was only peace.

The door opened with ease, just as it had the evening before, when she had come to sit and gather her thoughts. So many churches locked their doors now that being given entrance into this one, especially at this hour, was a little surprising. Yesterday, she had expected to walk in, given that it was Sunday.

So many people seemed to eschew religion for the new belief and theories in science. Olivia wasn't one of them—nor was she one of those who ridiculed Mr. Darwin's theories or other scientific revelations. She simply believed that there was truth in both science and religion. And while she believed that humans and animals evolved, she also knew that when life was difficult, it wasn't the Royal Academy she prayed to for comfort and strength.

The interior of the church was warm and golden with candlelight, and Olivia was over the threshold with the door closed behind her before she truly realized she was even inside. Right then, at that exact moment, she knew the meaning of sanctuary. Lightness filled her soul with every step she took down the aisle toward the front of the church, her footsteps echoing in the otherwise empty building.

"Good evening."

No, of course it wasn't empty. At least she hadn't embarrassed herself by yelping. Olivia stopped where she was, daring to glance at the priest. He wasn't the same one who had been there yesterday. This priest was younger, sharper. Would this one recognize her for what she was? It always surprised her, though less now, that these men of God didn't know a demon when they saw one.

And this one was no different. He smiled at her as though she was just an ordinary woman, nothing the least bit remarkable about her at all. Inside, a part of her collapsed with relief. She returned the smile. "Good evening. Is it all right if I sit for a moment?"

He seemed surprised that she would ask. "Of course, my dear lady." He even went so far as to gesture to the pew second from the front. "Please."

Olivia seated herself on the polished wood, waiting until the priest left her before opening up her thoughts. She didn't know if praying would help James. She didn't know if praying did any good at all, or if the Almighty still listened to her voice. But it made her feel better to sit in a house of God and ask for the strength she needed to get through an ordeal. Even when searching her own heart, the peace and tranquility of a quiet church buoyed her spirit and made everything seem so much clearer.

She was doing the right thing. Reign would never help her if he knew the kidnappers wanted him in exchange for James. No one in his right mind, unless he were a saint, would make such a sacrifice. And Reign was as far from saintly as a man could get.

No, she would deal with the consequences of betraying Reign when they came. For now her only concern was James and seeing him safe again. Still, she wished there was some other way to bring him home. One that didn't involve her husband at all.

The prayer book in the pocket in front of her had a slip of folded paper sticking out of it, she noticed, jarring herself out of her thoughts—which were becoming clearer and clearer as the moments ticked on.

Curiosity got the better of her and she picked up the paper, unfolding it as the church door behind her opened and then closed. Another late-night sinner, perhaps, she thought with a smile.

But her humor was short-lived. Her smile froze as she read the words on the paper. There, in bold script, she read:

Do not dawdle, Mrs. Gavin. James is depending upon you.

Dread filled her, yanked her to her feet.

The priest. He had specifically pointed out this pew.

Her jaw clenched as she crushed the paper in her fist. They were following her. She'd known it. And the priest was one of them, or at least had been influenced by them. She could kill someone.

"Olivia."

Her breath caught at that voice. Reign. He would help her. He would hold the false priest while Olivia tore him limb from limb.

"Did you see a man?" she asked in a low voice as she turned to face him. "A young man with reddish hair, dressed as a priest?"

He stared at her, obviously surprised by her predatory expression. "No."

"He might still be here, then." She moved her head to the side, trying to direct her hearing throughout the levels of the church. Rats scurried far below. Bats fluttered high above. Was that a tap dripping?

"Do you smell that?" Reign asked.

She held up her hand to silence him. And then she heard it—the faint beating of a human heart.

Olivia bolted out of the pew toward the sound. It was behind the pulpit. The coward was likely cowering there, hoping she'd take the warning and just leave. Reign was behind her as she moved, reaching the very front of the church a fraction of a second behind her.

But it wasn't the young priest behind the pulpit. It was Father Abberley, the elderly priest who had been so kind to her the night before. And he wasn't cowering, he was lying on the floor, his head in a pool of blood.

Chapter 4

"**D**o you think he'll be all right?" Olivia asked as they entered her suite through the tiny balcony's French doors.

Reign shrugged and straightened his coat. "I hope so. The doctor seemed to think he would be." A doctor glassy-eyed, though, from dipping into his supply of laudanum or some other equally as potent drug. Personally, Reign would be surprised if the old priest lived to see morning, which was fast approaching.

"Sometimes doctors lie." She yanked the doors closed. Olivia wasn't stupid. "Maybe he was lying. There was a lot of blood."

She felt responsible. That was the reason for all this fussing over the priest. "He took a cosh to the head, Liv. Those always bleed like a bastard." He didn't add that the wound was bad. In his own violent past he had seen many such wounds and there was no doubt in his mind that whoever attacked the priest, didn't care if the old man lived or not. In fact, Reign suspected the old man had been meant to die—a fact that made him more than a little uneasy.

"Are you going to tell me what happened?" As distraught as she was—or appeared to be—he was more concerned about why the old man had been attacked—and Olivia's part in it. She had recognized the priest, called him by name. Thank God, I'd followed her, otherwise she probably would have taken the old man to the hospital herself, and wouldn't that have been an amazing thing to see—a woman carrying a full-grown man like a child in her arms.

She turned to him. "That was you following me, wasn't it? You were the man on horseback."

He nodded. No point in denying it, and he wasn't about to apologize for it. He would have been an idiot not to follow her. His only thought was that he should have been better at it. Olivia was up to something—something that required his participation—and he hadn't survived six centuries by not knowing all he could about his enemies.

Olivia was his enemy whether he liked it or not. Until she was back in his bed and his life—until she trusted him and proved that he could trust her—he wouldn't treat her as anything else. For all he knew she might be planning to kill him, and this time she might be luckier than she had been thirty years ago.

He didn't blame her for despising him—hell, he deserved it. But he wasn't going to make it easy for her to have her revenge. As for his decision to help her . . . well, that was complicated. He owed her some kind of penance, and that's what he'd tell himself whenever he wondered why he had agreed. It was much more palatable than thinking she had some sway over him.

He was not going to think about that. "How could the kidnappers track you to St. Martin's?"

"I went there last night," she informed him, long fingers massaging her brow as she paced a small section of carpet. "That's how I knew Father Abberley. When I went there tonight there was another priest. I don't think he was really a priest at all."

"Why not?"

She stopped pacing. "He told me where to sit. I found this in a prayer book."

Reign took the crumpled, bloodstained paper she offered him and read it. If he had any doubts about the severity of her situation, they were gone now. He gave the note back to her, his jaw tight. "We'll find him, Liv."

A mixture of confusion, relief and consternation crossed her face. "Why are you helping me?"

After all the effort she'd put into convincing him, he was surprised she asked. "Would you rather I didn't?" She seemed angry that he was offering his help, even though she had come asking for it.

"I just want to know why you would help a woman who tried to kill you."

"You're my wife. I will always be there for you." To him that revealed more than he wanted, but there was only confusion in her gaze.

She looked away then. Guilty conscience, perhaps? Playing to her emotions was definitely the way to find out. Seducing her, body and mind, would lower her defenses, weaken her resolve. All he had to do was make her care for him again—make her think he still loved her, that he regretted all that had happened. Regret wouldn't be hard—he had an abundance of that, but love? No, he wouldn't be fool enough to allow that to happen again. Loving Olivia made him do irrational things, inane things, and that would be playing right into her hands.

"Thank you," she murmured.

"Hmm, that's twice now that you've thanked me this evening. Satan must be putting on his ice skates. Oh, was that a smile?"

The curve of her lips was gone as soon as it had come, but the sparkle in her eyes remained. At that moment Reign realized that he didn't want to manipulate her so much as he wanted to genuinely protect her. "Do not let it go to your head."

Somehow, he managed a wry grin. "I have to say, this is not how I thought we'd spend our thirtieth anniversary."

"We've been apart longer than we were ever together." She said it as though the thought had just occurred to her.

His smile faded, as did any good humor he might have felt. "Sad, don't you think?"

She nodded. "Yes." He watched in horror as tears filled her eyes, but they weren't for him, or even for them. "He's not even twenty, Reign. James is just a boy and these people have him . . ." The helplessness in her expression wounded him more than the blade she had shoved into his chest all those years ago.

Reign went to her, hesitating but a moment before he put his arms around her. She might think him a fool. She might hate him and be using him for her own means, but her tears were real.

He had only seen her cry once before and that was when he . . . betrayed her. He had thought the world was going to end with her tears. Olivia wasn't a woman who cried easily, especially not for herself. Her tears were reserved for moments when she honestly felt helpless and alone.

He could use this to his advantage. The thought came to him from the cold, untrusting part of his mind determined to have the upper hand. If he pressed now, could he wheedle the truth from her? Could he take her to bed, press her into the mattress and feel her body wrapped around his once more? She had haunted his dreams for years and he fantasized about her coming back to him. Sometimes she crawled, begging for forgiveness. Other times he found her and seduced her into coming home. And sometimes, he simply imagined what it would have been like had she never left. The one thing that always stayed the same in the fantasy was that she wanted him as much as he wanted her.

She let him hold her for a few minutes as she wiped the dampness from her eyes. The tears didn't even make it down to her cheeks before she ruthlessly pushed and blinked them away. Then she pushed Reign away as well—not forcefully, but it was obvious that she did not want his comfort.

Or perhaps she wanted it too much. It hardly mattered. There would be no pressing her into the mattress this night, and dawn would soon be upon them.

"They knew I'd go to the church. They're watching me," Olivia remarked as she put some distance between them. "Without my knowing. How is that possible?"

Reign remained silent. She didn't need him to answer. It was possible because like most preternatural creatures, Olivia fancied herself superior to all others. It wasn't that she held no regard for human life, but rather she thought she was above human intelligence. She was now learning how wrong that assumption was.

"If they're watching you it means they are not entirely certain you will do what they ask." It also meant that they knew about him but not, perhaps, what he was. Still he knew to be on guard. He wiped at a spot of dried blood on the top of his hand. It was from the priest. It didn't want to budge, a fact that annoyed him to no end. Finally he licked it. "We can use that to our advantage."

"How?" She scowled at him—at what he was doing. "How can I save James if they're watching my every move?"

Reign wiped the back of his hand on his trousers. It was a wonder he wasn't covered in the priest's blood, there had been so much of it. "Where there is an inability to predict the enemy there is fear. They're afraid of you, Olivia."

She made a scoffing noise. "They know I'll do whatever they want to free James."

"They know you'll do *anything* to free James. That's what scares them." It should scare him too, but he stopped caring for his own safety a long time ago. About thirty years ago, to be exact.

She nodded warily, not believing him—and he knew there would be no convincing her. Olivia would rather slit her own throat than admit that he might know something she didn't.

"It will be dawn soon," she reminded him needlessly. "You should go."

Reign laughed—a short, clipped bark. "Don't pretend concern for my person, Liv. Just tell me to get out."

A ghost of a smile danced on her wide lips. She looked sad and tired, and worst of all, resigned. "Get out."

"That's my girl." He continued to grin even as her smile faded. She didn't argue, however. She probably knew she couldn't change how he thought of her. "I will come for you tomorrow evening. We can hunt together." It was more than an excuse to be with her, it was a way to keep an eye on her.

"Hunt?" One dark eyebrow rose haughtily. "Are humans prey now?"

He backed toward the door of the room, not quite prepared to turn his back on her just yet. "They always have been, Darling. Always will be. That's why I always feed from strangers."

Her expression darkened. "Not always."

He might have smiled at the storm brewing in her gaze, were he not so conscious of the pain behind it. He did love baiting her. "There's an exception to every rule."

"Is that what I was?" Her hands fisted on her hips, the universal stance for the indignant female. "An exception to your rule?"

"You are my wife," he remarked, finally allowing himself that smile as he opened the door. "Rules don't apply."

Glib-tongued, deceitful, smirking bastard.
One thing Olivia had never liked about Reign—and unfortunately it had been just about the *only* thing she never liked about him—was the way he liked to pick at her, goad her until her temper

reared its head. He called it teasing. She called it torment, but that didn't stop him. He seemed to like getting under her skin, and thirty years and an assassination attempt hadn't changed that.

He only did it to people he liked. People he loved. That he continued to do it to her was even more aggravating than the behavior itself. Why could he not hate her? It had been easy for her to hate him. Apparently not easy enough, though, given that she felt more than a little guilt for leading him to whatever peril awaited him in Scotland.

Reign would survive. He always did. If she, a vampiress in the throes of fury, couldn't harm him, what chance did a few humans have? James, on the other hand, wasn't nearly as robust. James and his safety were all that mattered—more than Olivia's own life and more than Reign's. The two of them had both lived full lives. Hell, Reign had easily lived a dozen. James deserved the chance to live one. Olivia had tried her best to give him the best chance of that full life. If it hadn't been for her inability to travel during the day, Rosemary never would have died, and James wouldn't be held in exchange for the man responsible for Olivia's condition.

Was it unfair of her to blame Reign for so much? Probably. Did owning that ease any of her anger? Not one bit.

It had been twenty minutes since his departure and dawn was still safely tucked on the other side

of the horizon. She had time to go out and feed—
"hunt" as Reign liked to call it. She added *heart-
less* to the list of her husband's attributes.

Still, it was difficult to excuse her own actions
as anything but hunting. She left her room and the
hotel with the utmost speed and stealth, careful
not to be detected. It would raise brows, her going
out at such an hour, looking as she did, with her
hair mussed and bloodstains on her pelisse. No
one would care about her appearance where she
was going. Or rather, when she found the person
she was looking for, he wouldn't care.

The club on St. James's Street was less than a
mile from Claridge's. Hiking her skirts, Olivia
scampered over the tops of buildings and down
dark side streets to get there in a matter of minutes.
Reign was right about flying, it was too risky, and
sometimes running was easier.

She was perched on the roof of the club—she
didn't know if it was White's or Boodle's or some
other bastion of manly pursuits—when three
drunken young men staggered outside. Two of
them climbed into a waiting carriage. The other
continued around the building, obviously continuing onward to another haunt.

As quietly as a cat, she dropped to the shadows
behind the club and waited. A few moments later
the young man staggered into her line of sight. He
might have been four and twenty, and had dark
hair and a rugged face that would be handsome

once he reached full manhood. She could overlook that. It was the attitude that drew her in. He had that same kind of presence that made a person notice; a silent strength that pulled her closer. He was confident, perhaps even arrogant, this boy. Yes, he'd do.

He looked up as she came close, his eyes—they were light green—widening at the sight of her. This was St. James's after all, and women weren't terribly welcome on this historically male street.

"Are you lost, madam?" he asked. Oh, yes, he'd do. A nice low voice—not as gravelly as she liked, but delicious all the same.

"No," she replied, sliding her hand up his arm. She could feel the solid muscle beneath the dark fabric of his coat. "I've found what I was looking for."

It wasn't right, her stalking him this way, toying with him. But she wasn't thinking as a person at this moment. She was thinking with her hunger and her anger and her lust. She was hunting with all the shame that overtook her whenever she went looking for a man who suited her specifications.

"Come here," she murmured with a gentle tug. Drunk and unbalanced, he fell into her arms. She caught him—held him like a child. "Close your eyes."

He did so with a smile. "Are you going to ravish me?"

"Yes," she replied against the rough stubble of his throat. The young man moaned encouragingly when she touched his warm flesh with her tongue. Hunger and instinct rose to the surface. Her fangs lengthened as saliva filled her mouth and her tongue tingled with anticipation.

His arms went around her, tightening when her teeth pierced his neck. He was hard and young and warm against her, and she felt every pulse of his body reverberate in her own. He tasted of youth and whiskey and she drank deep, taking him into her, letting him fill her with all the sweetness flooding his veins.

Olivia closed her eyes as she fed, and glad that he was a stranger, pretended that he was someone else.

Pretended he was Reign.

Reign was by nature, a suspicious man. That suspicion was what made him write and leave a note for Saint. Last evening he gave it to a fence with whom the other vampire did business. Ezekiel would know where Saint was long before Reign ever did. They didn't communicate very often—not because they didn't want to, but because after six centuries of friendship, they didn't *need* to.

There was a sum of money tucked in the folded note—payment for a wager he and Saint made a long time ago. Saint had wagered that

Olivia would someday return, a notion Reign had declared utter shite. They had shaken hands, and Reign assumed they'd continue on their path toward eternity with neither of them ever becoming any richer.

Saint would have a laugh at his expense, of that there could be no doubt, but at least he would have an idea of whom to expect an explanation from if Reign failed to return from Scotland.

Did he honestly believe Olivia could kill him? The question voiced itself in his mind as he strode across the polished stone floor of his foyer, the tapping of his boot heels keeping time with the rattle of carriage wheels outside. He had finished the last of his arrangements and now all he had to do was await Olivia's arrival.

The answer was no. He didn't believe Olivia could kill him *herself*. If she hadn't done it thirty years ago, she couldn't do it now. But he had no such certainty when it came to allowing him to be killed by someone else. He didn't want to think her capable, but he had hurt her in the worst way, and it was possible that she truly hated him enough to hand-feed him to the lions.

All the more reason to keep a close eye on her and use whatever weapons at his disposal to uncover her secrets. After what he had done, he owed her his help in finding her nephew, but trust? No, he didn't owe her that at all. He wouldn't give her that until she earned it.

The fact that she had agreed to sleep with him proved that she wasn't to be trusted. No woman would give herself to a man she claimed to despise unless the end result was worth it. How in the name of holy hell would having sex with him help her get her nephew back?

Unless, of course, she was hoping to lull him into submission with her feminine wiles.

Feminine wiles. Did people use phrases like that anymore? Sometimes it was so hard to keep up with the ever changing English language.

And if that were true, why had she refused to go out with him the night before when he called on her? The thought of feeding seemed to bother her, or perhaps it was the thought of having him with her that made her so pale. He didn't understand it. It wasn't as though he had offered her his blood—that was far more intimate than sex and he knew she'd never agree to that.

Unless of course, it suited her schemes.

Regardless, trying to figure Olivia out was pointless until he knew more about what she had been up to the last thirty years. He'd tried in the beginning to keep tabs on her, but she kept sending his investigators back to him with broken bones. Finally, his pride—and pity for the poor investigators—forced him to give up.

"What have you found out?" he demanded as he swept open the door to his study. Clarke was there, waiting in a chair in front of the desk, just as

Reign knew he would be. There was also a bottle of brandy and two snifters on the blotter. Clarke knew him too well.

"A fair bit," the man replied, reaching forward to pour the brandy. "I'm not sure if any of it will be helpful to you, however."

"If it gives me any insight into my wife, it will be helpful."

Clarke smiled faintly, deepening several of the lines around his mouth and eyes. "So echoes the plaintive prayer of husbands everywhere."

Reign cocked both brows. "Spoken like a true, confirmed bachelor."

"I don't expect to be anything but, since they won't allow my kind to marry. Hell, after that mess with Wilde, I'm leery of approaching another man, much less engaging in a relationship."

"Wilde ended up where he did not because he likes boys, but because he liked the wrong one. Queensberry took the relationship as a personal affront, and that's what got Wilde in trouble."

"So, as long as I never fall in love with the son of a marquess, I should be safe?"

"Exactly."

They shared a small smile and that was the end of the conversation. Reign appreciated the unfairness of Clarke's plight. He just wasn't sure he could understand it. He could understand that it wasn't fair that vampires couldn't go out in sunlight, but having sex with another man? That was beyond him. Who'd want to lay with a man when there were such soft, supple, delicious women to choose from?

Reign seated himself on the other side of the desk, in the thickly padded chair that molded to his body, engulfing him in hedonistic comfort. He lit a cigar without bothering to offer one to Clarke—his valet didn't smoke—and took a drink from the crystal snifter as he braced the ankle of one leg on the thigh of the other.

"Are you settled?" Clarke asked with a smile. It was a joke to him how Reign liked to have everything a certain way before they began a meeting. For Reign it was practice in maintaining a façade of humanity. Clarke wouldn't find it nearly so amusing if that façade were to slip too far.

"I'm good," Reign replied. "What have you found?"

Clarke slipped a pair of spectacles over his ears and opened a small, leather-bound book. "It is true that she became guardian of her nephew James Andrew Winscott Burnley upon the death of his mother, Rosemary. A carriage accident."

Reign knew that. "What of the boy's father?"

Clarke shook his graying head. "I could find no mention of him. I can look into the boy's certificate of birth, see if it's listed there."

"Do that." If the father was still alive, he might be involved in James's disappearance somehow. Especially if the man was looking for a little revenge against the woman who had taken his son. He could speculate until the dawn and still not be any closer to the truth. "What else?"

"Young Mr. Burnley was a good student at school, but was sent down on several occasions for usual boyish mischief."

No doubt Olivia gave the boy a good head-reading for that. "What of his friends and companions?"

"He had a large circle of friends in school, but for the last year he's been spending more and more time with some young bucks from the upper classes." Clarke consulted the pages before him. "Misters Binchley, Haversham, and Dashbrooke. I believe you know Mr. Dashbrooke."

Reign nodded. "Portly fellow. Bald. Tried to talk me into investing in some gold scheme in the Americas?"

Clarke smiled, and Reign paused. Had he said something wrong? Damn, was *Americas* the wrong term?

"Yes," Clarke replied. "That's the man."

"Did anything come up about the boys or their fathers?"

"No. Only that they are wealthy, fairly powerful, and extremely lucky."

"Lucky?" Interesting. "How so?"

Clarke shrugged. "Horses. Political favor. Business. Either the men are very savvy or they're extremely fortunate in their choices."

"Or they have many friends willing to pull

strings in their favors. Perhaps James stepped on the wrong toes? What of Olivia?"

Another glance at the book. "She keeps a quiet existence wherever she goes. As of late she's been living in the south, in Clovelly."

Reign closed his eyes and drew a breath. Clovelly. Yes, he should have known. He opened his eyes to find Clarke watching him. "Do you know it?" the other man asked.

"Yes." They had taken a house there for a while. A little secret getaway where they didn't have to worry about gossip and society's rules. Olivia loved the shore, the smell and call of the ocean. At night they'd swim naked and make love on the beach, with the surf crashing around them. Stupid things Clarke didn't need to know. Fucking stupid things Reign didn't want to say aloud. "What else?"

"Well, of course I wasn't able to go there and talk to anyone, but my contacts didn't unearth anything. The only thing of interest is that Clovelly and its neighbors seem to have an awful lot of young men who go missing."

Damn. Reign raised a brow. "Dead—and-there-is-no-body missing, or 'Oh dear, we've misplaced Harold' missing?"

Clarke chuckled. "Disappear-at-night-and-wake-up-in-a-strange-place-with-no-memory-of-how-they-got-there missing."

"You think it's Olivia feeding?"

"I do."

"But only from young men?" Was that jealousy in his voice?

Clarke looked far too smug for a mortal. "I thought to ask if the young men had anything in common. Turns out that the majority of them were rugged young men with dark brown or black hair and gray or green eyes. Were she to have killed them, I'd say she was acting out her fantasies of you."

Reign looked away, his heart clenching too tightly in his chest for him to speak. He couldn't explain this feeling even if he wanted. An exchange of blood between lovers was so deeply intimate. He and Olivia had never had the chance to share such an experience. He knew what it was to pierce her flesh, but not the sublime pleasure of having her bite him. He thought of what that would be like often. To have her sink her fangs into his flesh rather than simply taking the flow of blood he offered.

He thought of her licking the blood from his lips in Mrs. Willet's parlor when they shared their first kiss in three decades. He had wanted her more than he could ever remember wanting her before. She had wanted him as well. Of course, sex had never been an issue between them. Sex had led to them falling in love.

Were Olivia's hunting choices revenge fantasies as Clarke suggested, or fantasies of another kind? And if she kept her word and gave her body to him, was there a chance that he might win her heart once more? Did he want to?

"Oh, and word came from the hospital," his friend remarked, his expression darkening. "The priest—Father Abberley is dead."

"Dead?" Christ, how was he going to tell Olivia? "Is that all?"

Clarke was watching him, his expression carefully blank. "For now. Shall I continue my investigation while you are gone?"

"Yes. Dig as deep as you have to. And quickly. I want to know what I'm up against."

His wording, and his timing, couldn't have been any more perfect, for at that exact moment, there came a knock upon the door and his housekeeper informed him that Mrs. Gavin had arrived.

"We'll be at the Edinburgh house before dawn," he remarked needlessly as he rose to his feet. Clarke was well aware of his schedule, having been the one to make the arrangements. "You know how to contact me."

His friend rose to his feet as well. "You will be careful, won't you?"

Reign made a scoffing sound. "Of course."

"No, I mean it." Reign hadn't heard such insistence in his old friend's voice in a long time. "Promise me you won't trust her—not before I can prove whether or not she deserves it."

Clarke's concern was touching, but unnecessary. Reign wasn't about to let his guard down. "I promise. I'll be in touch if I need anything. Send me whatever information you can as soon as possible."

They shook hands and Reign walked away, trying to ignore the worry in the other man's eyes. Honestly, sometimes Clarke was worse than a woman when it came to worrying.

He left the office and strolled to the foyer, where his wife was waiting. The wife he could see, could touch, could maybe even taste, but couldn't trust.

Not even if he wanted to.

Chapter 5

Haddington, Scotland

Reginald Dashbrooke turned away from the sun-dappled view of his window with a sigh. "I'm bored. Why does Binchley get to return to London and I don't?"

His father, bald, portly, with a face of a bulldog—*thank God, Reggie looked like his mother*—removed a much chewed cigar from his mouth with thick fingers. "Because our ranks are so thinned lately, we needed someone in London to make sure our friends there are doing what they ought."

His father was always spoke so cryptically, as though he suspected every conversation might be overheard. By what, Reggie wondered? Ghosts behind the walls? Pixies at the windows? At one time it might have been laughable, but that was before Reggie learned that vampires truly existed. Now, sometimes even he found himself wondering if he was being watched though there was no one in sight. "Are they? Doing what they ought, I mean?"

"The lady found what we left for her at St. Martin's. I expect that if she did not believe we were serious to begin with, she does now."

This was one of the moments when Reggie had to remind himself that these were vampires they were discussing, not actual people. Vampires weren't human and he shouldn't feel badly for them. Should he? He couldn't quite understand if the organization his father had brought him into hated vampires or revered them. Maybe both?

"Why do we have to bring them here?" Reggie asked, pouring himself a glass of port. "Why couldn't we have taken them in London?"

"Bringing them here was the only way we could ensure our complete control over the situation. Our numbers in England are greatly diminished at the present, you know that. It took a great number to seize the Cromwell entity and arrange its transportation. And now the London contingent is preparing for the Harvest."

Reggie didn't know what the "Harvest" detailed, or what was being harvested, but he was quite sure he didn't want to know. He was still new to all of this and had yet to embrace it as his cronies had.

But he knew that the Cromwell entity was a vampire. A very old and very dangerous vampire, whom his father's brothers in the Order of the Silver Palm somehow had managed to secure. There had been much celebrating that night when the news came that the one called Temple was in the Order's custody. Reggie couldn't help but wonder if the vampire had made it easy for them, if perhaps the very creature the Order thought they controlled was simply waiting for the change to rip them all apart.

"How is our young guest faring?" his father asked, sucking on his cigar once more. "Is he comfortable?"

"He acts like this is a big adventure." Reggie couldn't keep the distaste from his voice. James was his friend, and this entire situation didn't sit well with him, no matter how many times his father tried to make him believe it was in everyone's best interest. His father, Reggie had long ago decided, was not a trustworthy man, and while his praise and pleasure might be grandiose in nature, his cruelty could be just as overwhelming. Reggie had experienced that cruelty many times during his life.

His father chuckled. "It is! Perhaps you should look at it in the same light, my boy."

Reggie knew better than to shrug, so he nodded instead. "Yes, sir." But he couldn't resist adding, with just a hint of censure, "He doesn't realize that he's a prisoner."

"He's a *guest*, Reginald," his father corrected. "Our guest. Without him, this would not be possible, and we will reward him amply for all that he has given us."

Reggie turned to him, suddenly very anxious to hear the truth, no matter what. "And if this fails? If we fail, what then?"

Another chuckle, but there was no humor in his father's expression. "We will not fail."

He tried another route. Aware that he was risking his father's wrath and, surprisingly, nowhere near as frightened by that prospect as he should be, he asked, "What if he's no longer an asset to us? Would you actually kill him?" Now that he had asked, looking into his father's porcine eyes, he wished he could take the question back.

His father looked at him with a loving, almost teasing smile. "My dear boy, I'd even kill *you*."

"You have your own train car?" Olivia gazed around the opulent space with a mixture of awe and derision. Part of that derision stemmed from her own pettiness, she knew that.

"I'm forced to travel a lot," Reign replied easily. It was a simple explanation, not a defense. He obviously didn't feel that he needed to explain himself to her, after all, hadn't she been the one to point out that they had been separated far longer than they had been together?

She traveled often as well, but she didn't have her own train car. This was beyond luxury and extravagance as far as Olivia was concerned, with its separate sleeping area that housed a huge bed and chest of drawers, adjacent to a small bathroom with toilet, sink, and claw-foot tub. There was a dining area as well, plus a sofa and chair in shades of rich blue to complement the cherry paneling. A small bar sat against the opposite wall, and Olivia had no doubt it would be well stocked with the finest spirits.

All of the furniture was bolted to the floor to prevent it from moving with the rolling of the train. Heavy gold-, blue-, and wine-patterned drapes adorned the windows to block out the daytime sun. Polished brass sconces with crystal shades held lamps that burned sweet-scented oil. An Aubusson carpet in the same pattern as the curtains cushioned her every step. Oh, so opulent.

And she wanted one of her own, damn it.

Whenever she left a place she simply let the lease expire and moved on. She never purchased a home, never put down any kind of roots. She never saw the point. Obviously, Reign disagreed. It was easy to resent him for that. It was easy to resent him for almost anything she put her mind to.

Especially the fact that she could still taste him, even though nights had passed since the kiss they'd shared. He clung to her lips and tongue as though he had claimed them with his own just moments before. It had only been a drop. Just a drop. She had fed since then, on young robust men who had given her more of their salty sweetness than Reign had ever afforded. And now, standing here with him, in this . . . box, she was all too aware of the spicy, slightly sweet scent of him, the gentle heat of his body, and the overwhelming presence that was his alone.

That same presence that had overwhelmed her years ago, drew her out of her widowhood and overshadowed all memories, even the good ones, of her first husband. She had risked scandal on a regular basis with Reign and hadn't cared one whit.

Reign had closed the door behind them when they entered, and now he locked it as well. She was trapped with him now, and while her body might thrill at the idea of being so close to the one man who could make her quiver with just a look, her mind was as wary of it as a caged animal.

Her luggage had been loaded on by one of Reign's footmen and was neatly stacked in the bedroom area. The trip wouldn't necessitate her having to unpack as they would be in Edinburgh within a matter of hours. It was peculiar, however, seeing her cases set so neatly beside Reign's like they were part of a matched set. And they did match, odd as that was. That irked her as well. A reminder of how at one time she believed *them* to be a perfect match.

"A house in one of the most fashionable areas of London." She pulled off her gloves and tossed them on the sofa. "A house in Scotland and a private train car to get there. Do you have other addresses attached to your name? Perhaps an apartment in Paris, or a villa in Spain?"

He smiled slightly at her sarcasm. "I have a handful of permanent properties scattered across Europe and one in New York City. You may have a set of keys for the Paris apartment if you wish."

That was tempting. "Such extravagance," her tone was sweetly mocking. "And here I thought you were a simple businessman."

"I am a businessman," he replied smoothly as he stripped off his coat. "I've had the advantage of six centuries to learn the right ways to conduct my business and I've used that knowledge to my advantage."

"I wager you have." What angered her more—that he seemed so unruffled or that he looked so good in his shirtsleeves? No, it was the fact that she realized just how good he looked the less clothing he wore.

He had the audacity to laugh. "You needn't be so snippety, Liv. Everything I own is yours too."

That announcement hit her like a shove in the chest. "What was that?"

Oh, he looked so pleased with himself now. His eyes were bright and there was no trying to hide his smile. Big white teeth flashed in the lamplight. "Your name is on all my assets. Should I somehow manage to die one day, everything I own will be transferred to you."

For a moment, Olivia couldn't find her ability to speak, she was so shocked. "Why would you admit to that? Are you not afraid that I might kill you and stake my claim?"

He shook his head. A curling lock of inky hair fell over his forehead. "Besides assuming that you would want nothing to do with anything of mine? You're not a murderer."

Little did he know that she might very well be leading him to his grave by taking him to Scotland. The thought brought a peculiar tightness to her chest. "I almost killed you before."

"Had you truly wanted to, I think you would have succeeded, but perhaps that's just wishful thinking on my part."

"Why?" She shook her head, unable to comprehend his logic, or his smile. "Why would you want to make me your heir?"

"You're my wife."

"We've been apart longer than my life as a mortal, Reign. Surely there must be someone you would rather see benefit from all you've amassed? Someone else who could benefit from your generosity."

His expression changed. Gone was any trace of humor, replaced by an honesty and openness that made her wince inside. "Because you are still my wife, and as far as I'm concerned you always will be. Everything I have is yours—in life as well as death."

As Olivia's stomach lurched under the weight of his confession, the train lurched as well, beginning its trek north to Scotland. She stumbled into Reign, knocking them both against the wall so that her front was pressed to his. She lifted her chin and met his gaze, dreading but wanting to see the truth in his eyes. And there it was.

She was going to burn in hell for betraying him. They could burn together.

Reign's fingers wrapped around her upper arms—warm and firm. He could snap her like a twig and yet she had no fear for her life. No, there were other things she feared for. Like her honor and her soul. Her heart.

"You always did knock me off center," he mused softly, his voice a rumble that she felt through the layers of clothing between them.

She opened her mouth, not sure of what to say but determined to say something that would wake her from this dream, but nothing came out.

"Speechless," he mused with a seductive smile as he released her arms. "Imagine that."

The train was moving smoothly now, slowly picking up speed. She could have moved away from him and put a stop to the madness spiraling inside her, but she didn't. Instead she reached up and touched the tips of her fingers to the feathery lines fanning out from the corner of his eye toward his temple and cheekbone.

"You always complained that these made

you look old," she remarked, touching each fine furrow. "But I loved how they deepened whenever you smiled." *Back up. Back up and move away now, before you do something stupid like fall in love.*

His eyes were the color of thunderclouds as she met his gaze, and just as full of turmoil. She had agreed to share his bed once they had reached Scotland, and they were nowhere near Scotland just yet. Geography, she feared, mattered not at this moment. Not when he was lowering his head toward hers, and she was lifting hers in turn.

Reign's mouth could look so hard and unyielding at times, but when their lips touched, she sighed at the pliant warmth of his. Silky smooth and firm, they moved against her own, lazily caressing.

The hands that had held her arms just moments before came up to cup her head. His palms were large against her skull, long fingers massaged her scalp. Her eyelids fluttered at the deliciousness of his touch, and she let her neck relax, leaning into his grasp.

They were pressed together from breast to thigh. Every nerve in between tingled at the contact, despite the layers separating them. Olivia slid her hands down the solid shelf of Reign's chest, to his ribs. Beneath the silk of his waistcoat and the linen of his shirt, she felt the muscled plain of his stomach and stroked it with her thumbs.

When his tongue finally breached her mouth,

Olivia welcomed the hot, wet intrusion with a moan. He tasted her, nipped at her lips with his teeth. Olivia drew back from the sharpness of his fangs. He eased the pressure, but didn't let her go. Slowly, she eased back into his embrace. He wasn't going to bite her. Thank God. Her body, she would give him willingly, but she would not subject herself to the awful violation of those teeth.

His lips left hers to follow the line of her jaw to her ear. She gasped as he sucked at her earlobe and shuddered with delight as he moved lower, down the side of her throat to the sensitive hollow between her neck and shoulder. His breath was humid on her skin, his stubble a seductive rasp. Shivers raced down her spine. Her breasts tightened, her nipples hardening to the point of aching as a sweet throb began to build between her thighs.

God, how she had missed this.

She shoved herself away from him. His fingers pulled from her hair as she did so, yanking some of the pins out. She barely felt the pain. With her gaze locked on his, Olivia unfastened her pelisse and peeled the close-fitting garment off. Then, she turned her back to her husband.

"Unbutton me," she commanded.

Was that a chuckle she heard as he complied? Yes, nothing else could make her tingle like that. One by one, the many buttons on the back of her gown popped open with excruciating slowness. He was toying with her, damn him. Let him have his fun; she'd have him on his knees soon enough. Literally.

The last button slid free and the top of her gown gaped open. Rough fingers slid over her shoulders, sliding the silk downward, over her arms. More shivers. Her breasts wantonly straining against her corset, eager for his touch.

The gown slid to the carpet, pooling around her feet in a mountain of dark blue. Petticoats and bustle followed, and then he turned her around, picking her up as though she weighed nothing and moving her out of the pile of discarded clothing.

His hands slid around her ribs. His thumbs pressed, popping the hooks of her corset open. Was she really going to let this happen? Was she really going to give him her body and take his in return even as she worked toward betrayal? Yes. She didn't care what that made her. All that mattered right now was how much she wanted him. How much she needed to know the taste and feel of him once more.

Their gazes met and locked as he tossed her corset onto the sofa. His lids were heavy, the dark fringe of his lashes so impossibly thick as he stared at her with passion-bright eyes. No man had ever looked at her as Reign did. No man ever made her feel as sensual and powerful. She held that gaze as she raised her hands to the ribbon of her chemise. She tugged, shrugged, and then stood before him in nothing but her boots and stockings.

"Christ," he murmured, his hot gaze sweeping over her like a brush fire. He reached for her, but she pushed his hands away.

"My turn," she told him with a saucy smile as she loosened the knot of his cravat.

"Yes, ma'am." And he made her chuckle when he began yanking at his waistcoat, popping the buttons without a care.

How could he make her laugh and burn for him at the same time? How could all her resentment seem to fade with a touch? The question lingered unanswered until he yanked off his shirt, and was then forgotten.

He was golden and sculpted, and just as lovely as she remembered. The strong column of his throat gave way to wide shoulders, heavy with muscle and the sharp jut of his collarbones. Crisp, black hair began just below his neck and covered the hard wall of his pectorals, thinning as it trailed down the defined line of his stomach to disappear beneath the waist of his trousers.

Amusement curved his lips, tilting one corner upward. "Shall I continue?"

The combination of the sight of him, the sound of his rumbling voice, and her own heightened awareness served to drown Olivia in a wave of pure bliss.

"I'll kill you if you don't," she replied with a smile of her own.

Reign grinned, his hands going to the fastenings

of his trousers. "That would ruin my night." He bent at the waist and pushed the fine wool to the floor. He took the time to remove his boots as well before he straightened, revealing his full nakedness to Olivia's greedy gaze.

She started at his feet and moved upward past long, firm calves and muscular thighs. Such a beautiful man. The dark hair that dusted his legs thickened at his groin, where his erection stood long and hard and unabashedly aroused.

"Christ," she murmured, unintentionally mimicking him.

This time when he reached for her she didn't stop him. He took her in his arms and kissed her, filled her with his tongue as he pushed her backward, into the sleeping compartment. When she tumbled back onto the bed, he followed after, kneeling over her, dark and fierce.

"Next time I'll take my time with you," he promised roughly. "But after thirty years, I'm tired of waiting."

So was she, but she didn't say that. She'd rather slit her own throat than admit to wanting him as badly as she did, to missing him as deeply as she had, after all he had done to her.

Even as she realized this, her thighs parted, allowing him to slip between. His body was so hard and warm, the hair of his legs and chest prickly and wonderful against her sensitive skin.

The blunt head of his erection pressed against the

dewy lips of her sex. Instinct dug her heels into the soft mattress, made her want to shove down and impale herself on the hard length of him, but she waited, body tight and trembling, eagerly awaiting his invasion.

Reign braced himself on one hand above her. The other reached down, guiding his cock as he slowly flexed his hips, opening her slick flesh and pushing himself inside.

Olivia's body grabbed at his, her muscles twitching in anticipation as every inch of him filled her. She bent her knees, pulling them to her chest so that he penetrated her as fully as possible. Had it always felt this good to have him inside her? Had it always felt as though her body was made to house his?

She could feel the tension in him as he levered himself over her. He practically vibrated with restraint as she gripped his sides with her calves. She trailed her fingernails down his back and smiled as he shuddered.

He pulled out and then eased back in, sending a ripple of pleasure radiating through her. She ached with the promise his body offered. Arching her hips, she met his next thrust, gasping as the friction taunted her swollen clitoris with the promise of release. She wasn't going to last long.

Reign lowered his head and kissed her mouth before turning his attention to her breasts. He sucked one nipple then the other, gently biting and licking until she was writhing beneath him, grinding her pelvis upward, panting as orgasm neared.

Then she felt it—the graze of fang against her hot flesh. Her body shook and trembled at it even as her mind cried out in denial.

He was going to bite her. He was going to hurt her like he had hurt her years ago. Panic tore at the edges of her mind.

"Please," she whispered hoarsely. "Don't bite me."

Reign froze. He lifted his head and stared at her for a moment. God only knew what he saw in her expression, in her eyes. Whatever it was, it made his mouth settle into a grim line. But he began moving inside her again, his gaze locked to hers as he thrust inside her, deeper and deeper, faster and faster.

He was watching her, just as she had told him he would have to that night she first approached him. Was it meant as a mockery, or as a gesture of kindness on his part? It was so hard to tell. Reign's expression gave away nothing, cool and hot at the same time. Olivia clung to him, digging her fingers into the unyielding smoothness of his back as their bodies came together in hot, wet friction. Her spine arched, the pressure inside her building with every thrust, teasing her with the inevitable yet eluding her at the same time.

They were both breathing hard, a remarkable feat given that vampires didn't breathe as often as humans. The only sounds in the room were their gasps and moans and the sound of Reign's body driving into hers.

"Come for me," he commanded, his voice little more than a growl. "I want to watch you come."

He always knew what to say to send her over the edge and his words had the desired effect. He thrust deep and the pressure inside her rose to a crescendo, peaked and then imploded. Olivia's shoulders dug into the bed as she arched into her climax, crying out as pleasure tore her apart from the inside.

Reign quickened his thrusts and then stiffened, groaning out his own release as it filled her. His head was tossed back, the tendons in his neck standing out in sharp relief as the shuddering of his body eased to tiny shivers. When he collapsed on top of her, Olivia held him, savoring the weight of his body on hers, knowing that soon it would be gone.

She didn't protest when he rolled off her. Didn't say a word as he lay beside her, silent and staring at the ceiling. She remained silent when he pulled the blankets up around them. She was glad for the silence. If she spoke now she wouldn't be able to stop. There were so many things on the tip of her tongue, fighting to get out, insisting that she give them voice. Things that once spoken, she would never be able to take back. Things better left unspoken.

So neither of them said a word, but when Reign pulled her to him, pressing his chest to her back as he wrapped one strong arm around her, Olivia went willingly. And when he entwined his fingers with hers, she let him.

She told herself it meant nothing. That his tenderness was nothing more than a manipulative maneuver meant to throw her off her guard. He was using her just as she was using him, and all that mattered was rescuing James. And then she tried very hard not to cry.

Chapter 6

For what might be the second time in the entirety of his long existence, Reign doubted himself.

The first time had been when he turned Olivia into a vampire. He'd never forgiven himself for that, and neither had she, but until tonight he hadn't realized just how badly the event had traumatized her.

Her voice had *shaken* when she asked him not to bite her. Shaken, not with anger, but with fear. Of all the things he would have his wife feel for him, fear was not one of them. He'd rather she hate him than ever be afraid.

He stood by the bed, fully dressed, watching her sleep. The handsome lines of her face were softened by slumber, and in the soft light drifting in from the lamps in the other section of the car she looked young—far too young on a night when he felt older than hell itself. He hadn't felt young in a long time, and the last time had been on his wedding day.

He had revealed the truth about himself almost a month before the wedding. It wouldn't have been fair to her to wait any longer, and love had filled him with the burning desire to be completely honest with his bride-to-be.

At first she thought he was joking, then accused him of cruelly trying to cry off the engagement. He had to show her his fangs for her to finally believe. Her disbelief had lasted maybe ten minutes before she started sticking her fingers in his mouth to investigate his teeth and asking questions about what he could do. His relief had been so great he had been almost giddy with it. And then she had hugged him.

"What was that for?" he'd asked.

Wide brown eyes stared into his. "For having to be alone so long, and for trusting me with the truth."

Reign knew at that moment that he had found the woman he wanted to spend eternity with. He hadn't taken her feelings into account. He just assumed that she felt the same way. He *knew* she felt the same way.

They had been so happy, and not in a fairytale perfect kind of way, but in a real, enduring manner. Then he had gone and ruined it all on their wedding night.

He didn't want to think about it, not when the sting of Olivia's rejection was still fresh, not when he knew it would only make him feel dirtier than he already did. He wanted that former intimacy with her once more. Wanted that happiness, and it was so far out of his reach it might as well be on the moon.

Now, watching her as she slept, so peacefully, Reign rubbed the spot where she had plunged a dagger into his chest. The wound had long healed without a physical scar, but he still felt the tear inside, the searing realization that his happy life was over. She'd left before dawn, and he hadn't seen or spoken to her since—not until she showed up at Mrs. Willet's party and brazenly demanded to see her husband.

Was it coincidence that she had found him exactly thirty years to the day after his awful betrayal?

He had survived as long as he had by trusting his instinct and by being smart. He didn't trust anyone completely, because he knew any trust could be compromised by a threat to something the other person held more dear. For example, Olivia's nephew was the most important person in the world to her, and she would do anything to ensure his safety. Even with their past taken out of the equation, her devotion to James was reason enough not to trust his own well-being to her.

His own strange devotion to her was why he had agreed to help her find the boy. The need he had to somehow atone was what made him go against his own judgment and offer his assistance.

Instinct told him she was a threat. Instinct told him to put his hand around her throat and squeeze until she woke up in a panic and confessed whatever it was she was up to. She would have greater reason to fear him then, wouldn't she, as he crushed the life from her?

Who was he trying to fool? He could never intentionally hurt her physically, not like that. He would defend himself if she attacked him, but he could never instigate violence against her, despite what she may believe.

Although he sure as hell did a good job of hurting her.

If she was anyone else and made him feel this threatened, she'd be dead by now. But perhaps she was aware of that. Perhaps sleeping with him was all part of her plan to lull him into trusting her again.

Rubbing a hand over his jaw to ease the tightness there, Reign pushed these dark thoughts away. He had to keep his mind open and clear. Paranoia would only cloud his judgment and he couldn't afford such a weakness.

Not when his greatest weakness was gently snoring only a few feet away.

Everything about her was just as he remembered, only the reality was far more painful than memory. The feel of her, her touch and taste was so achingly potent. It hurt to look at her. This vulnerability was not welcome.

He took her by the shoulder and shook—perhaps a little rougher than he should have. "Wake up."

"Mmnn." She rolled away from him and burrowed deeper into her pillow.

Reign ground his teeth at the sight of her bare back, the gentle indent of her spine. Her skin was a soft rose-gold, soft and shimmery in the mellow light. His fingers itched to touch her, his tongue wanted to taste her—right in that little indent at the top of her arse. That perfect, heart-shaped part of her that filled both his hands.

He shook her again, and said loudly, "Liv, for Christ's sake, get up."

A deep scowl etched between her brows, drawing them close as she opened her eyes. "What?"

She never had reacted well to having her slumber interrupted.

"We'll be in Edinburgh soon," he informed her as he tossed several of her undergarments on the bed. "Get dressed."

Still scowling, she slid out of the bed. Her hair was a mess, most of the heavy mass having slipped from its pins, and she was still wearing her stockings and boots. One of her garters had slipped and the fine silk of one stocking sagged around her calf. She looked like a whore. She also looked so damn sweet he wanted to haul her against him and kiss her—touch her until she was wet and begging for his cock.

And then he'd tease her about it later just to see

the ire bright in her gaze. She hated when he teased her. She never quite understood what it meant. Neither had the girls in his village when he teased and tortured them mercilessly with boyish enthusiasm. That same enthusiasm had often earned his father's wrath.

"What time is it?" she asked as she stepped into her drawers. A thick lock of hair fell over her shoulder to curl around her breast, and suddenly Reign's trousers were becoming uncomfortably tight.

"Just a little past two," he replied, watching her dress despite the damnable erection he was sprouting. "We should arrive at my home around three."

"Long before dawn," she remarked—more to herself than him.

Folding his arms across his chest, Reign leaned his shoulder against the gleaming paneling. "And in plenty of time for you to make your rendezvous with the kidnappers."

She stiffened—just for a second, but he noticed it all the same. "Yes."

"And where is this meeting to take place?" Did he really think she'd slip and tell him something she didn't want to? Olivia was many things, but stupid wasn't on the list.

"It is not a meeting. They said they would leave instructions for me at the Wolf, Ram and Hart Inn."

Reign went perfectly still. "Wolf, Ram and Hart?"

Olivia frowned at him, but her gaze was puzzled, as she straightened her stockings and garters. "Yes, do you know it?"

"Yes. I've been there before."

"You don't own it, do you?" There was more than a touch of sarcasm in her voice, but she was worried too—worried that the inn might have been chosen for a reason. Chosen because of him. Now why would that worry her if the kidnappers knew nothing about him as she had insisted?

"No. Temple and I got into a fight there back in, oh, sixteen-forty-five? Some English showed up, acting as though they were all powerful. Scared a couple of the barmaids and bashed a few heads. We made sure they knew they weren't welcome."

"The memory of frightened barmaids and bashed heads makes you smile?" She had her chemise on now—more the pity.

He was smiling too. "No. The memory of the fight makes me smile. You know someone wrote a song about it."

She didn't look terribly impressed as she fussed with her corset. "Just what you needed—more reason to think highly of yourself."

Where the hell had that come from? "You think I'm conceited?" He crossed the short distance between them, turned her around and loosened the strings so she could fasten the hooks in the front of the garment.

She snorted. "I know you are."

"You know me so well, of course." Hopefully he sounded caustic to her ears and not as wounded as he felt.

Olivia glanced over her shoulder at him as she fastened the last of the hooks, her expression a mixture of sadness and mockery that stabbed at his heart. "There was a time I thought I knew you better than anyone. Perhaps I am as wrong now as I was then."

Only the tightness of her voice, the thinly veiled pain in her eyes kept him from lashing out himself. Hope flashed deep inside him. She wouldn't still carry so much bitterness if there wasn't some part of her that loved him still. He knew he shouldn't care, shouldn't wish for it, but he did all the same.

Perhaps that was her goal.

"Perhaps you are," he replied tonelessly, pulling the lacings tight once more. He used to play lady's maid for her quite often once upon a time. "I doubt you'll trust my opinion either way, so I'll keep my silence."

She looked away—the only indication that his words affected her at all. And when he finished with her corset, she tried to cover up her reaction to his words by making a show of pulling her gown over her head.

He watched her struggle with the garment. She wouldn't ask him to help her with it, but he would all the same. "Why did you come to me, Olivia?"

She shoved her arms into the sleeves. "I told you, I think the kidnappers know what I am."

"So I'm just added muscle?"

"And you have social connections in Edinburgh."

He stared at her. She held his gaze, but he could see the strain around her mouth and in the faint furrow of her forehead as she struggled with her hair, the unfastened gown gaping behind her.

"That's it?" He rubbed his hand over his jaw. "That's the truth?"

She laughed—a sharp, nervous sound. "What do you suspect me of, Reign, using my nephew's kidnapping as a convenient excuse to bed you again? I don't think such extremes would be necessary, do you?"

More cutting remarks that made his heart beat a little bit faster. How could one woman inspire so many emotions in him? Part of him hated her for being his weakness while another adored her strength and will. Another part of him wanted to strangle her and yet another wanted to tickle her behind the knees until she laughed so hard she cried.

Her reply was honest, but her demeanor was not.

"No," he replied. "Of course not." But he thought of those young men she'd fed from and how they had supposedly looked like him, and he wondered if they had been a way for her to have him, without having to admit that she wanted him.

"Good." She actually sounded relieved, like she thought she had persuaded him to believe her. "Now, be a good boy and button me up, will you?"

She turned her back to him, and just as he had unfastened these buttons earlier, he refastened them now. As he slipped the last one into place, he leaned down, putting his mouth near her ear.

"Are you trying to fuck me, Liv?"

Olivia shivered and stiffened. "I thought I already had."

The mockingly sensual lilt of her voice annoyed him. He caught her by the arms as she tried to move away. Her hair tickled his nose. Her scent made his head swim and his blood boil. He didn't need the extra heat in his blood. "You know what I mean."

Her head turned ever so slightly. The soft, fine skin of her cheek brushed against his mouth. "I just want to find my nephew, Reign. Help me do that and I promise I'll never darken your door again."

She pulled away and he let her go, watching as she walked into the tiny bathroom. He could see parts of her as she attended to her hair at the mirror.

He would help her find her nephew, because he wanted to help her. Let her think he was only doing it for the sex. If she was so foolish as to believe that was all he wanted from her, so be it. He could even let her believe that she had the upper hand over him.

But if Olivia thought that he was going to let her simply walk away from him when all this was done, when there was so much left unresolved between them, she didn't know him as well as she believed.

She didn't know him at all.

He had gotten her a maid.

The girl had been waiting in the bedroom. The housekeeper, Mrs. MacCoddle, introduced them. Olivia had been too busy gaping at the room itself to commit the girl to memory.

"I'm sorry, what was your name?" she asked as the girl began unpacking her luggage. Olivia sat on the huge sleigh bed, still in a bit of a daze, and gazed around at her surroundings.

"Janet, ma'am." She couldn't have been more than eighteen. Just a little red-haired slip of a thing. "This is my first position as a lady's maid, so I hope I don't disappoint you."

"I'm sure you won't," Olivia replied with a smile. The girl's accent was delightful. She'd always loved listening to how people spoke. Of course, Reign probably remembered that. He seemed to remember so much.

Like her favorite color. Surely it couldn't be a coincidence that this room had gilt trim on its pale green walls, or that the drapes were a rich shade of gold that matched colors in the carpet and the bedclothes? He had to have remembered that she loved the richness of gold, the brightness and the shimmer.

Her wedding gown had been a soft champagne-gold silk. He had told her how beautiful she looked in it.

Janet was watching her with a wide grin. "It's a lovely room, ma'am, if you don't mind me sayin' so. The loveliest in the whole house." Her smile faded just a bit. "Apparently the former Mr. Gavin—this one's da—had it made up special for his new bride thirty years ago, but she died before she could enjoy it."

"How . . . tragic." Olivia's mouth was suddenly very dry. Died? He had told the servants that she *died*?

"Aye, but good now that there's someone here to finally appreciate it." The girl flashed a broad grin that exposed healthy if not slightly crooked teeth. "If you don't mind me sayin', ma'am, it's awfully good to have you here."

"Thank you," Olivia replied softly. Then with more volume, "What happened to this other Mrs. Gavin?"

The maid shrugged as she added yet another wrinkled gown to a pile—presumably for pressing. "I'm not rightfully sure. It was well before my time, but a couple of the old servants say that the former master was so overcome by grief that he shut himself up in this room for a month and refused to leave."

"You don't believe that, do you?" It was too fantastical—too preposterous—to think that Reign would do that, especially when all she had done was leave him.

Janet moved on to tucking undergarments away in the many drawers of the large cream and gilt dresser. "You may think me a foolish romantic, ma'am, but I do believe it. I like the notion of a man being so distraught over the loss of the woman he loves that he locks himself in the room he made for her just so he can feel close to her again."

Olivia closed her eyes, her chest so tight she could scarce draw breath. She liked that idea as well. What she didn't like was knowing that Reign had done that for her. It had to be just a story. Exaggeration and nothing more.

But it fit the passionate man she had fallen in love with.

"Do you need help preparing for bed, ma'am?"

Bed. Dawn was still a few hours away, but it was obvious that this little girl had no idea that the former Mr. and Mrs. Gavin were now the present Mr. and Mrs. Gavin, else she'd know there was no way Olivia could be dead. And that meant that she didn't know that Olivia and Reign were vampires.

So Olivia needed to behave as humanly as possible around her new maid.

"Yes." She rose to her feet. "If you would help me out of my gown I can take care of the rest."

Janet complied with another toothy grin. "The housekeeper couldn't tell me what hours you like to keep, ma'am. Town or country?"

Oh God, this little chit expected her to get up during the day! Obviously Reign must have preparations in place, heavy drapes in rooms used during the day to protect them.

"Town," she replied, as the girl drew the gown— it smelled of Reign—over her head. "I'm a bit of a night owl, I'm afraid. And quite used to looking after myself. I'll ring when I need you." Quite used to looking after herself indeed, in so many ways since being on her own.

Janet dipped a curtsy. "As you wish. If that's all, I'll say good night."

Olivia nodded and the maid gathered up her laundry and gowns to be pressed. How the little twig of a girl managed to carry the heavy load, Olivia had no idea.

Alone, she stripped off the remainder of her clothing and set her underclothes aside for the laundry. She should have had Janet help with her corset as Reign had laced her in quite snugly. It took some struggling, but she managed to reach around her and loosen the ties, which made it easier to remove. Once she had the undergarment off, she put it in the drawer, then she donned a silky slip of a nightdress, perfect for this warm weather, and began plucking the pins from her hair. She was brushing the heavy mass, and cursing the tangles in it, when there came a knock on the door.

She didn't have time to ask who it was before the door opened and Reign strolled in.

Olivia paused in her brushing. "Just walk right in, why don't you." She didn't know what angered her more, that he didn't seem the least bit contrite or that her heart danced at the sight of him.

"My house," he replied, raking her with an indolent gaze.

She was far too old to be embarrassed, especially when he had seen her naked just hours earlier, but the urge to cross her arms over her chest was there all the same. She put her hands on her hips and straightened her shoulders instead. If he wanted to look, she'd give him a little taut silk over nipples to stare at.

"Mine too, according to you."

He jerked his shoulders in an abrupt shrug. With an amused glint, his gaze lifted from her chest to her face. "Then you can walk into my bedroom whenever you wish as well."

His bedroom. They had separate rooms, then? Why was that little tidbit almost as disappointing as it was pleasing?

"Was there something you wanted, Reign?" She tried to sound haughty, but it came out rather biting instead.

He arched a brow at her tone, but otherwise

ignored her reaction to him—another effort by him that she found both endearing and maddening.

He held up a crystal decanter filled with a rich, red liquid and two goblets that she hadn't noticed him carrying until now. "I thought you might be hungry."

Olivia's throat tightened, as did her brow. "Thank you."

Reign grinned rakishly, a bright light in his pale gaze. "Bet you damn near choked on that."

Whatever offense she might have felt quickly gave way to laughter. He was right, and she appreciated that he had the balls to crow about it—it made accepting whatever gestures he offered a little easier.

They shared a smile, the poignancy of which was not lost on Olivia. She didn't want to smile with him, didn't want to enjoy his company because she wanted to hang on to her hate. It made everything else easier.

She gestured to the pale green armchairs in front of the fireplace. It was such a warm night no fire had been lit, so they would be comfortable there.

Reign sat, set the decanter and goblets on the small marble-topped table between them and proceeded to pour them each a glass. The warm, coppery and slightly sweet scent of fresh blood teased Olivia's nostrils and sent a rush of saliva to her mouth. She slid into the chair across from him and accepted the goblet he gave her. The cut crystal was cool against her palm.

He lifted his glass. "Cheers."

Olivia mirrored his action and they both took a long swallow. No one had ever witnessed her drinking blood before, until now. It had always been such a private thing to her, and now here she was sharing it with Reign as though they were doing nothing more than having a glass of wine before bed.

They used to have wine all the time. They'd sit and talk—very much like they were now—and they'd share a bottle of Chianti. It usually took no more than three glasses for her to grow restless with conversation and throw herself on him like a cheap whore.

God, she had missed that. Missed feeling dizzy and wonderful after a small amount of wine and missed tossing herself at him and having him take full advantage of her drunkenness.

"I didn't tell you before we left," he began, not quite meeting her gaze, "Father Abberley . . . he's dead."

Anguish, guilt, anger—these emotions tangled together to vie for dominance as they swirled sickeningly in Olivia's stomach. "God rest his soul."

Reign didn't acknowledge her little benediction. "It's not your fault. You know that, don't you?"

She could argue, blame herself, but that only went so far. She felt awful that Father Abberley had been a victim of a scheme that involved her and James, and even Reign. But she could not have known that the old priest would have been killed or even injured because of a conversation with her.

"I know," she answered honestly. "But I regret it all the same."

He nodded, and a few moments of silence passed before he moved on to the situation at hand. "I sent word ahead of us to several acquaintances that we would be arriving today," Reign told her, wiping his mouth with the pad of his thumb. "As I predicted, we've received a handful of invitations already, one of which is for a party Friday night. If you want to ask questions about James, that would be a good place to start."

"A party?" Those were the only words that seemed to make it past the disorientation that clouded her brain.

"Sir Robert Anderson and his wife are the hosts. Their gatherings always draw a number of guests. Dashbrooke and his crowd would definitely be on the list. I'm sure someone there will have seen James before his disappearance, if he had been out in society at all."

Olivia stared at him, uncertain of what to do, or say or even think. When she had approached him with the appeal for help, it had been little more than a ruse, a way to persuade him to accompany her. She hadn't expected him to actually act upon it, even though he had promised he would. And now he had them invited to a party where the man who had brought James to Scotland might arrive.

It was all too much. Too much for her guilt-addled mind to accept. "Why are you being so nice?" she demanded, her voice cracking. "Why would you go to such measures for . . . for me?"

Reign's expression was sympathetic, a fact that fed the anger she was trying so desperately to hang on to. "You're my wife."

"Stop saying that!" The blood sloshed in her glass, coming dangerously close to spilling over the sides. "I was your wife for one night, hardly enough to warrant such devotion!"

"You were my lover for months before that," he reminded her, as though she needed reminding of those lovely nights. "And I've never claimed to be devoted."

No, he hadn't. But he had told her he loved her and she believed it. "Then why hold my comfort or my feelings in such high regard? Are you trying to make me regret my decision? Am I to be made to feel as though I was the one in the wrong?"

His smoky gaze bore into hers, suddenly as sharp as a hawk's. "Are you in the wrong?"

"No, damn it!" She would never admit to such a thing. She had been right then and she was right now. She was doing what she had to do, and she was not going to apologize for it! Not when she had yet to hear one word of remorse from his lips.

"Then you have no reason to feel any guilt."

"If either of us should feel guilty, it is *you*." Pain. Anger. Loss. They were combining inside her to form a dangerous chemistry. "I loved you. I trusted you, and you ruined that."

"Liv . . ."

She would not hear it. Her glass hit the table with a loud thud. "You raped me, Reign! For all intents and purposes, that's what you did when you bit me without my permission."

On their wedding night, no less. He had sank his fangs into her and when she struggled and pleaded for him to stop, he held her tighter. Olivia's hand went to her throat at the memory of the pain as he tore into her, drinking from the wound even as she sobbed in agony. And then, he had made her drink from a slash in his wrist, completing her transformation.

A transformation she would have made not only for him, but for herself as well, if he had only given her time. She would have had time to grow accustomed to the idea, to ask her questions and have some power over her own destiny.

If he had given her the choice.

"It was my decision," she ground out, clenching her jaw to fight back the tears of rage and betrayal as all the feelings came flooding to the surface once more. "It was *mine*, and you took it!"

Anguish played across the rugged plains and contours of his face, darkened his eyes and thinned his mouth. "I'm sorry."

Oh, it was like a kick to the chest, those simple words. They were too late. Much too late. She made herself believe that even as her traitorous heart burst with hope and longing.

"I needed your apology thirty years ago," she rasped coldly. "It's no good to me now." It was a lie and she knew it. Perhaps he did too.

"You won't even try to forgive me will you?"

The pain in his face was too naked and she looked away. "I don't know if I can."

He didn't try to touch her. He stayed as still as a statue, his heart beat low and calm while hers was practically human in its thumping. "Has your life been so awful? Has being a vampire been such a terrible thing?"

She thought about all the friends she had lost, and the family too. She thought about Rosemary and James, and she thought about all the days she had spent alone in her bed, knowing that she would spend the next day alone there as well. The dark-haired young men she had taken some comfort from, and she thought about the man sitting across from her, who had haunted her every minute of those three decades.

"Yes," she whispered. "Yes, it has."

Reign paled. The muscle in his jaw twitched as he ran his hand over his face. "It might not have been, had you stayed and allowed me to make amends, which might have done both of us some good."

There was truth in his words and it stung. Maybe she could have forgiven him if she had stayed and let him try to make it right. But how could he have ever accomplished such a feat? "If you wanted to make amends so badly, why did you never try before this?"

"I didn't think you would listen." His thick dark brows drew together. "I'm not so sure you're listening now."

She glared at him. "What the hell are you talking about?"

He rose to his feet, towering over her like some dark angel. She wasn't afraid. In fact, part of her wanted him to grip her by the arms and haul her to her feet as well. She wanted his anger to fuel her own. She wanted to fight him, physically and emotionally and then she wanted him inside her until they were too exhausted to think let alone fight.

"You are my wife, Liv. That means something to me, regardless of what it means to you."

Why did his words sound like a challenge? Or even an ultimatum?

He continued, "I'm tired of feeling guilty for what cannot be undone. I agreed to help you because I thought it might help mend things between us, that by offering you my trust I might lay claim to yours once more."

Olivia swallowed, but the lump in her throat made it painfully impossible to get any moisture to the dryness there. "What are you saying, Reign?"

"I want my wife back." He sounded almost angry at his own confession. "You either give her to me or get the hell out of my life for good. I'll give you until we find James to decide, but I won't be toyed with Liv, not by you or anyone else."

He turned on his heel and strode from the room, slamming the door behind him. Olivia stayed where she was, her mouth hanging open.

He wanted her back? No, that was too fantastic—too ludicrous—to be true. He had to be lying. He had to be playing with her, trying to rattle her for his own means. He didn't trust her—she didn't care what he said about offering her his trust, she knew the man too well, and he trusted her about as much as he trusted a coachload of cardinals armed with holy water and silver crucifixes.

But he had succeeded in rattling her, if only for a moment. For one brief second she had wanted to forgive him. She wanted to be able to let go of the past and start fresh. But she couldn't. Even if that foolish inclination had lingered, whatever new bonds she and Reign forged would be destroyed the minute she exchanged him for James. And she *would* exchange him for James. She had no other choice.

Unless she trusted him with the truth. If she did that, what then? Would he continue to help her, or would he turn his back on her and leave James to whatever fate awaited at the hands of his abductors. They'd kill him, of that she was certain. Anyone who could kill an old priest, wouldn't hesitate to kill a regular boy. No, she couldn't take that chance, no matter how badly her conscience prickled her. Reign might claim to offer his trust to her, but thus far, other than saying and doing a few pretty things, she had no real reason to trust him.

God, what had seemed such a small task, such a simple perfidy, now seemed so convoluted and uncertain.

Was she deceiving Reign? Or was Reign trying to deceive her?

Chapter 7

"Why can't I dangle him over the balcony by his foot until he tells us what happened to James?" Olivia inquired demurely.

Reign removed his discreet gaze from Dashbrooke, who was standing across the room deep in conversation with another man, and turned his attention to his wife, who was also watching the portly gentleman, a predatory, humorless smile on her face.

She was lovely, in a lethal sort of way. On the outside she looked like a normal woman, with her thick tawny and chocolate hair pinned and curled, her lovely figure clothed in a low-cut gown of wine silk. Her bosom was pushed high, her waist tightly nipped, and the saucy little bustle on the back of her gown exaggerated every sway of her round hips. But inside, Reign knew her to be the kind of woman who would kill if she had to. She had been that way even as a human. It had been something that had attracted him to her, that ferocity. But she rarely voiced it aloud.

"Tell me you are not serious."

"Of course not." She turned her gaze to meet his, a sliver of humor in her eyes, mixed with a healthy dose of mockery. "I merely thought perhaps we would look more like a happily married couple if we actually spoke to one another. Or do you plan to be silent all evening?"

He shrugged. "I have nothing to say."

She ran her palm down his arm, gazing at him as though he was the most fascinating creature she'd ever encountered. She was a good actress. "I doubt that."

"Nothing good."

The hand on his arm was suddenly gone, as was that expression of adoration. "So now, I'm the villain am I?"

Reign plastered a false grin on his face. He leaned in closer, as though he was about to say something charming, or perhaps apologize for making her cross. "One more word about how much I've wronged you and I'm gone. Understand? I will leave you here and return to London."

"You would do that?" Olivia's eyes were wide. He had surprised her. Good.

"In a fucking blink."

She must have sensed just how serious he was, because she didn't pursue the subject. Her mouth tight, she resumed watching Dashbrooke. "Are you going to approach him or are we just going to stand here all evening?"

He took a swallow of champagne. "Woman, you have as much patience as a horny sailor with his first whore."

That predatory smile was directed at him now. He could feel the tension vibrating in her tense form. When this evening was over they were going to either pummel each other or . . . well, sex was a bit like pummeling for them anyway. "You know, your charm was one of the first things that attracted me to you."

He lightly touched his index finger to the tip of her nose—a loving husband's teasing touch. "Just as your sweetness called to me."

She swatted his hand away. "Are you going to talk to him?"

"I want him to come to us. He won't be so quick to defend himself if we let him come to us."

"Defend himself?" Incredulity made her eyes round, but she kept her voice low. "You think the father of James's friend might be involved?"

He shouldn't feel quite so smug at having surprised her, but he did. "Darling, I prefer to suspect everyone and then whittle it down from there."

She snatched the champagne from his hand and took a sip. "Even me, I suppose?"

"No. Whatever your trespasses are, kidnapping your nephew isn't one of them." He stopped a footman for another glass of sparkling wine. Olivia finished the drink in her hand and took another from the tray before the footman walked away. She drank like a fish, his wife.

"How can you be so sure?"

"You would never hurt someone you love."

"I tried to hurt you."

He met her gaze with a wry one of his own. "Yes, I rather think that proves my point, don't you?" Olivia's smooth brow furrowed as she looked away, and hope, tiny and uncertain, fluttered in his chest. *Damn her.* He didn't want hope. This would be so much easier if he didn't want her affection. "Sir Robert and his wife are coming this way," he murmured. "We'll ask them about James."

"What would they know about James?" she asked.

"Probably nothing, but Dashbrooke will hear that we've asked."

She shot him a sharp glance. "Deception is a regular function in your life, isn't it?"

Her words stung—more than he cared to admit. "Right now that's a little like the pot and the kettle, darling . . . Sir Robert, Lady Anderson, good evening."

Robert Anderson was a baronet and quite possibly one of the tallest men of Reign's acquaintance. Being of good Scottish stock, the baronet was six and a half feet of ruddy-cheeked, bright-eyed good humor. His wife, Heather was tall as well, slender with classical features and a quick grin. Both were so open and good-natured that they were impossible not to like, and for that reason Reign was loath to introduce them to the wife they never knew he had.

"Reign, my lad!" Sir Robert clapped him heartily on the shoulder. "What a surprise to see you in this part of the world again so soon."

Reign smiled at the larger man. "Thank you. May I present my wife, Olivia?"

"Wife!" Lady Anderson cried, echoed by her husband. "You sly dog. You never told us you were engaged."

How lovely of her to give him a convenient way to lie. "It was rather unexpected. Once I met my Liv, I knew I had to have her." He put his arm around his wife's shoulders and squeezed. He knew she'd love to smack him, but she smiled instead and took Heather's extended hand, murmuring an appropriate greeting.

"So you're here on honeymoon, then?" Sir Robert inquired.

"I wish the occasion were so happy, but I'm afraid I'm not here for pleasure, Robert."

The big Scot frowned. "What's the matter?"

Reign gestured to Olivia. "My wife's nephew recently disappeared from Edinburgh. We fear he may have been abducted."

The baron and his lady were honestly horrified, that was obvious. "Oh dear lord." Heather shot Olivia a sympathetic gaze. "Is there anything we can do?"

Reign smiled slightly, as though their generosity came as a bit of a surprise. "Perhaps you might let it be known that we are inquiring after James Burnley of London? He would have been out in society. Perhaps you have acquaintances who might have useful information."

"Of course," Sir Robert agreed. "Burnley, you say?"

Olivia nodded. "Yes. James."

The Scotsman nodded. "I believe I met the young man a fortnight ago. He seemed in very good spirits and company. You say you believe he's been abducted?"

The hopeful expression on Olivia's face broke Reign's heart, so he tore his gaze away from her and concentrated on Sir Robert instead. "We have every reason to believe just that, yes." He didn't want to reveal anything too particular. The less he gave away, the more anyone with connections to the crime might then reveal.

"We will certainly let our acquaintances know and encourage anyone with information to contact you." Lady Anderson's expression was both determined and sympathetic. "Meanwhile, if there is anything else we can do, please let us know."

"You're very kind," Olivia replied, her voice soft and hoarse. "Thank you."

After a few more moments of conversation and making Reign promise that he and Olivia would call some evening, the Andersons left to chat to other guests. They would be true to their word and mention James's disappearance, Reign would bet on it.

"Are you all right?" he asked his silent wife once they were alone again.

Olivia glanced up at him, a little too surprised by the question for his liking. "Do you care?"

"Don't play with me, Liv." It came out gruffer than he intended. "Do you think I'd even be here if I didn't care?"

She tilted her chin defiantly, and he knew her silence was about to come to an abrupt end. "I thought perhaps guilt was your motivation. Or is it having me in your bed once more?"

Truth came easily to his tongue. "Neither would be half so motivating, if you didn't mean something to me."

She looked away, her hand pressed to the delectable swell of her breasts. "I'd really rather you wouldn't make such confessions."

Reign studied the delicate lines of her bare throat, how they convulsed when she swallowed. She was not immune to him. He would have thanked God if he didn't think the old bastard would smite him with a lightning bolt. "Then perhaps you shouldn't ask."

They stood in silence for a little while longer until a few couples decided to take advantage of the string quartet the Andersons had hired and began dancing.

"Care to dance?" Reign asked.

A self-conscious chuckle answered him. "It's been a very long time since I danced."

"All the more reason to do it now." He offered his arm. "Shall we?"

It was a country dance called The Tartan Plaid. As most country dances, it didn't have much time for closeness, but that wasn't the reason for dancing. Reign simply wanted to see Olivia smile. Dancing always made her smile.

It worked. By the end of the dance she was smiling, and there was a brightness in her eyes he hadn't seen since their wedding. They danced so much that night.

They participated in another country dance called the Irish Washerwoman, which neither of them were terribly familiar with. They were both smiling at the end of that one.

So when the music started for a waltz, it seemed only natural for Reign to take Olivia into his arms—in proper form, of course.

"I had forgotten how well you dance," she remarked as they glided gracefully around the floor. They certainly looked the doting married couple now, he'd wager.

He smiled wryly. "I think you've forgotten a lot of my good traits."

Her lips quirked, as did one brow. "It does make it much easier to remember all the bad."

Reign laughed—and *she* chided him for blunt

confessions! He would rather trade insults with this woman than be flattered by any other.

When they had finished their waltz, Reign went and fetched them both a glass of champagne. He hadn't been back a full minute when Dashbrooke approached.

"Gavin, by all that's holy, what are you doing here?"

Six centuries might not have made Reign any wiser, but they had made him smarter. For example, just as he knew Olivia was keeping secrets, he knew that Dashbrooke was not the least bit surprised to see him. That might be because he had seen Reign earlier in the evening, or perhaps heard of his arrival the day before. Or, it might be for another reason—one that it wouldn't be wise to attempt guessing at this point.

"Dashbrooke," he greeted with a smile and handshake. "Allow me to introduce my wife, Olivia."

Was it Reign's imagination, or did Dashbrooke's astonishment ring false once again? "Wife? Deuce take it, man. You weren't married three weeks ago!"

"We eloped," Olivia lied—and with surprising jocularity. "It was a whirlwind courtship." She giggled.

Giggled. It was the oddest sound Reign had ever heard, but he realized what she was doing, and he quickly fell in line. "Once I saw her I knew I had to have her."

A hint of a leer colored Dashbrooke's grin as he gazed at Olivia. Reign stiffened, but didn't act upon instinct—which made him want to rip the fat bastard's throat out.

"Actually, I believe you are acquainted with my nephew, Mr. Dashbrooke," Olivia went on, seemingly oblivious to the fact that the old cur was practically salivating over her breasts. "A young man by the name of James Burnley."

Instantly Dashbrooke's expression became one of sympathy. "Of course I know the boy. He and my Reggie are thick as thieves. Tell me, Mrs. Gavin, have you any word from him? We haven't heard from him in days. Reggie's quite convinced he's run afoul."

Most of the color Reign worked so hard to put into Olivia's cheeks drained at the callous remark. "I have not, sir. I was rather hoping you might have some clue as to my nephew's whereabouts."

Dashbrooke shook his head. His jowls made a faint slapping sound. "I am truly sorry, my dear madam. One morning he was there at the breakfast table and by that evening he had disappeared."

"Perhaps your son might know something?" Olivia wrung her hands, giving away her fear though she kept her voice calm. Her eyes were calm as well. Damn it, she wasn't as fragile as she let Dashbrooke—or Reign—believe.

Their companion shrugged. "Perhaps. I'm afraid Reggie isn't with me tonight."

Reign could take no more of Olivia's distress, real or otherwise. "Perhaps your son might call upon us at my town house?" Reign suggested. "I beg your pardon, Dashbrooke, but I really must take Olivia home."

Dashbrooke said something, but Reign wasn't listening. He took Olivia by the shoulders and steered her toward the exit. He didn't even bother to bid good night to Sir Robert and Lady Anderson. He would send them a note tomorrow. Right now, all that mattered was his wife.

Thankfully his house wasn't far and leaving the party early helped them avoid heavier traffic. They were home within twenty minutes.

"You must think me so weak," Olivia whispered, standing in the hall, her shoulders slumped and her gaze sad. "I feel weak."

"No woman who can handle me is weak," he informed her. He took her by the arm and led her to the stairs. "You are afraid. There's a world of difference."

"I am afraid." The confession seemed to surprise her. "I didn't want you to see it. I thought you might use it against me."

Jesus. Was her opinion of him truly that low? At the top of the stairs he stopped and turned to her, making sure her gaze met his before speaking. He wanted her to see the truth in his eyes. "I might use many things against you, Liv, but fear will never be one of them."

"So blunt." A ghost of a smile curved her wide lips. "So honest. I always admired that about you."

The admiration was mutual. "Stop it. You'll make me blush."

She laughed, and his heart thrilled at the sound. "You? Impossible!"

"But it is." Reign placed his palm over his heart in a dramatic gesture of sincerity. "I'm so dreadfully unaccustomed to compliments and you've given me several tonight."

She poked him lightly on that same hand. "I also gave you several set downs, so that should keep everything even."

They shared a grin—just for a moment—before the ease and humor faded.

"We'll find him." He wasn't sure why, but he needed her to know that he had every intention of finding James.

She nodded. "I know."

Her certainty should have strengthened his resolve, but it didn't. In fact, it made the back of his neck feel cold. For a second he suspected that she already knew how these events were going to play out. But how could she, when he was without a doubt convinced that she wasn't involved in her nephew's disappearance?

"There's blood in the cellar," he told her, jolting them into new territory before the air could thicken with tension once more. "Help yourself. I know you haven't fed tonight."

Olivia looked down at the floor, then back to him. "Perhaps tomorrow night you could show me a good place to . . . hunt?"

Did he want to do that? Could he watch her drink from some mortal man when she had never bitten him? When she wouldn't allow him to bite her?

"Of course." He could do it and he would, because she had asked, and that meant something. "I think I might retire."

She glanced toward the window at the far end of the hall. It was black as pitch outside. "But it's early yet."

Yes, yes it was. He didn't say anything. For once, words eluded him.

A long, warm hand closed around one of his. "Come to bed with me."

She wanted him. God, he couldn't begin to describe how he felt. Excitement. Fear. Uncertainty. Bliss.

Reign allowed her to lead him into her bedroom—the bedroom he had specially decorated for her just before the wedding. Thirty years later, did it meet her approval? He shouldn't care, but he did.

She didn't turn on the lamp. They didn't need the light to see each other perfectly. The faint gloom shining through the window was more than ample.

Reign helped her undress and then she played

valet for him. Soft warm hands caressed every inch of him, high over his chest, and low to the eager length of his cock. Olivia kissed him, touched him, sank to her knees before him and took him into her mouth. He gasped at the exquisite heat of her mouth, the skill of her tongue. He came with his hands in her hair, rasping out her name.

Then he swept her into his arms and carried her to the bed. He kissed every tanned inch of her, explored every curve and contour. She was so strong. So smooth and perfect. Her breasts were firm, her nipples like tiny pebbles against his palm and tongue. He licked them, sucked them until she squirmed beneath him, trying to maneuver his body so that it was between her thighs.

But he wasn't done with her yet. Tonight was about Olivia. She was afraid for the boy she thought of as a son, and she was uncertain of Reign, untrusting and rightfully so. Neither of them was right. Neither wrong, but the only way Reign knew to show her that she was not alone, no matter what else might lay between them, was to give her as much pleasure as he possibly could.

So he went down between her splayed legs, to the damp heat of her cunny and he used his fingers to open her for his mouth. He licked her slick, salt-sweet flesh, flicked the tip of his tongue against the tight crest that made her moan and arch against his face. He made her come, in great noisy shudders, and then he leaned back on his heels, his face wet with her juices.

Olivia was gasping for breath, her expression soft and sated as she came upon onto her knees after him.

"Turn around," he ordered softly. "On your hands and knees."

He saw her shiver, smelled her heat and musk. She knew what he had planned and she wanted it as much as he did. She used to love it when he took her this way. It always gave her so much pleasure, and whatever gave Olivia pleasure pleased Reign as well.

He ran his hands over the soft indent of her spine, down to the full curve of her buttocks as he positioned his cock at the soaked entrance to her body. Olivia moaned as he slid inside, and Reign couldn't help but groan himself.

"Christ, you feel good."

She chuckled, and pushed back with her hips, taking all of him inside with a gasp. "So do you."

If those words were meant as encouragement, they worked. Reign thrust inside her with smooth, measured strokes. He reached beneath her and took a breast in one hand and her cunny in the other. He squeezed her puckered nipple as his fingers found her sweet spot once more. Her body clenched at his as she moaned, her knees spreading so she could take him even deeper inside.

Nothing in the world felt like Olivia. No other woman, no fantasy, no pleasure was as delicious and perfect and right as she was right now. Reign didn't even want to think about what that meant. Not now. Probably not ever.

He quickened his thrusts as familiar pressure—a growing tightness—unfurled between his legs. One hand left her breast to grip her waist and his other rubbed ruthlessly between her plump lips. Her back arched, her thighs locked and trembled against his, and then she was crying out in release as damp heat flooded his cock. Her internal muscles clenched at him like a humid vice, pulling his second orgasm from him with an intensity that made his balls ache.

They collapsed together on the bed, falling naturally into a spoon position on their sides. Reign pulled the quilt over them before tucking Olivia against his chest.

"That was one thing we always seemed to get right," she remarked with a trace of laughter in her husky voice.

"Mmm," he agreed, closing his eyes. It wasn't dawn for hours, and yet he could fall asleep like a baby right then. "There were other things too."

Olivia sighed and wrapped her hand around his forearm. "Well, at least we still have something."

Something inside him splintered at the bleakness of her tone. "Yes," he murmured roughly.

It was worse than nothing.

* * *

When Olivia awoke late the next day, Reign was gone.

Her room was shrouded in darkness. He must have gotten up before dawn and drawn the curtains—fortunately for her. She should be pleased by his attention. There should be some satisfaction in knowing that he retained some feelings for her— whatever they were. The side of her that needed retribution for what he had done to her should be positively thrilled that she had some power over him.

But she wasn't pleased. She wasn't thrilled. In fact, she felt rather dirty. Once she exchanged Reign for James there would never be any hope for a reunion between them. And not because she thought Reign might be killed. No, he would escape any situation, but he would know what she had done and he would despise her for it.

Olivia didn't want him to hate her, but she didn't truly hope for reconciliation, did she? That was . . . disconcerting. Certainly not something she wanted to entertain.

Throwing back the quilt, she climbed off the bed and padded across the pretty carpet to the attached bathroom. Cool stickiness between her thighs reminded her of the pleasure she'd taken in Reign's arms. Her body hummed faintly with the memory.

Her mind would be much clearer if he would

just be an arse and stay that way. When he did things like hire a maid for her, or make her remember how much she loved dancing, it was damned difficult to also remember that he was her enemy.

She shouldn't be remembering all the things she loved about her enemy, she acknowledged as she turned the taps to fill the porcelain tub. And there had been a lot to love about him once upon a time. They had been so similar in manner and pursuits. He indulged her every whim, but there was real value in every gift—value beyond mere expense. He had taken her places, taught her new things. Oh, and his acerbic wit made her laugh. His strength made her swoon. And his gentleness . . . well, there might be scarcely one woman out of a hundred who didn't appreciate sensitivity from a man built like a gladiator.

A man who, even though he shouldn't trust her, asked if she was all right after a difficult night of searching for her nephew.

Her nephew. James. She was to go to the Wolf, Ram and Hart this evening for further instructions. Would the kidnappers tell her where to meet them? Or would they keep her dangling a little while longer?

As she poured a little amber-scented oil into her bath, Olivia had a thought that gave her a slight glimmer of hope. If James's abductors sought to make her wait, she could use that time to try hunting James down. If she and Reign found him, she wouldn't have to lead Reign to the villains. He might still despise her for her original plan, but at least she would have a clear conscience.

As if her conscience mattered when James's safety was at stake.

She tried not to think about it anymore as she climbed into the tub. It only made her anxious and short-tempered.

Olivia bathed quickly, washing away the residue of lovemaking from between her thighs. She didn't even know if vampires could procreate. She hadn't had regular monthlies since he turned her, but every once in a while she did. Was there a chance she could become pregnant?

One more thing she was not going to think about at present. Not because it frightened her, but because she didn't want to hope for such a gift. A vampire child—one she could be a real mother to, and not some pale imitation.

A child who would forever be a reminder of how she had betrayed the man she once loved. God only knew what kind of monster it might be. What if she had a baby that never aged?

"Oh, this is foolish!" She yanked the stopper out of the drain and jumped to her feet, spilling water over the side of the tub. "Would that my mind could just stop!"

"Talking to yourself?" came Reign's amused voice from the doorway. "They say that's the first sign of madness, you know."

Olivia started. She hadn't heard him come in. She had been so deep in her idiotic thoughts that he had snuck up on her. That had been happening a lot lately. One look at him told her that he wasn't as amused as he sounded. He had heard her outburst—the suspicion in his smoky gaze was proof of that.

"Then I have been mad these past sixty years," she replied, forcing herself to calmly reach for her towel. "I've talked to myself since I was old enough to talk."

"Brilliant conversation, I assume?"

Her lips tilted self-deprecatingly. "Usually exactly what I want to hear." She could admit that to him, but never to anyone else.

He nodded, his gaze never leaving her face despite her scantily clad form. "Once you're dressed we'll leave for the inn."

There was something strange about him, something removed in his manner and person. He was not his usual self, overwhelming her with his passion and presence. Something had happened. What?

He looked . . . almost sorrowful. Was that sorrow for her? Or for himself? And damn him, she wanted to take it away from him, even when part of her insisted she should enjoy the sight of it.

"Are you all right?" she asked, stepping out of the tub. "You seem odd." In the outer portion of the room, she heard a knock and then her door opened. *Janet.* Reign must have sent the maid up to help her get ready.

"I'm fine." Of course, that was a blatant lie. He didn't even bother trying to disguise it. "I'll wait for you downstairs."

"All right." She watched him go with a haughty lift of her chin. She wasn't going to whine, or insist that he confide in her. His counsel was his own, and distancing himself from her would only make things easier for her. It was good that he was treating her like someone he barely knew.

Unfortunately he knew her better than anyone ever had. And better than anyone else ever would.

Chapter 8

The Wolf, Ram and Hart Inn was located in the part of Edinburgh known as Old Town. On the ride there, from Reign's town house in the surprisingly named New Town, Reign told Olivia of how amazing the tall buildings of Old Town had once seemed, so fantastic to him and his cronies. Now buildings of thirteen stories didn't seem that amazing at all, but Reign smiled as he recounted how he had marveled at the sheer engineering feat of it.

Olivia had seen many changes during the course of her life as well. Thirty years ago who ever would have dreamed that people could whiz about in motorized carriages and speak to each other over great distance via a telephone? She could only imagine the amount the world had changed during Reign's life.

"It must seem so incredible to you at times."

He glanced at the windows of the shops closing for the day and the pubs readying themselves for the evening's business. "Sometimes, it's just sad."

"You think progress is sad? People today survive things that would have killed them in your time."

"Maybe some of them shouldn't," he replied drily. "Not all progress is bad, no. Though I think the ruins of a Roman temple destroyed to make way for some monarch's new monstrosity should be criminal."

Olivia watched him for a moment, unsure of what to think. She had never seen this side of him before. What else did she not know about him? Enough to fill at least a century or two.

"Anything destroyed for the sake of something else is generally unpleasant," she agreed.

Reign's eyes narrowed in the coach light. "Another thinly veiled barb aimed at me?"

"No." How did he always know exactly how to put her on the defensive? "Why must you assume everything I say is an insult to you?"

His lips formed a thin, grim smile. "Because it usually is."

She scowled as she settled back against the padded cushions, putting more distance between them. That wasn't true, was it? "Not this time. Besides, it would take worse than you to destroy me."

His smile grew, curving his well-shaped mouth up on one side as he glanced out the window. "My apologies, then."

"You don't believe me?"

"Don't get all huffy, Liv. We both know you

don't trust me, so it would be stupid of me to trust you."

"I'm not huffy." Her tone alone betrayed her as a liar.

Reign sighed and ran a hand over his jaw. "Darling, you're using me—no, don't deny it. The fact that I'm allowing you should tell you something, doesn't it?"

Was she that transparent? Dear God, he knew her better than she thought. "What should it tell me? That you feel guilty for something?"

"Oh, for Christ's sake!" He fell back against the seat with a loud thump. "Let's stop rubbing salt in each other's wounds, shall we? Just for tonight?"

Guilt. She was right. It was guilt that drove him. That should please her, but like all expectations she'd harbored of him recently, it did not. She would much rather he didn't talk about caring for her—it only made her feel all the more terrible and twisted for planning to betray him.

It had seemed so simple, this diabolical plan of hers, and in less than a week she doubted it, doubted herself. She questioned everything, including the last three decades of her life. She didn't want to question anything. She just wanted her life to be simple again. And it would be, once she knew James was safe.

The carriage stopped, and the tension Olivia felt toward Reign was replaced with another kind. Would the kidnappers actually be here tonight? She assumed they would be too smart to approach her. Even in a public place she could find subtle ways to hurt them. No, they wouldn't come to her themselves, but they would be there watching. They would have a messenger come to her and they would watch her reaction from a safe distance.

"Ready?" Reign asked, opening the door.

Olivia nodded. "Of course."

They stepped out onto the street in front of a large, old building made of weathered stone. Mellow light brightened the windows, accentuating smudges on the glass. It might have been a lovely prospect at one time, possibly even cheery, but now it seemed decrepit and lecherous—like an old rogue who didn't realize his days of seducing virgins were long over.

Good thing she had worn a simple gown of fine, dark blue calico. It was light and allowed her to move freely, and she wouldn't be terribly upset if it was ripped or ruined by bloodstains.

Music drifted outside—rambunctious and lively. A couple of fiddles playing a reel, the kind of thing that made Olivia's toes tap despite her edginess.

"Do you know who you are supposed to talk to?" Reign asked as he placed a hand at the small of her back and nudged her toward the entrance.

"They never said. I will ask the innkeeper if there is a letter for me."

He merely nodded, and with the hand that wasn't warm and comforting against her back, pushed open the heavy oak door.

The noise and smells rushed at her like a wave crashing to shore. Over the years she had trained herself to ignore many of the things that assaulted her sensitive ears and nose; she'd trained those senses to rise when needed and lay partially dormant when not. But at times like this, when there was just so much going on in an enclosed space, her senses were too overwhelming to ignore, just as it was at the hotel in London.

She lurched to a stop just over the threshold, too bombarded to go any farther. The sudden movement forced Reign to bump into her, his chest hard against her shoulders. His hand slid around to her waist, steadying her. Curious gazes passed over them, some with brief disinterest and others with more lingering disdain. Aggression brought out the beast inside her, made her want to retaliate with aggression of her own. Her gums twitched in anticipation.

"It's all right," Reign murmured for her ears alone, his strong fingers lightly stroking her corseting waist.

Damn him for knowing exactly what had happened. And damn him for knowing just how to calm her. But most of all, damn him for making her want to turn around and cling to him for support and strength.

His breath fanned her ear. "Do you want me to ask the innkeeper?"

Was he reading her mind? She stiffened at the thought. "No. Thank you."

Lifting her chin, Olivia made her determined way through the drunken, rowdy crowd that filled the tavern area to the bar—the surface of which was almost as rough and scarred as the man standing behind it.

Small, suspicious blue eyes raked over both of them with narrow intensity. "Wot?" was all he said.

She could reach over that bar, grab him by the throat, and shake him like a rag doll. That would teach him a thing or two about manners. Instead, she fixed him with a contemptuous gaze of her own.

"I was told there would be a message left here for me. Under the name of Gavin." She could feel the overpowering presence of her husband behind her. Was he pleased that she continued to use her married name? Or did he find it a painful reminder of what might have been, just as she did?

The innkeeper's expression never changed. "I'll check."

He turned his back on them to sift through a selection of tiny boxed shelves on the wall, but his reflection in the mirror betrayed that he didn't take his attention off them for long.

Olivia smiled sweetly at him. He'd piss himself if she flashed her fangs.

When he turned to face them again, he had a thick envelope in his hands. He shoved it at her. "Here."

Olivia took it and, out of habit, checked to make sure it was indeed her name scrawled elegantly on the front. "Thank you."

The man said nothing, but he caught the coin that flew over her head with quick fingers. She hadn't thought of paying for such treatment. Obviously, Reign thought the services deserving of a gratuity. She was tempted to snatch the coin back.

"Do you know who left it?" The deep rumble of her husband's voice startled her.

The barkeep pocketed the coin. The money seemed to have loosened his tongue and softened his disposition. "No, sir. Fancy gent who thought himself too good for the likes of us." The glance he shot Olivia said he considered her of the same ilk. "He dropped off the letter, gave me a few shillin's, and then left."

"Do you remember his hair color?"

"He was wearin' a hat."

"Anything stand out?" Reign sounded so calm. Maybe a hard slap to the side of the head would help the barkeep's memory. Olivia wouldn't mind doing the slapping.

"He had a scar on his forehead, like someone had bashed it open once."

That was something—something that they could use. And they had only discovered it because

Reign had thought to ask. She would have taken the letter and not asked about the messenger at all. God, what was wrong with her? She wanted to find these men and make them pay—didn't she? Or was some part of her content just to hand Reign over and walk away?

Reign tossed the man another coin, ignoring Olivia's disapproving glance. "Much obliged."

As they turned away, Olivia started to tear the envelope open, but Reign stopped her. "Not here. In the carriage."

"Why?"

He kept his gaze fixed on the exit. "They may be watching for your reaction."

Somehow, she resisted the temptation to look around and see for herself if anyone was watching. "So?" She simply wouldn't give them one.

"That," he nodded at the item in her hands, "might be intended to get a reaction."

The way he said it, made her guts churn. "Good Lord, Reign. What do you think is in here?"

"I could think of a hundred possibilities that could be as equally right as wrong, and none of them are good. Open it in the carriage, where it's just you and me."

She would rather the entirety of this inn witness her distress than he alone, but he was right, of course. Wasn't he almost always?

They left the inn and climbed into the carriage that had stood waiting for their return. Once inside, Olivia gave in to her screaming nerves and ripped the envelope open.

"It's an invitation," she muttered, pulling the heavy cardstock from inside. Quickly, she raked her gaze over it. "A dinner party hosted by Mr. and Mrs. Hiram Dunlop. It's for two nights hence. It's for both of us. You're mentioned by name."

Reign didn't look the least bit surprised, although there was no way he could have foreseen this anymore than she could. "They have done their research."

A wave of panic swept over her. What if he figured it out? What if the kidnappers underestimated him and Reign figured it out? He'd leave her in Scotland, just as he threatened. God, she'd be lucky if he didn't kill her. She certainly wouldn't blame him if he did, and James would be . . .

She drew a deep breath. "Shall I accept?"

He arched a brow. "I don't think we have much choice."

"No, I suppose not." Her gaze drifted toward the window. She didn't have a choice. That's what she had to keep telling herself. Anger took hold in the pit of her stomach. She hadn't had a choice when Reign made her a vampire—and she didn't have one now. The next person who tried to take control of her life was going to get their heart ripped out, no question about it. She was so tired of being someone else's puppet.

Silence stretched between them, not strained but

pervasive all the same. It went on for a long time as Olivia counted the clip-clop of the horses hooves to keep herself from thinking.

Suddenly, Reign knocked on the carriage roof. They eased over and rolled to a stop.

Olivia turned to him. "What are we stopping for?" They weren't home, they hadn't gone far enough.

"We're getting out," Reign informed her, rising to his feet.

"Why?" Even as she asked, she was following him out into the night once more, the invitation left behind.

He took her hand. "We're going hunting."

She protested but he didn't listen. He instructed the driver to go on home and then tugged her along behind him as he entered another pub, this one much better kept than the Wolf, Ram and Hart.

"It's called The Bucket of Blood." She'd read the sign with some astonishment. "Who would give a tavern such a name?"

"I would," he replied with a quick grin. "I own it."

Oh hell. Why was she surprised? No wonder he'd seemed amused when she asked if he owned the Wolf, Ram and Hart. "Of course you do."

Instead of being hit with a wall of sensory offenses upon walking in, as she had been at the Wolf, Ram and Hart, Olivia found the Bucket of Blood to be much more pleasing to her nose and ears. The music was more subdued, though still lively, and the patrons imbibed a higher quality of spirits. A faint whiff of cigar smoke drifted high on the air, mixing with various colognes and perfumes—all expensive. The bodies were washed and well groomed, and there for amusement rather than trouble.

"Some of these people are vampires," she whispered to him after surveying the room.

"A few, yes. No doubt just passing through. This is a safe house for our kind. They can come here and find shelter and sustenance, but humans are welcome as well."

"Like your whorehouse in London." Both his brows shot up and Olivia allowed herself a small smile. "What? Did you think I wouldn't find out?" At the time it had been one more thing to despise him for, but later it seemed the perfect front for a vampire hideout.

"I didn't think about it at all. Yes, this place is similar, only the only thing for sale here is whiskey and the like."

"Do they have blood here?"

"Usually, yes."

"Then why are we hunting? Why not simply get a bottle?"

Shrewd gray eyes locked with hers. "Would blood from a bottle satisfy you right now?"

Subtle heat rose in her cheeks. "No." She wanted that thrill of choosing prey—the satisfaction of her fangs piercing flesh.

"Then pick someone. Someone who has maybe had a little too much to drink, who won't remember in the morning that a beautiful woman nibbled on his neck tonight."

His words sent a little tremor through her. There was no way he could know that was how she chose her victims. She shouldn't be excited, but she was. Already her skin was tingling as she glanced around the room, looking for someone to taste.

Then she found him. He was young, but not too young, and he was slouched in his chair with a glass of whiskey on the table beside him. "Him."

Reign bent down slightly, and followed her gaze. He was standing so close she could feel the brush of his lapels against her arm. "The fellow in the corner?"

Olivia nodded.

Sharp stubble brushed her jaw, the side of her neck. She shuddered, tilting her head slightly as her gaze locked on the young man. It was an invitation and she knew it, even as the idea of Reign's teeth puncturing her flesh sent a flutter of fear through her. Fear wasn't the only emotion she felt at that moment. Desire was there as well.

"He looks like me." Reign's voice was a delicious, velvety rasp, mocking and seductive at the same time. "A little bit, don't you think?"

Her heart hammered against her ribs. "No." But she was lying and she was certain he knew it.

"Go get him," he urged. "I won't watch, I promise."

She felt him slip away, gone after prey of his own, she assumed. What were they doing? This was wrong, she knew it, and yet she was so very hungry and it had been days since she fed from a person and not a bottle. Blood was what kept their kind alive, what gave them peace and comfort, just like hot buttered bread used to when she was a normal woman. She still took comfort in it now, but it wasn't the same.

She wouldn't hurt the young man, and she did need to feed. With that thought in her mind, she fixed a smile on her mouth and put a sway in her hips as she approached.

He didn't look like Reign at all. What was he getting at? This man was nowhere near as tall or rugged. His eyes were blue, not gray. And his hair was brown . . . bloody hell. He looked like Reign.

That didn't stop her from joining him at his table. She was too hungry, too fixed on the game, on proving something to Reign—although she wasn't certain what she had to prove. The idea of him watching her with this man aroused her, and that was disturbing, but she pushed past it. Reign said he wouldn't watch.

"You're nice," the man practically sighed at her after a few moments of drunken conversation. "You smell pretty."

"So do you," Olivia purred. "Would you like to

come outside with me?" Outside to the alley. She had done this before so many times over the past few years. There was always an alley.

Her companion needed no further encouragement and followed her like a hound out the back of the building. There, outside in the cool air, in the narrow alley that smelled faintly of garbage and urine, she pressed her prize against the wall, skillfully avoiding his clumsy attempt to kiss her. Her fangs slid from the sheath of her gums and she sank them into the warm flesh of his throat, moaning in unison with him as his sweetness filled her mouth. His heart beat against her breast. His hands held tight to her waist as he uttered little sounds of pleasure into the night.

She took only what she needed. Any more and he would be noticeably weakened, and that wasn't right. He had already gone lax in her arms, a combination of sensual pleasure and too much whiskey. She ran her tongue over the holes in his neck, felt them begin to close, and lowered him to the alley floor.

It wasn't until she straightened that she realized she wasn't alone. Reign was there, and from the heat of his gaze she knew he had watched her feed. And she knew from the woman in his arms, that he was about to do the same.

Olivia froze. He said he wouldn't watch, damn him.

Was it a coincidence that he had chosen a woman

with coloring very similar to hers? No, it wasn't. No more than her meal had been. He knew. He knew that she purposefully went looking for men that reminded her of him, and now he was giving a little of that back to her.

The woman had her back to his chest, and was running her hands languidly over every inch of his magnificent body that she could reach. She was drunk—as drunk or drunker than the man on the ground. Her head lolled to the side as her mouth slackened. Reign held her with one arm around her waist. His other hand held her head, kept the hollow of her long, slender throat open and vulnerable.

Olivia's own neck began to tingle. Her nipples tightened and a slow burn built between her thighs. Even as her body reacted, memories of the one time Reign had bitten her came rushing back. The fear. The pain. And yet, she couldn't look away.

His gaze locked with hers as his lips parted, revealing the full distension of his fangs, glistening in the silver light. His head lowered. Olivia swallowed hard. She could see the woman's throat, see it indent slightly in two spots. A tiny trickle of blood ran down the white flesh toward the low neckline of her gown, slipped between the tight cleavage of her breasts.

The woman gasped and moaned, pressing herself against Reign. Her hips undulated, making the skirts of her gown rustle softly. Was Reign hard? Did knowing she was watching arouse him as it aroused her? There was nothing painful or traumatic about this embrace. The woman loved the gentle pull of his mouth as he drank. She wanted more, wanted him. Soft cooing sounds slipped from the woman's plump lips, her cheeks flushed with pleasure. She moved her hips against Reign in blatant invitation. God help her, Olivia couldn't blame her.

She wanted him too. Wanted him to puncture her flesh and take some of her into himself. She wanted him to make love to her as he fed, make her come as he drew her into himself. And she wanted to bite him back. Oh, sweet Jesus, she wanted to bite him so badly.

He released the woman. Her wound was already healing as he gently set her against the opposite wall. She and the man would wake up soon, or in a bit the inn staff who had seen them leave with her and Reign would come out and take them back inside. They would wake up with little but a fuzzy memory of the strangers who had given them pleasure.

Reign licked his lips as he looked at her, his eyes bright as silver coins. She shuddered, so close to orgasm that it would take little more than a touch to send her over. Never had feeding been such a sexual experience for her.

"Let's go," he rasped.

Olivia followed readily. When he vaulted into the sky, she went with him. They arrived back at his house within minutes, and let themselves in through the garden door.

Lifting her skirts, she hurried up the dark stairway behind him, eager to get him naked and inside her, and not the least bit bothered by it. She would have started disrobing on the return flight if it had been at all possible.

She flung open the door to her room and stepped inside. She whirled around, expecting to be swept into his embrace.

But he didn't embrace her. He just stood there, so close she could touch him, and stared at her as though she was a stranger.

"Aren't you coming in?" she asked, and then hated herself for asking.

"I'm tired, Liv."

"Then come to bed." She was hot and needy and wanted him inside her so bad she was ready to explode from it. Pride didn't matter. She had no problem admitting that she wanted what he could offer.

"No." He shook off her hand as she reached for him. "I'm tired of these games we play."

Olivia stilled, the heat in her blood rapidly turning to ice. "Is that what your little display at the Bucket of Blood was about?"

"Yes." He wasn't the least bit contrite either, the ass. "You can pick men that look like me, but they're not me."

"I know that." Could he hear her heart pounding? Why was he doing this now? Why do it at all? Was his pride bruised? Or was this just a way for him to take a swipe at her? "And I don't pick anyone because they look like you." *Liar, liar.*

He didn't believe her either, she could tell from the sardonic twist of his lips. "How did you like my choice?" Bitterness tinged his low tone. "Did you wish she were you?"

"No," she lied again. Oh yes, she had wanted it. Wanted it so bad she was half sick with it.

It was the wrong thing to say if she hoped to make him give in. "You lie, even when admitting the truth would give us both what we want. And you do it because you don't want me to be right. You want to resent me even as you want me to fuck you."

She blinked at his coarseness, even though she should be used to it. "That's not true." But it was. So twisted and perverse, it was.

"I watched you bite that boy. I saw the pleasure on your face, and I know you pretended he was me, just as I let myself believe every strong brunette I bite is you."

Olivia's eyes widened. "You do?" Good Lord, they really were perverse. Beyond perverse. Deviants.

He rubbed his eyes. Weariness radiated off of him. That was her fault. "I'm tired of hoping you'll smile but expecting a scowl. I'm tired of hoping you'll forgive me. I'm tired of wondering just what the hell you're doing here."

She was tired of all their conversations seeming to come back to the same spot. She was tired of him treating her as though she was the one who should apologize. She had yet to see any proof of regret from him, and until she did she would keep her forgiveness close. "You know what I'm doing here." Had he actually asked for her forgiveness? No, but he expected it all the same.

"I meant with me, Liv." He raked a long hand through his hair. "What you're doing with me."

"I don't understand." And in truth, she didn't. Oh, she knew what she had been told to do with him, but that had nothing to do with her feelings or what she wanted. One minute she managed to hold on to her bitterness and the next it slipped away, leaving her vulnerable and so damned needy—for him. Just for him.

"That doesn't surprise me. When you do understand, let me know. Good night."

He walked away, leaving her frustrated and cold, her body humming with a mixture of need and shame. She should be glad he was walking away, that she didn't have to play the eager wife. It would be good to have some distance between them. Smart. Necessary.

Now if she could just make her heart believe it.

Chapter 9

What the hell was he doing?

Reign spent the remaining hours before dawn lying naked on his bed, the sheets a tangled mess around his legs. He was too warm, despite the gentle breeze drifting through the open French doors; and too agitated, despite the relative stillness of the street outside. Both conditions could be blamed on the woman in the room adjoining his more than anything else.

After leaving her he had gone to his room, stripped, and lain down on the bed. Then, not caring if Olivia heard him—in fact hoping she might—he wrapped his hand around his stiff prick and stroked himself to a quick and violent orgasm. At the moment he came he could have sworn he heard a tiny sob of release from Olivia's room as well. The thought of her fingering herself, rubbing her slick, hooded nub, while thinking of him was as mentally satisfying as it was physically frustrating. She deserved to be as horny as he was, but, damn it, if she would just give in, they could have come together rather than in different rooms.

He had to be mad for letting her draw him into her game. If it were simple attraction he could laugh it off as being ruled by his cock, but while that particular part of him would certainly go wherever Olivia led, that was not the reason he put himself through this torture. In fact, he had walked away from her earlier because he didn't want her to use his desire for her against him anymore. Or use her own desire for him as a convenient distraction to keep from telling him the truth.

And he didn't want to face the guilt of knowing he was to blame for all of it.

He was worried about her. He laughed to himself at the absurdity of it. The lies and the games, those were only part of the problem. There was something other than kidnapping afoot and Olivia either knew what that was, or had an idea. Regardless, she wasn't going to share with him. Either because she didn't trust him, or . . . Or what? He had absolutely nothing to do with James and hadn't been in Liv's life for three decades. What other reason could she have for not telling him? Fear? Another man? Was her lover involved somehow?

The idea of there being another man in her life—especially when she had agreed to share his bed—made him want to growl and bristle like an old dog. *Idiot*. He hadn't been chaste these long years, he'd be stupid to think she had been.

No, it wasn't the fact that she might have had a lover that bothered him. It was the fact that she might care enough about that lover to come to him for help—something she had vowed never to do.

Christ. He sat up and threw his legs over the side of the bed. He was not going to lie here and ruminate over this as though he was some unsure, infatuated boy. He was acting like a woman, thinking too much when he should act instead.

The night wasn't over yet. He hadn't checked for news from Clarke, and if that proved fruitless he could always break into Dashbrooke's and see what he could find there. Anything to make him feel as though he had some control.

A dark wine silk brocade robe lay at the foot of his bed and he slipped it on before leaving his room and silently striding downstairs to his study.

Despite being a nocturnal creature, he allowed most of his servants to have evenings off. Only those he trusted with the knowledge of his true nature kept similar hours to his own. In London, one of those few people was Clarke. Here, it was Watson, his butler.

The house was relatively silent. Reign could hear Watson singing to himself below stairs as he readied for bed. In his thirties, Watson had learned all there was about looking after Reign's household from his father, a good man unlike Reign's own, who had retired several years before. Watson would go to bed and sleep until the afternoon when the rest of the staff arrived. No one questioned a wealthy gentleman keeping such hours—after all, weren't all privileged people lazy and decadent by nature, sleeping half the day away?

These arrangements assured that an unsuspecting servant would not walk in on Reign while he slumbered and risk injury should he wake. A surprised vampire was as volatile as a nest of hornets and a thousand times more deadly. And it ensured that Reign had his privacy should he come home with bloodstains on his shirt—his own or someone else's.

In his office, he turned on the desk lamp and sat down in the softly cushioned chair. The only modern convenience missing in his Edinburgh home was a telephone. There was rarely any need for one in his life. The people he wanted to speak to were usually with him, or didn't have a telephone of their own. And he sure as hell didn't want people thinking they could ring him anytime they wanted.

On the top of the desk was a small pile of correspondence. A couple of envelopes obviously held invitations. He'd look at those later. One was a letter from a business associate in Massachusetts who always sent his letters to Edinburgh to be forwarded to wherever Reign was, and the last two were telegrams from Clarke. One was dated yesterday, the other early that very day.

He opened the earlier one first. It was short and

to the point. Apparently James Burnley had an acute interest in vampire lore and was part of some society that got together for lectures on the occult and supernatural phenomenon. The boy had also been overheard boasting to a friend at Boodle's that he was very much looking forward to his trip to Scotland as he expected it would change his life forever.

Interesting. What had the little snot-nosed git been into?

The second telegram was unrelated, but the news within it was even more of a shock—an awful one at that. One of the girls at Maison Rouge, the brothel he owned in London, had been murdered in a brutal fashion shortly after Reign's departure for Scotland. So soon after that it seemed impossible that it could be a coincidence, but that was just his suspicious nature talking. Anything else was too fantastic to entertain.

He looked up as a familiar scent brushed his nostrils, soft at first then growing stronger as she approached. He took a deep breath and then she was standing at the threshold. "Couldn't sleep?" she asked.

He shook his head. "No." She looked so beautiful standing there, arms over her chest, with her long hair mussed about the shoulders of her thin cream silk wrapper.

"Good." Lowering her arms she walked into the room. "It's your own fault, you know."

Despite his better judgment, and the hollowness in his heart over the news from London, Reign allowed himself a small smile. Obviously that was as close as she was going to come to discussing their mutual "frustration relief." "I know."

Sighing, she slowly lowered herself into the chair on the opposite side of his desk. "Any news?"

"One of the girls from Maison Rouge was murdered."

Olivia pressed the fingers of one hand to her mouth as she gasped, her doe eyes widening in horror. "Dear God."

That hadn't been his first reaction, but good enough. He was a little numb actually. Couldn't quite believe that something like this had happened to someone under his protection, his care. How *could* it have happened?

He chose his words carefully, watching for any change in her expression as he spoke. "I'm going to compose a telegram for Clarke before bed, but I may have to return to London for a few days."

Panic flickered in her eyes, followed by . . . anger, then shame. She didn't like it at all, but even she knew death took precedence when all James's captors seemed to want to do was toy with them. "Of course. When will you know for certain if you are needed?"

"As soon as tomorrow evening I hope."

She nodded. "Is there anything I can do?"

It was a simple question, one that almost anyone

would have asked under the circumstances, but it pierced his heart all the same. He might have answered, if he had only known where to start. Instead, he shook his head.

Another nod before her gaze flickered downward. "You have two telegrams there."

"Yes. Another from Clarke. He's been looking into James's recent activity."

Her chin snapped up, all sympathy erased from her features. "You've had James investigated?"

Such vehemence. Was there something about sweet baby James that she didn't want him to discover? "Of course. Are we not trying to uncover why he was abducted?"

That took some of the starch out of her, but not much. She still looked cagey and coiled like a cobra ready to strike at the slightest twitch. "Well? What has your spy learned?"

Reign propped his elbow on the desk and rested his chin on his palm, tapping his fingers against the side of his face. "What is it, Liv? Does he like boys and someone found him out? Did he kill someone in a fit of passion?"

She scowled at him and he smiled. She had a magnificent scowl that never failed to let him know when he had crawled under her skin. "Of course not. Don't be an arse."

She could also rival a fishwife when he pushed her too far. But that would have to wait for another time. This was too important and he was still too shocked by the news from Maison Rouge to engage in petty amusements at his wife's expense.

Reign leaned back in his chair, crossing his legs at the ankles as he regarded her carefully, watching for any deception in her expression. "Has James told anyone in his little group that you're a vampire?"

"What group?"

He consulted the telegram once more. "The Friends of the Glorious Unseen."

"I've never heard of them." She spoke as though their existence relied on her knowledge.

"He's vice chairman." Her blank expression continued, so he pressed on. "He's never told you about them?"

"No." Now she looked miffed. James hadn't told her he was coming to Scotland, hadn't told her about this organization of his. No doubt she was wondering what else the boy hadn't told her, and just what the little wanker had gotten himself into. "What are they?"

"Apparently they have a keen interest in the paranormal, especially vampires."

The subtle widening of her eyes, the startled catch of her breath could not be false. "Do you think the kidnappers might be part of this group?"

"Possibly." He shrugged. "If it weren't for the dead priest in St. Martin's, I'd wonder if this was all some elaborate ruse for James to show off his vampire auntie to his cronies."

Her scowl was back full force. Luckily for her vampires didn't develop frown lines or she'd have ruts to rival a dirt lane after a heavy rain. "James would never do such a thing."

"No?" He wasn't quite so sure that her nephew was as saintly as she believed. "Has he ever asked you to turn him?"

She didn't have to answer. Her face lost all color and she averted her gaze with a quick jerk of her head. "Yes. The first time when he was fifteen. I don't see what that has to do with this situation whatsoever."

Fifteen. Just a boy. A child. "When was the last time?"

She pressed her white knuckles to her mouth. "Last month." Despite her obvious distress, she raised her chin to a defiant angle. "I suppose you think I should turn him."

Laughter, harsh and sharp rushed from him. "Not in bloody hell! He's too young."

"That's what I said." She leaned closer, her fingers gripping the edge of his desk so tightly the heavy wood groaned. "I told him I would never do it. He doesn't know what it means."

"Please don't break my desk. He knows what it means, Liv—he's been around you his entire life. He probably doesn't even mind the idea of drinking blood. It's the spending eternity looking too young to have hair on his scrot that should give him pause."

She stared at him as though he was the most stupid and repulsive of men. It was a first, even for him.

At least she had released his poor desk—but not before leaving slight indentations in the polished surface. "You've been a vampire so long you've forgotten what it is to be human." A faint sneer curved her lips. "That's why you try so hard to appear human in public, and live by human rules, because if you didn't, there'd be no humanity left in you."

Her words stung, but only because they were partially true. It was a fear he had, losing himself completely to the beast inside, but he had yet to face that fear in over six hundred years.

He kept his face impassive. "Meanwhile you cling to your lost mortality, afraid that if you embraced what you are you just might like it."

Her lips tightened. *Touché*.

Unfortunately, just as they knew how to wound each other, they also tended to immediately regret the hurt they inflicted. Of course, cutting out their own tongues was preferable to apologizing, so Olivia moved on.

"James thinks only of the strength and keen senses. I would not have him know the fear of those first few moments as the change overcomes him. I would not have him know the horror of drinking too deeply and accidentally becoming a murderer the first time he feeds."

Horror froze him in place, made his voice deceptively calm. "Is that what happened to you, Olivia?"

Her answering nod was so slight, so stiff, he almost missed it. "I know what you are thinking, that it would never have happened if I had stayed with you instead of running away. I've told myself the same thing a thousand times."

Christ. How could he ever make this up to her?

Rising from his chair, Reign came around the desk to kneel before her. He didn't touch her, but he held her gaze firmly with his own. "If I had been patient and allowed you to become comfortable with turning, you wouldn't have had to learn on your own. I should have been a better sire. I should have been a better husband, and for that I am truly sorry."

The soft tips of Olivia's fingers brushed the ridge of his cheekbone like the brush of a feather. This was when she was the most beautiful to him—when he said something that resonated within her and she let that show on her face. When she let him know that he hadn't ruined everything.

"We can't live on what-ifs, Reign," she murmured, rising to her feet. "I've spent a long time learning that. I'm going to bed."

On his knees, Reign watched her leave. He stayed like that for some time before standing. He turned off the light and returned to his room, closing the French doors and the heavy drapes over top of them just as the first gray light of dawn appeared on the horizon.

Naked, he crawled into bed once more and in the darkness of his room, he stared at the ceiling and contemplated what was perhaps the biggest difference between him and Olivia. He didn't live on what-ifs.

He lived *for* them.

Would tonight be the night she had to betray her husband?

Not for the first time that evening, as she prepared for the party the kidnappers demanded she attend, Olivia ruminated over that very question. If James's abductors chose this night to demand their ransom, she would hand Reign over and walk away. She would. She had to.

And yet, she had dressed for Reign's approval and his alone. Her gown—gold embroidered gauze over ivory satin—had large silk flowers on the left shoulder of the tiny puffed sleeve, that trailed along the low neckline to just above her left breast. Matching flowers decorated the hem and train. Her gloves were the same delicate shade of ivory, reaching past her elbows. Gold slippers with low, curved heels, and pearl inlaid buckles adorned her feet.

She had even had Janet style her hair in the way that Reign preferred, a mass of artfully arranged curls on top of her head that allowed a few soft tendrils to curl around her cheeks. Not the most fashionable of looks, perhaps, but flattering.

And for what purpose, she asked herself. So she could be a pretty Judas?

God, she hoped the kidnappers did want to make the exchange this night. Then she could take James home and resume her life.

And hope that Reign survived whatever they did to him, because living with the guilt of his death might prove too much—even for her. Just when he did something crass or bullyish and she thought she could hang on to her bitterness and hatred, he did something unexpected, something sweet that made him strangely vulnerable.

He didn't humiliate her when they had sex, but he humiliated her by rejecting her when she practically offered herself up like a bitch in heat. He insinuated that James might have played a part in his own abduction, as if James would ever do such a thing to her. And then he expressed such sincere regret for having brought her over as he had. If he would just stop being so unpredictable this would be so much easier.

God, the horror of when she killed her first victim—how hollow it had left her. How could he take that away with an apology? But he had taken it away—or at least diminished it. Those days of hiding from the awful sun in crypts and cellars didn't seem so awful now. Feeding on drunken men—some clean, some not—didn't seem as horrible as she had once thought either. Only the loneliness of that existence continued to haunt her. Until she reunited with Rosemary and became part of a family again. Rosemary had accepted her for what she was, and entrusted the welfare of her only son to her. That boy, that baby, was what kept Olivia from walking out into the first sunrise she found after the death of her sister.

James had given her hope. "You're going to wear a trench in the marble."

Olivia lurched to a stop. She hadn't realized she'd been pacing until that exact second. She looked up, and saw Reign regarding her with blatant amusement as he came down the stairs with the lazy gait of an arrogant male.

He was beautiful as usual. Black and white were perfect colors for him, bringing out the tan of his skin, the paleness of his eyes and the richness of his thick, wavy hair. His face would never be pretty, but that was only because it was such a patently male face. That little smile of his, the one that crinkled the skin around his eyes, was enough to bring even the most hardened of women to her knees. Tonight, it made that hardened woman want to beg for forgiveness while she was down there.

"I had to amuse myself somehow while you made me wait," she replied with more humor than she felt. "Pacing seemed the logical choice."

His smile grew sympathetic. Of course he saw

through her façade to the fear and worry beneath. Thank God, he didn't see the deception as well. "As long as we do what they tell us, James is safe, Liv. You have to believe that."

She nodded—too hard. "I know. I'm just anxious for this to be over."

"Patience is your best weapon."

A tiny bubble of hysterical laughter caught in her throat. "Oh, God."

He came to her then, as he stepped off the last stair. It was all she could do not to push him away. Comfort? The last thing she wanted was his comfort.

"They will be watching tonight," he surmised, brushing his palms lightly down her arms. "Don't let them see your fear. Think of James."

"You are right." It was not a difficult acknowledgment, and the low rumble of his voice took much of the tension from her. All she had to do was concentrate on James and everything else paled in comparison. She would do whatever she had to do to get her nephew back, and for that reason she had to be strong.

"That's my girl. Now, where's your wrap?"

She retrieved the prettily embroidered ivory shawl from the table where she had set it and stood stiff, and close to coming out of her skin, as he draped it over her shoulders.

"It will all be over soon," he told her, his breath warm against her ear. "I promise."

Olivia closed her eyes. She could do this. She had to.

It was a half-hour trip to the Dunlop's home. They shared a bottle of blood in the carriage to dull any hunger that might arise from being in the company of a group of humans, and made little conversation. Reign didn't seem any more eager to talk than she was, and for that Olivia was grateful. The last few nights they had both said more than enough—more than either of them should have.

How easy it was to fall into intimacy with the man who had put her life on this path. And far too easy to forget that if not for him, James wouldn't be in trouble in the first place. This was all his fault and he deserved everything he got.

And so did she.

"You look beautiful," he commented, bringing a lengthy silence to an end. "I should have told you earlier."

She shrugged, trying to ignore the thrill of pleasure his words wrought. "You don't have to tell me at all."

He didn't seem the least bit offended by her snotty tone. In fact, he grinned at it. "I wanted to tell you before we left, but you were gazing at me with such adoration I couldn't think straight."

"I was not." But her words had no effect as he laughed. As much as she wanted to hit him, she wanted to thank him for irking her. She preferred annoyance to guilt anytime.

He leaned back against the seat, lazily sprawled like a sultan in the carriage light. The very picture of masculine indolence. "I took it as a compliment, Liv. As should you."

"I should be flattered that you believe I adore you?" Any cattier and she'd sprout whiskers.

All humor disappeared from his mouth and eyes. "That I was so dumbstruck by your beauty that I couldn't put it into words. Even now I cannot, and I've had this long to think upon it."

Oh. Olivia's mouth opened, but nothing came out. Fortunately, the carriage slowed and gently lurched to a stop, effectively saving her from trying to respond. And Reign, to his credit, did not mention it again.

Hiram and Rosamund Dunlop greeted them immediately after they were announced to the other guests assembled in a pretty little blue parlor. Hiram was a tall, stocky man with red hair and a clipped beard. Rosamund was almost as tall with hair that was as black as pitch and bright green eyes. Both of them were fair with rosy cheeks and bold, jovial personalities. Olivia liked them instantly. Rosamund reminded her of her own mother, who had been a little boisterous in life. She'd also had a temper that would frighten Lucifer himself.

Sir Robert Anderson and his wife Heather were in attendance and Olivia found herself being drawn into conversation despite her nervousness about the evening. Through the baronet and his wife, and their hosts, she met several other guests, all of whom seemed far too pleasant and open to be involved in James's kidnapping.

"We're so delighted that you accepted our invitation," Mrs. Dunlop gushed, handing Olivia a glass of wine. "When we didn't hear immediately, we thought you would not be able to join us, and then poof! There was your reply just in the nick of time."

Olivia forced a smile. "Thank you for inviting us." Obviously the kidnappers had intercepted the invitation. Was it someone in the Dunlops' employ, or had they watched for the post to be delivered to Reign's town house and nabbed it there? Whichever it was, they were arrogant. And she was going to beat them within an inch of their lives if she ever found them.

The rest of the evening followed without incident. Olivia kept watching, her gaze darting from guest to guest, servant to servant. Her attention was rarely held by one person for long, but she managed to participate in some conversation and somehow avoided making a fool of herself.

Reign, she noted, was much more subtle in his surveillance. He could seemingly keep track of all conversation while still keeping an eagle eye on everyone who came and went during the course of the evening.

Nothing happened. No one looked at her with a meaningful gaze. No one made any cryptic or thinly veiled remarks. In fact, it would have been a perfectly pleasant evening were she not constantly waiting for *something*.

Dessert followed the meal, and then the ladies left the men to their port and took tea in the parlor. Olivia would rather have had the port. Once the men joined them, several of the ladies indulged in a little sherry. It did nothing to dull the rawness of her nerves.

They stayed until the rest of the guests began to leave. In fact they were the last to leave, but only by a few moments, after it became clear that neither their hosts nor anyone else had any information to offer them. Hiram and Rosamund were obviously tired and ready to retire for the evening. Olivia and Reign had no choice but to take their leave.

"It was so delightful to meet you!" Rosamund punctuated the announcement with a brisk, tight hug that might have bruised the ribs of a lesser woman. "Please come visit with us again."

Olivia hated to lie, but she replied that she would gladly return in the near future. She would never return here. Even when she found James, she could never return to Edinburgh, coward that she was.

If she found James. Her anger at his abduction was rapidly turning into stark terror. They had come to the party as instructed. Now what?

"What happened?" she demanded as they stepped outside into the balmy night to wait for their carriage to pull up. She spoke softly so none of the others could hear, but it was very difficult to keep the despair from her voice. "Did they change their minds?"

She snuck a glance at Reign. His mouth was grim, the spot between his dark brows furrowed. "I don't know."

"Was it all a ruse? Did I do something wrong? Is James dead?" Her voice might be low, but the agitation in it wasn't.

Reign took her by the arm and guided her to the far end of the portico. No one seemed to notice their odd behavior.

"You did nothing." As always, his mellow voice soothed her. "Their plans might have been thwarted, or my presence might have kept them from getting close to you."

There was concern—real concern—in his countenance. Instead of worrying that he was right, Olivia instead wanted to ease his mind. "No, they would have found a way to get to me. Either you are right and their plans were thwarted by an outside force, or the bastards are having a bit of fun at our expense."

At James's expense.

Their carriage pulled up behind one belonging to Sir Robert and Lady Anderson. Reign led her down the steps toward it, calling out their farewells to their hosts and the few other guests that were waiting for their conveyances.

"Pardon me, sir?" The driver—whose name

Olivia did not know, but he was the same man who drove them every evening—beckoned for Reign to approach.

"What is it?" Reign asked. Olivia chose to watch the exchange rather than climb into the carriage.

The driver leaned down. "I joined some of the other lads belowstairs for some supper. When I come back to the stables, I found this—" he held out an envelope "—on me bench. It has Mrs. Gavin's name on it."

Olivia's chest pinched in anticipation, but she managed to keep silent, remembering earlier Reign's supposition that the kidnappers would no doubt be watching her. The pointed glance he slid in her direction was proof that he was thinking the same thing.

"You were right to give it to us now," Reign informed the man, who couldn't have very well come into the party looking for them. "Thank you."

He turned toward her and Olivia finally took the footman's hand and stepped up into the carriage. Reign followed. Once the door was shut behind them, and the carriage in motion, he gave her the envelope. As commanding as he could be, he wasn't so heavy-handed as to open something meant for her.

Olivia held the envelope in her lap and stared at it. It was roughly the same size as the one she had received containing the invitation to the dinner. Was it a demand to attend yet another party?

"Are we to be led on a merry goose chase?" She raised her gaze to Reign's. "Why have us come all this way just to leave this in the carriage?"

Reign's face was impassive, but anger burned in the sooty-ringed pale depths of his gaze. "Because they wanted you to fret and worry all evening."

"Bastards."

"Yes. They like feeling as though they have power over you."

And they did. They did, damn them. She would hunt them down and rip them to shreds were it not for James. If somehow she and Reign managed to discover some hint as to their identities or whereabouts, she just might do it yet. Whatever sins Reign might have committed against her, what she was being asked to do to him was worse, and if she could turn circumstances to her favor then she would. She owed the kidnappers nothing. Her debt to Reign was quickly amassing into something she could never repay.

She slid her thumbnail under the flap and tore it open. Inside was a folded piece of paper with something inside it.

It was a lock of hair. James's hair. She could smell the soap he used. It was enough to bring tears to her eyes. She clutched the dark silky strands in her fingers and forced herself to abstain from crying long enough to read the accompanying note.

"Three evenings hence," she read aloud, her voice strained by the tightness in her throat, "come to the Wolf, Ram and Hart at midnight if you want to take your nephew home." Relief and disbelief took hold at the same time. She didn't dare trust it. And she was ashamed for looking forward to it all the same, especially since Reign was watching her with such an attentive gaze.

"That gives us two nights to find him," he announced, determination clearly etched in the lines of his face. "Everyone leaves a trail, we just have to find theirs. We'll rescue James and then we'll teach these little pricks a lesson they won't live to forget."

Olivia bared her teeth—a predatory imitation of a smile. "I like that idea." And she did. She liked it so very much. Finding James on their own meant she wouldn't have to betray him. And it meant she would be there to see the look on the kidnappers' faces when they realized their plan had gone straight to hell.

And then she'd personally send them there.

Chapter 10

She hadn't told him what they demanded for ransom.

That little neglected piece of information occurred to Reign as they returned to his town house after receiving instructions from the kidnappers. Olivia hadn't told him and he, idiot that he was, hadn't asked.

That he allowed himself to be so deliberately obtuse where she was concerned should worry him more than it did. He didn't trust her, but he would never forgive himself if something happened to her when he might have prevented it.

Plus, if she wanted him dead, she would have tried killing him by now. That didn't mean that she didn't have some part for him to play in this charade. If he knew his wife, she was saving whatever she had in store for him till last.

Six hundred years of living had made him rather blasé about life. It wasn't that he looked forward to death, but it didn't drive him like it used to when he was human and lived every day like it might be his last. He wasn't totally stupid, however. When Olivia started acting really strange, he would know to be on his guard. And in his heart he hoped that she would have second thoughts before that became necessary.

Watson attended them in the foyer. He was a thin man of medium height with curly blond hair and bright blue eyes. Reign always thought he was too good-natured to be a proper butler, but the boy had proved damned good at his post.

"There's a young man waiting for you in the parlor, sir."

"At this hour?" Reign scowled at his pocket watch. "Who the hell is it?"

"Mr. George Haversham, sir."

Olivia clutched at his arm. "That's one of boys James was with when he was abducted."

One of Dashbrooke's group, then. They had yet to call on Dashbrooke, and he had not been in touch. Perhaps Haversham was there to ferret out information.

"Thank you, Watson. We'll join him." He cast a glance at Olivia who was still holding the envelope found in their carriage. "Give that to me. I don't want Haversham to see it."

She didn't question him and he hadn't expected her to. She simply passed the envelope to him. Ornery and difficult she might be at times, but she had sense. He tucked it inside his waistcoat. "Let's see what young Mr. Haversham wants."

"Do you think he has information about James?" Olivia asked, taking his arm as they walked down the corridor.

"I doubt it. More he wants to discover what we know—find out if we blame Dashbrooke."

"You think he's a spy, then?"

"Yes."

He saw her watching him out of the corner of his eye. "I think you are more suspicious of people than I am."

"Perhaps I lost my trust when I lost my humanity." He had not forgotten the remark she made to him about trying so hard to remember what it was like to be human. She was probably right, but he wasn't going to admit to it.

She turned her attention to the wall closest her, obviously pretending to study the painting hanging against the thinly striped sage-and-cream wallpaper. "I apologize if my remark hurt your feelings."

Reign snorted. "It would take a lot more to hurt me." Bravado, all of it. She could hurt him with the flick of her little finger.

She stopped, and turned her entire body to face him. Years of habit made him pause as well. "Have the centuries made you impervious to pain as well?"

He couldn't tell if she was teasing or making a dig. He smiled at her all the same, self-awareness lending a crooked tilt to his lips. "Your leaving me just set the bar a little higher, I guess."

"It hurt me as well."

"I know." He had handled things badly and they both paid for it.

He didn't wait for her reaction. The baring of his soul was not something he wanted reflected back at him.

She was two steps behind him when he entered the parlor and found Haversham sitting on the cherrywood and ivory brocade sofa. The young man rose when he saw them. He was thin and had yet to outgrow the lankiness that some young men developed in their formative years. "Mr. and Mrs. Gavin."

Christ, that sounded good. Reign wanted to like him based on that alone. "Mr. Haversham."

"I apologize for such a late visit, especially as no formal introduction has been made between us, but I thought perhaps my friendship with James might grant me a little familiarity."

Well spoken, and said with just enough genuine nervousness that it didn't sound rehearsed. The boy fidgeted a little, regarding both of them—especially Reign—with something that looked strangely like awe.

"Of course," Olivia assured him. "Please, sit."

Knowing his manners, Haversham waited until she had sat down on a nearby chair before seating himself once more. Reign followed suit, frowning slightly under the eager glances the boy kept shooting in his direction.

He knows. This certainty had no grounds, but Reign didn't need them. Every instinct he had was screaming that Haversham was well aware of both his and Olivia's true natures. He knew they were vampires.

And he was more awed by that than frightened. *Christ, James had told.* The little bastard had betrayed his own aunt for popularity with a group that no doubt believed that immortality was all gothic romance, dark sighs, and forbidden hungers.

Reign hoped James's kidnappers had a penchant for buggery.

"Have you information regarding James's disappearance?" Olivia asked, her gaze flicking back and forth between them. Could she not tell what her nephew had done? Surely she didn't think Haversham looked at everyone he met with this much wonder.

"No, ma'am." He switched his attention to Olivia. Reign saw the boy's eyes widen just a fraction. He might laugh were this the least bit amusing. Christ only knew what James had told the boy about her. "Reggie mentioned you were looking for James. I rather hoped you might have news for me."

Spy. Too bad he couldn't enjoy being right. "Unfortunately we've yet to learn anything," Reign answered before Olivia could give information away.

The young man looked crestfallen. "Oh."

"Tell me, Mr. Haversham," Reign leaned back in his chair, crossing one ankle over his thigh, "why did none of you go to the authorities when you noticed James was gone?"

Olivia looked very much interested in the answer to that as well. Haversham regarded them both with wide-eyed innocence.

"Until you two showed up, no one thought he was missing. We all thought he up and went back to London. He took all his things."

In his peripheral vision, Reign caught Olivia looking at him in confusion. She was a smart woman. She knew no one packed for an abduction. So had the kidnappers taken his things to make it look as though James had simply left? Or had James staged his own kidnapping?

Or was Mr. Haversham spouting bullshit.

"How interesting," Reign allowed. "That's a nasty scar on your forehead, sir. Mind if I ask how you got it?" He cast a quick glance at Olivia. From the glint in her eyes he knew that she was thinking about the barkeep at the Wolf, Ram and Hart, and the scar he'd told them the kidnapper's messenger had on his forehead. It might be a coincidence. Haversham was jittery, but he didn't seem the coldhearted abductor type.

The young man touched the scar, his expression one of fondness, oddly enough. "Cricket ball a few years back. We won the match, regardless."

Reign smiled politely. "Congratulations." He paused. "You don't by chance know anything about the Friends of the Glorious Unseen?"

Haversham laughed, not at all thrown by the question. Had he been expecting it? "You mean that group who believes in ghosts and goblins? I've heard of them. James talked about them all the time." His humor died quickly. Too quickly. "Do you suspect that they had something to do with his disappearance?"

Reign smiled tightly. "I'm told that I am suspicious by nature."

Young Mr. Haversham didn't quite seem to see the relevance in that statement.

"So you don't belong to the group, then?" It was Olivia who asked.

The boy shook his head. "I don't believe in such stuff—no offense to James, of course."

Of course. The little bugger was lying through his teeth. He believed all right. Not only believed, but he *embraced*. If Reign rose to his feet right now, offered the boy his hand, the foolish git would no doubt drop to his knees and press his forehead to Reign's knuckles.

He could think of a better use for his knuckles.

"Is there anything you can think of that might help us find James?" Reign tried to keep his voice low, gentle even, with just a hint of weariness. He wasn't about to sit around all night with this tosser.

Haversham thought for a moment. Then his face brightened. "He did tell me about a chum of his from that Unseen group. Fellow by the name of Allbright. Maybe he knows something."

An expression of such hopefulness bloomed in Olivia's countenance that Reign nearly threw Haversham through the wall for putting it there.

"Thank you for stopping by, Mr. Haversham." Reign rose to his feet. "You are a good friend to James." He lied so easily he almost made himself believe it.

They shook hands and Reign saw him out. When he returned to the parlor, Olivia was standing by the window, with her face lifted, just as she had been that night when she first came to him in London. Praying.

"Has He answered yet?" he asked roughly, rubbing his hand over his jaw. He needed to shave. He needed to get the hell out of this situation.

Her head lowered, but she didn't turn. Ignoring his barb she spoke softly, "You think Haversham was lying, don't you? About all of it."

He wasn't going to lie to her. "Not all. Most."

She touched her fingers to the glass. "I wish James had run off with friends. I could be angry then, instead of so worried."

"Liv, we don't know that he didn't run off."

Now she turned, whiskey eyes flashing. "But you saw what they did to Father Abberley!"

The priest had been a bit extreme, but the old

man hadn't been worth something to them. Now he lied to her. "That might have been an accident."

She made a huffing noise. She didn't believe it anymore than he did. "People don't accidentally bash someone's skull in, Reign."

He could. So could she, if she didn't think about how much force she was exerting.

"And I resent you insinuating that James might be involved." Color rose high in her cheeks as her voice gained strength. "He would never put me through this!"

When he thought of all the worry and heartache he had put his own mother through, Reign knew he could argue her logic, but he didn't. Arguing wouldn't make her see anything but what she wanted. Right now she needed to believe that her precious little boy—and there was no doubt that she thought of James as her own son—was exactly what she wanted him to be.

"George Haversham knows I'm a vampire—it was all over his face. If he knows about me, he probably knows about you as well." No "probably" about it. "Either James told him, or someone James told decided to blab as well."

She shook her head, jaw set. "James wouldn't do that."

God, he could shake her for having such faith in the boy. A boy that age would do and say damn near anything to impress his friends. Why couldn't she have such faith in him?

Time to try another tactic. "What did they ask for as ransom?"

"They didn't."

He arched a brow—something he seemed to be doing a lot lately during this unbelievable excursion. "Doesn't that strike you as strange?"

Her gaze averted, Olivia shrugged. "I haven't had much experience with abductions."

Vague comments. Hidden gaze. Christ, did the woman actually think he believed any of this? Did she think him that much of a fool? Or was she hoping he'd realize she was playing him? Why the hell couldn't she just be honest?

"They want you to meet them. They're willing to kill to bring you to them. What does that tell you?"

Her gaze snapped to his. Her expression was cool now, even remote. She'd taken great pains to make it that way. "It tells me that my nephew is in serious danger."

"What else?"

She pushed away from the window, shoving the sofa out of her way as she approached him. "That it was a mistake to ask you to come with me. You want to make James a criminal, when he is the victim!"

She probably wouldn't believe that her precious boy gambled, drank, or whored either. Beautiful little idiot.

"It tells me that they want something, Liv. You."

She gaped at him. "Me?"

Why was that so hard for her to comprehend? "Surely you must have begun to wonder once we learned about the Friends of the Glorious Unseen?"

"You're talking madness."

Again, she avoided his gaze as she shook her head. "They have made demands, haven't they?" Again, it was instinct that drove him to that conclusion. "Do they want you to turn them all into vampires? Do they want your blood? Is that why you brought me? Am I supposed to save you, or give my blood as well? What do they want from you?"

She stilled, only her eyes lifted. Something awful flickered in her gaze—disgust perhaps. Or maybe fear. Or guilt. He had struck a nerve there, but with what? "I told you, they've made no demands."

"Jesus, Liv." His hands tore through his hair before he thrust them in the air in frustration. "What are you hiding?"

"Nothing." She moved past him, shoving a chair aside and sending it skittering across the floor on its side. "Will you leave it alone?"

He grabbed her arm, swinging her around to face him. "Liv, tell me. You can trust me."

She jerked free with a force that shocked him. "No, I can't!"

There it was. Out in the open like a whore's drawers on a Friday night. What was this emotion?

Shame? Surprise? Whatever it was, it was followed by a strange numbness that started in the middle of his chest and radiated outward.

There was really no point in continuing, was there?

"Fine." Pivoting on his heel, he headed toward the door.

She followed after him. Christ, would she not give him a moment's peace? "Where are you going?"

"The Bucket of Blood. There's someone there I need to see." After what she had just said, that was all the information he was going to offer.

"Your victim from the other night?"

He stopped and glanced over his shoulder, his jaw tight at her snide tone. She pressed her fingers to her lips, as though she wished to take the words back.

Would that she could take them back and choke on them.

"Someone else." It was more than she deserved, but he wasn't going to let her think he was going there to get off when he was trying to find her damn nephew.

She took another step forward, as though she was afraid to approach, but too stubborn to let him see it. "If it's about James, I want to come with you."

He shrugged. "Do whatever you want. I don't fucking care." But he did, he silently admitted as she followed after him. After all he had done to try and win her trust, it hadn't been enough. It would never be enough.

If he thought she had broken his heart when she left him, it was nothing compared to what she was doing to it now.

"Reign, please listen."

He didn't stop, and if he was listening he didn't let on. Even as they exited the attic and climbed onto the roof of the town house, he refused to acknowledge her.

He had told her he didn't care if she came with him and that was the last he had spoken. She chased after him, trying to apologize for her callous outburst, but he refused to hear it.

"You have no right to be angry!" she exclaimed, following him to the edge of the roof. "Why would I trust you after what you did to me?"

He met her gaze with one so cold and remote it chilled her to the marrow. "Because I agreed to help you find James even though I knew you weren't telling me the entire story. Because I'm still here trying to help you even though you lie to me every chance you get."

When he phrased it like that, it made her sound like such a bitch. It made her feel . . . wrong. "Why *are* you still here?"

"Because once this is done, you'll leave again and I'll have some peace." There wasn't one flicker of emotion in his voice or expression. "Rest assured, darling, I won't spend the *next* thirty years wishing you'd come back."

It was just as well that she didn't know what to say, because he didn't give her a chance to say anything. He simply vaulted off the roof into the sky.

The man who took his coach everywhere, was flying—and he didn't seem to care if anyone saw him or not.

Hell and damnation. She really had pissed him off.

No. The realization hit her as she took to the sky after him. He wasn't angry. He was hurt. She hadn't meant to do that. He had started saying those things about James, making her wonder if the boy she thought of as her own son could possibly turn on her like that. Of course, he couldn't, but it made her think about how she had brought Reign to Scotland for the sole purpose of betraying him and it made her sick with shame.

All she wanted was James safe. But now, there was a voice in the back of her head asking, what exactly did James want? How could she doubt her own flesh and blood?

Whatever the answer to that question might be, Olivia didn't have a chance to ponder it further. Reign was descending toward the buildings of Old Town, and if she wasn't careful she might lose him amongst the narrow alleys and have to track him by smell—something she wasn't terribly good at.

They touched ground in the alley behind the Bucket of Blood, the same place where he had made her watch as he fed from a cheap imitation of herself. Made her want to be that woman. A shiver racked her at the seductive memory.

Reign leered at her over one broad shoulder, his face shadowed in the darkness. "Maybe your hunt from the other night will be here."

She lifted her chin at his obvious attempt to needle her. "Yours as well."

He didn't blink. "I'm not hungry."

This was too much. "Reign . . ." She'd barely said his name before he was on her, carrying her backward until her shoulders hit the rough stone wall. A cough of mortar dust rose up around them from the impact. His mouth captured hers, his lips and tongue assaulting her with dizzying thoroughness. She clung to his shoulders, digging her fingers into the soft wool of his coat. He smelled divine. Tasted heavenly and felt deliciously sinful. Her body instantly reacted to his touch, tightening and warming in all the right places.

And when he pulled away, every inch of her cried out in grief.

"You say you don't trust me," he rasped. "Your body says something else."

She opened her mouth, but he stopped her by placing a rough finger over her lips. "One is a lie, Liv. Don't say a word until you figure it out."

He left her standing there as he turned and

walked away. She hesitated a moment, pulling herself together. God, the effect he had on her. Worse, he knew it.

When she entered the pub, the smells of cigar smoke and ale greeted her. The music was little more than a lone fiddler on a stool, tapping his boot in time to the lively tune he played.

Reign was at the far end of the room, talking to a short, heavily muscled man who stood behind the bar. He was not the same one who had been there the last time they visited. She approached, in time to hear the man speak, "There was a kid in here a week or so ago, lookin' for you."

"A kid?" Olivia moved to stand beside Reign. She couldn't stop from casting a hopeful glance at him. He stared straight ahead. "Was his name James Burnley?"

The man behind the bar studied her the way one might study a painting or a tree. "You Olivia?"

Her brows shot up. "Yes. Have we met?"

The man shook his head. "Naw. The kid mentioned you too. Said he thought he should get acquainted with the place since his 'uncle' Reign owned it." He shot Reign a bored glance. "Thought he was cock of the walk, that one."

Reign looked grim. "Don't they all. What else was he saying, Mac?"

The barkeep leaned forward over the thick forearms he rested on the polished oak. When he spoke, his voice was low, for their ears only. "He was talkin' loud about vampires. Tellin' his friends stuff he should have had sense not to tell."

Olivia bristled a bit, but it didn't last. James should have known better. He had lived with her secret for most of his life. She thought he respected her enough to keep it.

Perhaps when it came to James and Reign, she was putting her trust in the wrong man. She shook that thought off as soon as it came. James was family. Reign was . . . her husband. Damn it, this wasn't helping. She turned her attention back to the man in front of her.

"Then he got all belligerent when one of his fellas asked when was he going to become a vampire. They rode him hard for a bit after that, about how his auntie wouldn't turn him unless he ate his peas or said his prayers—foolishness." He turned to Olivia. "If you don't mind me saying, ma'am you ought to have beaten that boy more."

Olivia's lip curled. What the hell did this man know of being a woman alone trying to raise a child? She had done the best she could despite that she could never be a proper mother—could never run with him in the sun. Never take him to the shore.

"I do mind," she said softly.

Reign placed a hand on her arm and she looked up. There was no sympathy in his cool gaze, but there was something there that told her he understood how hard it had been for her. Slowly, she relaxed.

Mac watched her warily, but he didn't apologize. "That was the first and last time I saw him, but a couple of his friends have been in since."

"Any trouble?" Reign asked.

"Naw. Come in, have a drink and left. Got the feeling they were waiting for something." He shot a pointed gaze at Reign. "Or someone."

Reign shifted beside her, his attention still focused on the shorter, stockier man. "That's very interesting. Did you happen to hear any of these boys mention a group called the Friends of the Glorious Unseen?"

Mac chuckled. "They did. The four of 'em were right enthusiastic about it too. Said they were senior members. Left me a pamphlet for a meeting they planned to have here in Edinburgh."

"May I see it?" Reign asked.

Mac turned to sort through a pile of papers on a shelf behind him. While he was distracted, Olivia turned to Reign. "George Haversham said he didn't belong to the Friends."

He tilted his head. "Makes you wonder what else he was lying about, doesn't it?"

It did. It also made her wonder just what sort of "friends" her nephew had fallen in with.

"Here it is." As he came back around to face them, Mac offered Reign a folded piece of paper. On the front was the title: "Mating Habits of the Vampyre: A discourse on the male and female of the species."

"Oh, Christ," Reign muttered. Olivia shook her head in agreement as she perused the leaflet from her spot beside him. "Thank you, Mac."

They pulled away from the bar. Mac waved farewell and went off to attend to a thirsty patron.

Olivia glanced at him as they walked across the wooden floor. "There's a lecture scheduled the night after next. Shall we go?"

Reign, pamphlet in hand, stuffed the paper inside his coat, where he had stored the note from the kidnappers earlier. He barely looked at her. "Of course. It may lead us straight to James."

"And then you'll be rid of me." The words leaped out before she could even think of stopping them. Before she could think at all.

"Yes," he agreed, moving toward the exit like a big cat prowling his territory. "Then we'll all be happy, won't we?"

Oh yes. She'd have her nephew and her life back. She could go back to Clovelly and try to spend the next few decades forgetting what she had done—forgetting Reign. Of course she would be happy. And the wetness burning her eyes? Those were tears of joy.

Chapter 11

William Dashbrooke was not stupid. He knew better than to visit his "guest" in the evening. He went during the day, when the sun was high in the sky and no vampire could survive for longer than a few minutes.

He couldn't risk the operation by having Reign or Olivia —he had studied them so long he thought of them by their Christian names—follow one of them from his Edinburgh address to this little country cottage just a few miles outside the city. An unexpected visit could lead to catastrophe, and the vampires would be the victors.

No, it was imperative that they draw the vampires to them at the right time, when they would be able to capture the pair of them, hopefully with few casualties. They had lost several men in England taking Temple. That vampire had seemed to expect them, despite the fact that they had purposefully timed their efforts with an archaeological dig. The chalice he protected was long gone, the pieces scattered to the rest of his brethren. Snarling and terribly strong with feral strength, Temple had killed two men before they could get one dart into him. It took three darts of the poison designed for vampires to bring the creature to his knees.

Amazing beings, these vampires. Demi-gods and they didn't even know it. The five of them, and their women would be a glorious sacrifice—and a necessary one.

Now with so many members of the Order awaiting the arrival of the other vampires, it was increasingly important that everything here go according to plan.

But there was a backup just in case. Always a backup. Vampires were fast and strong and practically invulnerable. The only way to beat them was to be smarter. Fortunately, vampires weren't very smart. Immortality tended to make them comfortable and lazy—they thought of themselves as invincible. They would go wherever the Order wanted, assuming they could fight their way out of any situation.

Not this time.

As he entered the cottage, he thought of how fortunate he had been to have young James Burnley fall into his hands. The lad saved him so much work, and provided the perfect situation for bringing Reign right to them.

Reign would never resist Olivia's call, and Olivia would not allow anything to happen to her precious nephew, blaming herself for the boy's lack of a mother.

Perfect, really.

He found James in the little, sunny dining room, just sitting down for luncheon with Reggie. His son was proving to be less of a disappointment than usual.

"Good afternoon, lads," Dashbrooke greeted them heartily as he sat down with them. "How are you this fine day?"

The young men made their replies and offered him some of their meal—good boys that they were.

"Have you seen my aunt?" James asked, spearing a thick slice of cold ham with his fork.

Dashbrooke regarded the boy with a smile. James looked very much like his aunt in terms of coloring. He was tall and thin, with a handsome countenance that Dashbrooke's own son Reggie coveted. Poor Reggie. He took after his grandfather.

"I have," Dashbrooke replied. "She's very anxious to see you again."

James smiled, but there was a hint of anxiety about it. "She's going to be so angry with me."

"Tell her you had no choice. She'll forgive you."

"Once she brings Reign to you, you'll keep your end of the bargain?"

Dashbrooke nodded. "You'll get exactly what you asked for, dear James. Small payment for all you've done for us."

James's grin grew.

"What about me?" Reggie demanded.

Dashbrooke humored his son with a wide grin. "You too, my boy."

He wasn't about to inform Reggie that once this was over the boy would be heir to more power than he could ever imagine. In the same vein he didn't have the inclination to inform James that while he intended to keep his bargain all right, it would no doubt end in the boy's death.

No, he hadn't the inclination at all.

Just minutes after midnight, Reign and Olivia entered William Dashbrooke's house via a second-floor balcony.

"Are you certain Dashbrooke is out for the evening?"

Olivia's voice was an erotic shiver down his spine as Reign closed the doors behind them. She had a low voice, rich and lush, and when she talked softly like this, it was like being stroked by velvet. "Yes."

Reign had never been much of a housebreaker or thief—that had been Saint's job. His own special talent seemed to be being able to discern when a situation was as it ought to be or if there was something underhanded afoot.

And he *knew* that Dashbrooke's house was completely empty save for the servants belowstairs, just as he knew that Olivia was warring within herself. Over James, and over him. He told himself he didn't care about the outcome.

He'd been a damn fool to think he could win her back. A damn fool to want her.

He wanted her still.

"Reign, this is ridiculous. What are we looking for?"

"Anything that looks important." He didn't bother to look at her. It hurt to look at her and he was getting tired of hurting. He should be harder than that.

He heard her sigh behind him. "That's so helpful, thank you."

He looked at her now, numbing himself against the sight of her face in the gloomy night. "We both know Dashbrooke and James's friends are involved somehow, or at the very least know more than they're telling. If we're going to find any clue as to what happened to James or where he is, we'll find it here."

Her expression softened, and with it went his heart. "All right. Where do you want to start?"

"The bedrooms. Anything of personal value will be there."

The room they were in was obviously a guest room. It had been cleaned and made up neat and tidy for a future guest. There was nothing there. Still, Reign would be remiss if he didn't give the room at least a cursory examination, so he checked the closet and the chest of drawers as well as under the bed. Just as he expected, there was nothing of consequence.

The next room—down the narrow hall and on the left, belonged to George Haversham, proven by the monogrammed underdrawers draped over the back of a chair.

"Disgusting," Olivia griped as they stepped inside.

Reign had to agree. The room had obviously been tidied by the maids that morning, but Haversham had left clothing scattered all over the place. And a used, uncovered chamber pot sat near the bed, lending a particularly pungent aroma to the room.

Quickly, they picked through the dresser, armoire, and small writing desk. They even searched his luggage. All they found was a leaflet for the Friends of the Glorious Unseen, and a pair of women's drawers.

Reign held up the flimsy linen undergarments with one finger and chuckled. "Think Haversham got these from an obliging tart? Or does he wear them himself?"

Olivia grinned. "Either way, I don't want to know."

For that second, they were as they had been before he'd ruined everything, and the memory of those days sliced through him like a blade. His smile faded and he tossed the drawers back into the dresser where he had found them. "We're done here."

The next room was Reggie's. It was notably

cleaner and more pleasant smelling than Haversham's. Reggie also had a leaflet for the meeting
of "The Friends." On it he had drawn pictures of
little vampire faces. The fangs, tiny v-shapes.

"Obviously he missed his calling as an artist,"
Olivia quipped, and Reign allowed a smile.

Reggie kept a notebook. Every page was a
new list with titles ranging from, "Things not to
say to Young Ladies" to "Ways to be Less of a
Disappointment."

"That's a little sad," Olivia remarked. "Look.
Number twenty-three: 'Try to be less of a nitwit.'
Poor thing."

Reign rolled his eyes. "Every boy his age is a
nitwit."

"Were you?"

He thought about it, but it was so long ago, not
many memories came forward. His only memories
of having felt like an idiot where when his father
called him one. Fortunately, the centuries had
dulled those to the point where they seemed to be
the memories of another man.

"Undoubtedly," he told her. "I just didn't realize
it at the time."

She set the notebook back in its place. "Someone has made certain Reggie knows it."

Reign closed the armoire door. "Probably his
father." He was aware of Olivia watching him
closely—too closely. He left the room to avoid
conversation.

She followed.

The next room was another guest quarters. "This was James's room," Olivia whispered, as she moved toward the chest of drawers.

"Do you smell him?" It would be faint after so many days, but it was possible.

"No, but this is his." She held up a fine, dark brown beaver hat. "This proves that he didn't leave here on his own."

"It's just a hat. He could have forgotten it." Christ, he had been known to take off and leave everything he owned behind.

Her mouth thinned. "I gave him this hat. There's no way he'd simply forget it."

She sounded so sure—or rather she sounded like she *wanted* to be sure. Reign wasn't. Instinct told him that James was a brat, who resented Olivia for being immortal while he wasn't. The boy resented her for a number of things, he imagined. Boys generally did. The fact that he had left his hat meant nothing more than he hadn't cared to take it with him.

There was a shirt and a pair of shoes in the closet as well, as well as an umbrella in the corner. "He certainly didn't pack all his belongings and leave as Haversham would have us believe."

Olivia's expression was grim. "Let's move on to Dashbrooke's room."

The master bedroom was a large, opulent space that suited Dashbrooke. It was decorated in a decidedly haughty style that was ill-suited to the simple architecture of the house. It was the room of a man who thought very highly of himself, and felt the need to prove it.

They searched the adjoining bath and found nothing. The armoire contained a red sash with a ruby pin, that seemed ceremonial, but nothing out of the common way. In fact, Dashbrooke's room was void of anything too personal. There was a small pile of stationery in the desk, but no letters.

There was, however, a small pile of ash in the grate of the fireplace. A tiny corner of paper, unburned and blank sat amongst them.

"He burns his correspondence," Reign mused aloud. "Interesting."

"Look at this." Olivia came to him holding a small, open ring box. "I found it in the dresser."

Inside, on a bed of red velvet, was a silver signet ring with a chalice on it. It was new and shiny— the kind of gift a father gave a son, or an underling who had performed a duty well. The top of the ring was movable. Reign took a pencil from the desk and used it to turn the ring over. The silver would burn him as surely as sunlight.

What he saw on the other side made his heart stop cold.

"What is it?" He could hear the frown in Olivia's voice.

He stared at the embossed image of a hand,

palm up on the small, polished surface. "I've seen this before." Seen it. He'd borne that mark many times, had it bruised into the side of his face.

"You know someone who had a ring like this?" Olivia obviously thought this was a significant piece of information. "Who?"

Reign closed the lid on the box and thrust it back at her. "My father."

"This can't be a simple coincidence. Can it?" Olivia waited until they were back at their . . . *at Reign's* house to ask. She'd let him have the trip back here to ruminate, but now they needed to talk.

Reign shook his head. While she paced, he lay sprawled on the sofa, one arm across his stomach, the other above him on the cushions. "James's kidnapping, Dashbrooke having the same ring as my father. The murder in London happening just after I left. I can't believe any of it is simple chance, and the one connection between them is me."

Olivia's heart quickened until he added, "But my connection to James's kidnapping is slight to say the least." At least he hadn't mentioned her return to his life, otherwise he very well might start putting the pieces together. She almost wished he would, then she might have a better idea of just what James had gotten them into.

She didn't believe that James had knowingly involved himself in something underhanded, but he certainly seemed to have fallen into a fine mess.

"I have to send word of this to Clarke. Maybe he can uncover what the symbol means."

"You don't know?" *How could he not know?* And if he didn't know, how were they going to ascertain what this group wanted with James? And with Reign himself?

"No. My father wasn't very . . . open." He rubbed his jaw. "I don't know what's going on in London either. Christ, I can't go back there now, not after this."

He looked so torn, she couldn't help but comment, "You care about those women, don't you?"

"Of course. They're my responsibility."

It was said so matter of factly that Olivia could do little more than gape at him in response. Was that how he looked at her? Probably. That was why she had convinced him to help her so easily. He saw her as a responsibility to be fulfilled.

If that were true, why would he have insisted on having sex with her? Of course, they hadn't shared their bodies for several nights now. In fact, this exchange about his father and his own confusion was the deepest intimacy they'd shared since she told him she didn't trust him—on that night when he'd looked at her as though she'd just kicked his favorite puppy.

"You don't trust me either," she blurted.

His head turned, and his bewildered, but annoyed, gaze locked with hers. "What has that got to do with Dashbrooke's ring?"

"Nothing." She had stepped in it, so she might

as well see how deep she could sink. "But I'm tired of your sulking over what I said when you feel the same way about me."

He sat up, swinging his long legs over the side of the sofa. Slightly rumpled, and devilishly appealing, he let his hands hang between his knees. "You're right. I don't trust you, but I came to Scotland regardless. I've done all I can to help you find your nephew despite the fact that you refuse to be honest with me. I've asked for your trust and you refused me, whilst demanding my own." He rose to his feet, an angry flush coloring the bold jut of his cheekbones. "So if you're tired of my 'sulking,' give me a fucking reason not to."

"How can you ask me to trust you after all you've done to me?" Even as the words left her mouth, she wanted to yank them back, she felt so awful having said them.

"Not this shit again." Harsh laughter contorted his face. "I thought you might make an effort, Liv. After all, it's been thirty years."

He was right. She should make the effort, and if circumstances weren't what they were, maybe she would.

She studied the tips of her shoes. "Sometimes it feels like thirty days."

"If your life has been so awful, why haven't you ended it?"

Horror jerked her gaze to his. "You mean kill myself?"

He shrugged. "It would end your suffering. You have suffered greatly, have you not?"

The mockery in his tone was lost in the truth of his words. If her life had been so awful, why hadn't she put an end to it? James was almost grown now. He didn't need her. His father's family would make certain he was looked after. So why did she continue on if she hated what she was so much?

Because if she killed herself, she would never see Reign again. And that awful truth lodged in her throat like a piece of dry bread.

How could she have these feelings and betray him like she was going to? There was little chance of them finding James before the meeting with the kidnappers. Two nights, that's all the time they had. Just two nights before Reign realized that he should never have thought of trusting her.

"What?" he taunted. "No biting retort?"

Wearily, she gave her head a shake. "None. Happy?"

"I haven't been happy since our wedding day."

Olivia turned away from the brutal honesty in his pale gaze. "Don't say things like that."

"Why not?" She could feel him moving closer. "You think I ruined only your life that night? I ruined my own as well."

Oh God. She closed her eyes. *Give me strength.* "I don't want to hear this."

Solid heat met the chill of her back. She could just let herself go and sag into his arms, let his warmth and strength envelope her. She went rigid instead, her muscles trembling with the effort as he leaned in over her shoulder, tickling her ear with his breath.

"It might have saved us both years of misery if you had only stayed, Liv. You would have forgiven me. I would have made sure you forgave me."

Olivia shivered. He would have, she knew that. Her body hummed with tension as he stroked his long fingers down her arm.

"I would have done everything in my power to make you happy."

She knew that too. The shiver turned to trembling as he wrapped his arms around her, bringing her back against the full length of him. His jaw scratched hers as his lips touched the side of her neck, where the blood rushed and pulsed with need.

"But you ran away." His tongue traced tiny circles on her throat. "I would have welcomed you back at anytime, but you stayed away. I would have begged you to come back if I'd thought it would work."

Sighing, Olivia leaned back against him, her body so ecstatic to feel his again that it would allow him almost anything. Reign's hold on her tightened, and her eyes snapped open at the roughness of it.

"So if you want to blame someone for your misery, my darling wife, blame yourself."

She struggled against his hold and he let her go easily, as though he'd never really been holding her at all. Heart pounding in shame and anger, Olivia whirled on him, fists clenched.

Reign arched a dark brow. "Going to hit me because I'm right? Go ahead then, Liv. Hit me. I'll still be right."

That was all the invitation she needed. Olivia swung, but he knew it was coming and he caught her fist in one large hand. Using the momentum of her body against her, he hauled her against him, this time so that they were chest to chest, belly to belly.

They stared at each other, bodies tight and humming like strings, color high, breath shallow.

"Christ, I want you." His voice was a rough rumble that snaked down her spine, tightening her nipples and swirling liquid heat between her thighs. "How can I be so angry and want you at the same time?"

"I don't know," she answered honestly. "How can you?"

He laughed, his breath a warm brush against her cheek.

There was no humor in his eyes, only something raw and vulnerable that made Olivia's stomach flutter.

"And you want me too, admit it."

"Yes." There was no point to denying it, even if she wanted to. "I do."

"What is it between us, Liv?" He released her

clenched fist and cupped her cheek tenderly with that same hand. "Why do I only feel alive when I'm with you?"

He couldn't have robbed her of breath any quicker if he'd choked her. Oh, she knew then that she was so much more than a mere responsibility to him. "I . . ."

And then his mouth was on hers and he kissed her with a desperation matched only by her own. His lips, his tongue, his teeth were ruthless against hers and she was equally aggressive in return. The taste of him filled her, rich and salty, with an underlying spice so exotic it made her head swim.

It was his blood. And she wanted more of it. Grasping his lip with her teeth, she suckled gently as her fangs ached to extend and sink into him like she truly wanted.

Reign groaned against her mouth, pulling her tighter against him. Their breathing quickened, became more shallow as the heady taste of him filled her mouth, filled her with such strength and longing that she wanted to weep with joy. She loved the feel of him, the smell of him, the taste.

She wanted to bite him, and she wanted to feel his fangs in her as well.

And that awareness hit her like a slamming door. She released his lip, and pushed him away, licking the last traces of him from her own mouth.

He watched her, his eyes heavy with desire and hunger, his mouth red. "What is it?"

She could hardly tell him the truth, because as much as she wanted it, she was still afraid of it. Her ears picked up a soft and distant sound, and she grasped at that instead. "Someone's coming."

Reign pulled a handkerchief from his pocket and wiped at his mouth. He wasn't bleeding anymore that she could see, and when the knock on the door finally came, he looked perfectly normal, except that he hid the lower half of his body behind the sofa.

"Come in," he called.

The door opened and Watson stepped inside. Olivia liked the fair-haired man. He never seemed to pass judgment upon her as Clarke did, but this time his blue gaze passed shrewdly between her and Reign. She couldn't tell what his thoughts were, but it was bad enough that he knew something lingered between them.

"Please excuse the interruption, but a telegram from Mr. Clarke just arrived. I thought that given the hour it might be of some importance."

Reign came forward, hand outstretched. "You were right to bring it to me. Thank you, Watson. You can retire now."

The butler sketched a small bow. "Of course. Good night, sir. Madam."

Olivia watched him leave before returning her attention to Reign. He was reading the telegram with a grim expression.

"What is it? Is it something about James?"

He looked up, and for a moment she thought

he was going to say something biting. That's when she knew the telegram had nothing to do with her nephew, but rather contained news that affected Reign deeply.

"It's about Maison Rouge, isn't it?" she asked, her heart filling with unease. "There's been another murder?"

He nodded. "Yes, goddamn it. Clarke asks that I return and do something about the situation. Madeline, the mistress of Maison Rouge is not handling this well."

"She couldn't be expected to." Olivia knew how awful she felt with James missing, she couldn't imagine knowing that one, let alone two people she cared about had been murdered.

But she knew how she would feel if she learned that the people who wanted Reign had hurt him. Or worse, killed him. God, just the thought felt like claws ripping at her soul. Panic seized her, and this time it had nothing to do with James and everything to do with the man in front of her.

"You should go," she said, her voice more steady than she would have dared hope.

He looked surprised at her words. She was too, if she was honest with herself. It was an awful feeling, knowing the risk she was taking with James's safety at that moment, but all she knew was that she could not betray Reign, nor could she tell him the truth.

She could not bear to have him hate her.

"What about James?" His gaze narrowed. "You cannot meet the kidnappers on your own."

"I can. Probably there will be nothing more than another note waiting for me. Like you said, they like having me in their power."

"Liv, these people are dangerous."

She tightened her jaw. "So am I. Go to London, Reign. Do what you can for those poor women. Maybe you are right and none of this is a coincidence. I will handle things here."

He watched her strangely, as though seeing through her bravado, to the heart of her desperation. "No. I'm not going to leave you. For all we know that's what they want. I'll telegraph Clarke details of what we've discovered here. He can look into the murders. Until I know for sure that there is something sinister afoot, I will stay here."

"Until you know? Reign, two girls have been killed!"

The gaze that met hers was calm and resolute. "In eighteen-forty, two girls were shot to death by men jealous of their other clients. Another was robbed on her way to visit her mother, and stabbed when she wouldn't hand over her reticule. People are fragile, Liv. They die. I don't like it, but right now I have no reason to return to London except to comfort an employee and old friend, and give financial support to the families."

"And is that not reason enough?" She couldn't believe he could be so cold.

The muscle in the side of his jaw ticked. "Not when it means abandoning my wife, no."

All Olivia could do was watch him turn away and go to his desk. He sat down and began composing his reply to Clarke, and she stood there like an idiot, silent and watching. Why, when she finally wanted him gone, would he not leave? It was for his own safety, damn it! Why did he have to play her hero now? Why did he have to go and say such awful, wonderful things, and put her above all others?

And why did she have to love him so much for it?

Chapter 12

It was the vampire's curse to be shunned by daylight. When Eve hid the children of Lilith and the fallen angel Sammael from God's sight, did she know that she was cursing them to an eternity of darkness? And when the Almighty had deemed that those hidden should remain so, had He meant to punish or protect those who would have been hated and hunted for being powerful and different?

Reign refused to believe he was damned simply because he was vampire. Yes, he lived off the blood of Christ's children, but he was not a murderer. He was not cruel and he allowed his conscience to dictate his behavior. His soul was his own, and when he died—and someday he would—he was not worried for his eternal rest.

But he'd gladly shave some years off the rest of immortality for the chance to find out where the older Dashbrooke went during the day. Since that was impossible for him to do, he had Watson follow the portly Englishman instead. Of course, the portly Englishman had chosen to stay at home today.

The symbol on the ring he'd found at Dashbrooke's home haunted him. He needed to know about the connection between the two men. Needed to discover what his father had been part of and . . .

He tried not to think about his father. A bitter man six centuries dead did not deserve to wield such power.

Nevertheless, Pierre Gauvin lingered in the back of his son's mind as Reign and Olivia arrived at the public meeting room in New Town where the Friends of the Glorious Unseen were offering their latest lecture, titled: "Revered, not Feared: Dispelling the Myth and Superstitious Belief that Vampires are Inherently Evil & Soulless Creatures."

"I should have worn black," Olivia remarked, smoothing the skirts of her dark green evening gown. "And made myself look a little more like a blood-starved fiend. What do you think?"

"I like that dress," Reign replied, slouching in the corner of the carriage seat. "It displays a lot of breast."

She chuckled and he smiled, far too pleased with himself for having amused her. He liked it so much better when there was ease and comfort between them.

"It is unfortunate that we missed the lecture on the mating habits of vampires," she remarked, still smiling. "You might have learned something."

Reign laughed. "How would you have fared sitting through two hours of how the male is the dominant of the species."

She scowled at him. "That's not true."

"Of course not," he replied with false accord.

"Perhaps we should volunteer to say a few words, show off our fangs and assure everyone that we are peaceful creatures," she suggested with the same light mockery in her voice.

"Easier to do now that we've fed," he replied. "I don't think we'd appear very peaceful amongst all those humans when the hunger comes upon us." His gaze drifted to the rise of her breasts, magnificently displayed by the neckline of her gown. He'd gladly let Olivia nibble on him, if she'd let him nibble on her. But that was unlikely to happen. He'd traumatized her when he turned her. She wouldn't let him bite her any more than a woman who had been raped would make love to her attacker.

If he could change one thing in his life, it would be his wedding night. He'd even pray if he thought it would do him any good.

Olivia had been acting strangely lately—more so than usual. Whatever she had weighing on her mind, it plagued her. She looked tired—weary even, as though something was draining the strength from her, her very life. He couldn't force her confidence, and she wasn't about to offer it, so he could only suppose that he was part of her dilemma. He wished he could feel badly about that, but he really couldn't. If she was conflicted, that meant she still felt something for him, whether she admitted it or not, and he'd cut out his own tongue before he'd feel badly for that.

What did she have planned for him, his sneaky little wife?

The carriage came to a stop and the door opened. Reign stepped out, and offered his hand to Olivia. Her gloved fingers were strong and light in his. He didn't have to worry about hurting her because she wasn't some dainty human. She was his match in every way a woman could be. His equal.

His.

Her face lifted to the night, she glanced around their surroundings. A few other carriages were pulled up along with theirs and men and women of various ages and social spheres walked past them, up the steps into the meeting rooms. The night was alive with the scent and sound of horses, laughter and conversation, and a frisson of energy that came from a group of like-minded people coming together.

He offered her his arm and she took it. They strolled up the steps together, just another wealthy couple attending an interesting lecture.

"We could be walking into a trap," Olivia murmured. "This could be exactly what they want."

Reign had already considered that. "Are you worried?"

Her answering chuckle brushed over him like

a soft caress. "No. Call me a fool, but I am not. You?"

Smiling, he took a second just to enjoy looking at her. "I've called you worse. And, no. I'm not."

Inside the hall, it soon became apparent that the Friends of the Glorious Unseen were no threat to them whatsoever. The air rung with a feeling of genuine excitement and felicity that was nothing if not positive in nature. There might be a few rotten apples in this organization, but most of those in attendance that evening were far from evil.

Reign and Olivia took seats at the back of the room near the exit—just in case—and waited for the event to begin. They didn't have to wait long. A middle-aged gentleman walked to the front of the room where a podium sat on a raised dais, and welcomed everyone.

"I'm so pleased to see so many eager faces," the man said with a smile. "It is so very wonderful to know that our glorious friends—those who walk unknown amongst us—have such support in Edinburgh. I'm Walter Allbright, president of the Scotland chapter." He held up his hand at the thunderous applause that followed that announcement.

Olivia glanced at Reign. "That was the name Haversham gave us."

Reign's gaze flickered from the older man to her. "Do you want to speak to him?"

She studied the older man carefully. "It wouldn't hurt, but I don't think he'll have much information for us. I think Haversham gave us Allbright's name as a diversion."

He had to admit, her perception surprised him. Suspicious little minx. She relied on her instincts almost as much as he did.

What did her instincts tell her about him?

Allbright continued speaking, "I want to welcome you all to the second in our series of lectures and thank you all for the overwhelming response we've received. But you didn't come here tonight to listen to me prattle on. Please join me in welcoming our guest speaker, all the way from London, Mr. George Haversham."

As polite applause echoed throughout the hall, Reign and Olivia shared an arch look. George Haversham, who claimed to know nothing about the Glorious Friends of the Unseen, was their special guest.

Was the boy particularly stupid, or did he think they were? He had to know that they would discover his lie, especially since they had made a point of asking about the organization.

"Perhaps he wanted us to discover the truth," he murmured for Olivia's ears alone.

She shot him a dry glance. "I wouldn't give him that much credit."

Reign inclined his head in acknowledgment of her words. "It certainly lends strength to your theory about Allbright."

At the front of the hall Haversham thanked the

man for the introduction and took his place at the podium. He looked fresh and confident—not at all a stranger to public speaking.

"Thank you. I'm very grateful for the opportunity to speak to you all this evening. Before I begin I would like to thank all of you who have inquired after my good friend James Burnley. I'm sure James is off having one of his grand adventures and that he will return soon, eager to tell us all about it."

There were a few murmurs throughout the crowd. Reign reached over and squeezed one of Olivia's hands. To most, Haversham's words sounded like those of a hopeful friend, but to Reign—and undoubtedly to Olivia—they sounded careless and unfeeling.

"I know James would want to be with us tonight, as he shares my passion for our nocturnal friend, the vampire." Reign rolled his eyes. If Haversham started spouting Byron, or anything remotely like poetry, he was leaving.

Fortunately, the young man avoided poetry— mostly. His words were full of praise and romanticism. He dwelled on the mysterious, making vampires sound like dark heroes—an evolution of the human race, rather than a separate demonic species. Around them, the crowd nodded and murmured in agreement with his statements, their excitement rising as Haversham placed vampires higher and higher on a verbal pedestal.

It was more than a little disturbing. Not that

Reign minded being discussed in such a flattering manner, but it was odd knowing that these people thought so highly of his kind, and coveted his "affliction" for want of a better word, that if he were to walk to the front of the room and offer to turn all who were willing, there would be a line out into the street. And not one of them would think of the consequences, or how their lives would be forever altered.

And James, were he here, would be at the front of the line. Not only did Olivia have to worry about getting James back, but once she had him she was going to have to watch him grow old and die—unless she gave him the "dark gift" he so desired. To deny him would earn his contempt, and possibly push him to find another route. Could she accept that, regretting her own change as she did?

"Bram Stoker's portrait of the vampire is not accurate," Haversham was saying. "He would have you believe all vampires are murderous fiends, twisted and ugly." Reign had to nod. Whoever Stoker had based Dracula on had been one poor example of their kind. Probably some syphilis-affected aristo who was on his way to becoming Nosferatu—a monstrous strain of vampire.

"In truth," Haversham went on, "most vampires look no different from you or I when the lust for blood isn't upon them. You might dance with one at a ball, or frequent a pub one of them owns. Why"—Haversham swallowed as his gaze met

Reign's. Smiling coolly, Reign nodded at the young man, who continued, his voice slightly wobbly— "you could be sitting next to one right now."

Reign stifled a chuckle. It didn't say much about him that he took amusement from intimidating a young man, but he enjoyed it regardless. Had Haversham truly thought they wouldn't discover his lie?

Haversham composed himself and continued to speak for another half hour. Every once in a while he would glance in their direction and Reign would glimpse the excitement in his eyes.

He's going to expose us. Perhaps he was overly suspicious, but Reign could feel the young man's exhilaration. Buoyed by the crowd and swept away by his own beliefs, he might very well lose all reason and reveal Reign and Olivia as vampires to the entire room. And then what? They could deny it, but if the room closed in on them, all those hearts beating wildly just might send Olivia, a much younger vampire compared to Reign, into a blood lust, and that could prove dangerous.

Haversham was watching them with a wild gleam in his eyes as he delivered his closing remarks. People began raising their hands for questions, and it was obvious Haversham was torn between wanting the attention of his audience and wanting to give them living proof of vampires.

"Let's go." He took Olivia by the hand and pulled her to her feet.

"Wait!" Haversham cried from the front of the room. No one seemed to notice where his attention was focused, or that his expression was one of near desperation.

Reign did something then that he hadn't done in over four hundred years of trying to blend with humans. He bared his fangs—just a little—in the unmistakable hiss of a predator about to strike. Haversham went white, but he said nothing.

Turning on his heel, Reign tightened his grip on Olivia's hand and pulled her toward the door. Neither of them spoke until they were outside.

Olivia broke the silence. "He was going to tell them all that we're vampires, wasn't he?"

"Yes." They hurried down the steps toward the street where their carriage sat. "Bloody idiot."

"He talked about us like we were gods. Do you think he believes all of that?"

Reign shrugged, as he followed her into the coach. Within seconds they were in motion. "People believe in God without proof of His existence. Young Mr. Haversham has been given proof of ours—by someone with firsthand experience." He didn't have to tell her who he thought that informant was.

"Those fools." Olivia's voice was soft yet harsh. She ignored his remark, but the stiffness of her posture told him that she had understood—and that she knew he was right. "They have no idea what it is to be a vampire. They're like children believing in unicorns and mermaids. Nothing they believe is anything like the truth."

Something inside Reign snapped. The near debacle at the hall had frayed his patience and brought his need to protect Olivia to the surface. Now, all that energy needed to go somewhere and she had just offered him the perfect outlet. "For Christ's sake, how many times do I have to apologize?"

Olivia gulped. "What was that?"

He sat in the corner, every muscle in his body tense and ready to pounce. "I'm sorry I ruined your life. I'm sorry for everything you've endured. I'm sorry we ever met!"

She stared at him, her whiskey eyes wide. "I only meant—"

"I know what you meant." His jaw tightened. "You've made sure I've known ever since you waltzed back into my life. If I hadn't made you a vampire, your sister would never have died and James would have known his mother. You wouldn't have killed the first person you fed from. You would know what it was like to feel the sun on your face. You'd be sixty now, and maybe even have a couple of grandchildren if not for me."

"Reign . . ."

He ignored her. "I made a mistake. Don't you think I've paid for it? My actions cost me the woman I loved and whatever future happiness I thought of having. I've lived with that every day since you left, knowing that I had ruined not only my life, but yours as well. I am sorry. What more do you want?"

"You loved me?"

He scowled at her. "Of course I loved you. I would never have tried turning you if I didn't. It was because I loved you that I made such a mess out of it."

"You tore into me because you loved me?" She made a small scoffing noise.

Her dismissal struck him hard. He lunged forward and grabbed her by the jaw, holding her face so she was forced to look at him as he spoke, and see the truth in his eyes. "I lost control because I was afraid of losing you. You were so human and fragile. You remember how you tripped over your wedding gown and almost fell down the stairs?"

She nodded slightly, her chin pressing into his palm, but she said nothing.

"That terrified me." He had never admitted this before, not to her, not to anyone. "I realized at that moment how easily you could be taken from me and I knew I couldn't let that happen. I would *not* let that happen. All I could think about was making you like me so illness and physical harm couldn't touch you. Death, I determined, would not easily part us.

"I was afraid, Liv. That's why I did what I did. I thought you wanted it. I thought you understood." And then he let his pride go and admitted what he swore he never would, "I thought you loved me as much as I loved you."

The light in her eyes mellowed. Was that understanding or pity he saw there? Disgusted with himself, Reign let her go and turned away. He'd rather stare out the window at nothing than face his wife. Still, once the flood gates had opened, he found himself loath to close them again. It felt good to tell her this, to bare his soul. Maybe it would make it easier when she was gone once more.

"To you, being a vampire is a curse." A harsh laugh tore at his chest. "I suppose it's been that to me as well on occasion, but when I met you it became a gift. A chance to spend forever with the woman I loved. Yes, I ruined your life. But, woman, losing you destroyed mine."

A soft gasp filled the carriage and Reign briefly closed his eyes as his heart leapt at the sound. Soft fingers touched his arm, but the carriage rolling to a stop in front of his house saved him from having to face her. He had fought to the death many times during the course of his life and none of those battles had ever scared him as much as the woman beside him.

"We're home," he said, and opened the carriage door. He stepped out into the cool night and strode toward the house without a backward glance, like the coward that he was.

Olivia knew what she had to do, and by the time she reached Reign's room later that night, she knew how she was going to do it.

She was still dazed from his earlier confession, and still so deliriously happy and terrified that she couldn't find words to articulate her feelings. But she knew how she could express herself to him, now that she understood that all that bitterness she'd carried for so long stemmed from mistaken belief. She hadn't thought he loved her. In fact, she'd thought that her feelings didn't matter much to him at all. She had no idea he had felt so strongly for her.

Her mind tried to grasp it all. Her heart recognized it as true, but she'd held on to the bitterness for so long it was hard to accept anything else. But she let her instincts drive her. She'd made a choice and now she had to follow through with it.

She knocked on his door and turned the knob before he could respond.

Reign turned toward her as she crossed the threshold. Clad only in his trousers and shirt-sleeves, he was tousled and golden in the glow of a single lamp. He was barefoot, and the crisp white of his sleeves was rolled back to reveal strong forearms. He had a glass of whiskey in his hand.

"Have any more of that?" she asked, nodding at the glass.

Reign stared at her, his gaze bright as it lazily drifted from her head to her feet and back again. She was wearing nothing more than a seductively flimsy nightgown and a wrapper that was little more than gauze. Judging from the heat in his expression, she assumed he liked what he saw.

He gestured toward a bottle and extra glass on the top of the desk near the wall. "Help yourself."

Olivia moved across the room with deliberate slowness, giving him plenty of time to watch her, and giving herself the opportunity to visually explore his bedroom.

The room was large, but not opulently so, with plush gold and ivory carpet, and cream walls. The furniture was dark and simple, very masculine. The only art on the wall was a melancholy painting of a knight and his lady on a bed of grass so dark it was almost black. He loomed over her, his intent clear in the sharp lines of his face. Her surrender was just as obvious. They were fully clothed, but the image of his big hand on her bodice, just below her breast, gave Olivia a little shiver.

Below that sensual scene, lurked a heavy, four-poster bed. It was fairly plain, the wood darkened with age, but it was sturdy and dressed in sumptuous fabrics in shades of cobalt and gold.

"Does the room meet your standards?" he asked wryly as she poured herself a splash of whiskey.

She glanced at him over her shoulder as she replaced the stopper in the bottle. "It suits you."

He seemed amused, but genuinely interested. "How so?"

She turned to face him, leaning her hip against the desk, dragging her gaze around the room before letting it meet his. "It's strong, sensual, and utterly masculine."

Reign cocked a brow, a small smile curving his lovely lips. "Are you trying to butter me up?"

"Mmm, butter." She smiled against the rim of her glass. "That's one we've never tried."

The smile melted from his face. "What do you want, Liv?"

Olivia downed the contents of her glass in one swallow, delighting at the way it burned all the way down to her stomach. She set the empty glass on the desk and moved toward him with slow, purposeful strides. "You."

He tensed as she approached, but he didn't move. Silently, he watched her, as though he couldn't quite trust his own eyes.

When she reached him, Olivia reached out and took his shirt in both hands, pulling the tails free from his trousers. Then, she seized the hem in her fists and tore the fine linen right up the center, baring his torso to her gaze.

"Christ!" he swore, looking down at his ruined shirt. His laughter told her he wasn't angry.

Placing her palms on his chest, she pushed him backward so that she had him pinned against the wall. His skin was warm beneath her hands, the hair there coarse and springy against her fingers. He was so muscular, so wonderfully solid.

Stepping forward, she pressed herself against him, burying her face in the hollow of his neck. She breathed his scent deep into her lungs, let it fill her until her head swam.

Olivia had never felt more powerful and alive in her life and she had barely touched him.

Grabbing the torn edges of his shirt, she yanked the soft fabric down over his shoulders so she could run her hands over the knobby bones of his shoulders, the sleek muscles between those and his neck, and down to the firm, gentle curve of his pectorals.

"Liv." She could feel the rumble of his voice under her palms. "What are you doing?"

Olivia lifted her head, trailing her lips up the side of his throat. She nipped at his jaw, delighting in the rasp of stubble against her lips. "I thought it was obvious. I'm trying to seduce my husband."

The word "husband" made him shiver—just a little, enough that she'd notice. God, knowing that she had such an effect on this man, this incredible, amazing specimen of a man . . . it was as exciting as it was humbling.

And it pushed her onward. "I want you, Reign." She ran her hands upward again, so that she could tangle her fingers in the thick silk of his hair. "I want you inside me. I want your hands on me, and I want your blood on my tongue. And I want mine on yours."

He stiffened and for one terrifying second she feared he might push her aside. But then his hands closed around her waist and he lifted her, swinging her around so that now she was the one against the wall. Her legs went around his waist, bunching her gown and wrapper around her hips. Her hands clutched at the sleek muscles of his back as he pressed deeper between her thighs, the wool of his trousers scratching her delicate flesh, tickling her most intimate recesses.

His eyes were like silver, bright and dangerous in the tan of his face. Olivia cupped his jaw with her hands and pressed her lips to the fine lines fanning out toward his temple, high on his cheekbone. She loved those beautiful lines that creased when he laughed and smiled.

Reign's hands were between them, yanking at the sash on her robe, pushing the flimsy fabric aside. Hot fingers slid up her ribs to cup her breasts, teasing her nipples into tight, aching peaks that he squeezed until she gasped at the intensity of it.

He yanked the neckline of her nightgown down, so that her chest was exposed to the cool night air and applied his mouth where his fingers had just been. Olivia squirmed at the moist, heated strokes of his tongue, the sweet pressure of his lips. Arching her hips, she pressed against him, increasing the damp ache between her thighs. It felt so good to have him touch her like this, to give herself to him.

He shifted and she felt his hands on the underside of her buttocks, fumbling with the fastenings of his trousers. Tightening her thighs around him, she lifted herself upward so that he could better maneuver. When the hard length of him brushed her skin, she shuddered, pressing her shoulder blades into the wall so that she was angled to receive him.

Reign lifted his head from her breasts as he guided the head of his erection to the entrance of her body. Olivia held his gaze as her body thrummed with want, opened her mouth in silent invitation so he could see her fangs, distended and wet and ready to sink into his flesh.

He was inside her with one slick upward thrust that lifted her up the wall and had her trembling with satisfaction. She was stretched and full and so eager for him she shook with it, could barely contain it.

And when she looked at him, all heavy lidded with points of sharp white visible between his parted lips, she knew she would never feel as alive and vibrant as she did with this man.

"I want to taste you," she whispered hoarsely. Did he realize what her words meant? Did he know she forgave him?

He thrust deep, drawing a gasp from each of them. "Do it." His palms hit the wall on either side of her and he leaned forward, head slightly bowed and to the side so that his throat and shoulder were open to her.

Yes, he knew.

Olivia didn't hesitate. She lowered her head to that heated hollow and ran her tongue along the sensitive vein there. Reign shivered and she smiled against his skin. Then, she placed her fangs against the salty sweetness of his throat and bit.

He stiffened, groaning in pleasure as she pierced his flesh. Olivia moaned in response as he filled her mouth, shuddering as the intoxicating taste of him flooded over her tongue.

Nothing could have prepared her for this. More intimate than sex, this was the epitome of trust. He gave himself freely to her, without pause, and when she felt his mouth on her own throat, his tongue stroking her in tandem with his cock filling her, Olivia wasn't afraid. She dropped her shoulder to give him better access. He wasn't going to hurt her. Not this time.

The sensation of his fangs entering her was unlike anything she had ever felt before—an exquisite blend of pleasure and pain that made her gasp and shudder and arch into his embrace. The pull of his lips brought tears of pleasure to her eyes, deepened the pulsations between the lips of her sex. Olivia ground down and Reign quickened his thrusts, bringing her closer and closer to climax.

Olivia didn't lift her head, didn't stop drinking until the pleasure became too much and she had to let it out. She threw her head back, mouth wet, and cried out as orgasm tore through her.

Reign's hips pumped once, twice, and then he growled against her neck as he emptied inside her. Limp, held up only by his strength, Olivia felt him run his tongue along her neck to close the wound, and lowered her head to do the same to the small holes in his neck. He shivered at the touch of her tongue.

She ran her fingers through his hair as she straightened, kissed his forehead and temple. "You know, if you had done it like that thirty years ago I never would have left."

He stilled and for a moment she feared she had ruined the moment, but when he raised his head there was a smile on his lips that softened his features and damn near broke her heart.

"You're not going to try to kill me again, are you?" he asked in a low, velvety tone. "I don't want to die with my trousers around my ankles."

It was such an absurd image, that Olivia couldn't help but chuckle, and soon they were laughing together. She was still laughing when Reign kicked the offending trousers to the side and carried her to the bed.

It didn't take long for her laughter to subside when he began to kiss her again. And for the rest of the night, Olivia didn't think about what could happen or what the future might hold. She thought only about how sweet it was to be in Reign's arms and be his wife. She was determined to enjoy it for as long as she could.

Because she knew there was no way it could last.

Chapter 13

George Haversham's head snapped back as pain exploded through his face. His lip was split and he tasted blood. It was coppery and warm on his tongue, and through the relief of ebbing hurt, he hoped that blood would taste better once he became a vampire.

"You almost ruined everything, George," Reggie's father said to him, wiping George's blood from the back of his hand with a snowy white handkerchief. "Now the vampires know that we are aware of their true nature."

"I'm sorry, sir." George accepted a similar square of linen from Reggie—who looked deuced uncomfortable—and dabbed at his cut lip. "But I'm afraid I don't understand. How are they ever going to turn us into vampires if they believe we are unaware of what they are?"

The older Dashbrooke gave him a withering glare. "Because, you simpleton, if they think their secret may be compromised, they will kill to protect it!"

George shook his head. Until now he had believed everything Reggie's father told him, but not this time. "I don't think so, sir."

"You don't think so?" Dashbrooke's face was purple as he advanced on George once more. This time George was braced for the blow. He was more than willing to take the abuse if it brought him closer to his goal. He, James, Fitz and even Reggie had shared this dream ever since James first revealed that his aunt Olivia was a vampire. When Reggie came to them and told them that his father had a plan to make their hopes a reality, the four of them leapt at it. All they had to do was exactly what Mr. Dashbrooke said.

George had broken one of those rules with his enthusiasm over Reign and Olivia the night before. The fact that Reign had bared fang at him seemed to anger Mr. Dashbrooke, but it gave George hope. Surely Reign wouldn't do something so revealing if he didn't think George worthy of seeing his true nature.

The older man stopped but a foot away from him, his hand poised in midair, but he didn't strike. "It's not a good idea for you to be in Edinburgh anymore, George. I think you should retire to the country with James and wait for us there. You and Reggie both should go and be with your friend."

George knew he should feel ashamed. He should at least feel badly for acting as he had and risking their plans, but he didn't. If anyone should feel foolish it was Mr. Dashbrooke, who had told George to lie about being part of the Friends of the Glorious Unseen. Now Reign and Olivia knew the truth, and they would be looking for George for answers. That's why Dashbrooke wanted him in the country.

George had sat in the same room as *two* vampires. Olivia wasn't that old—enough to be George's grandmother, but Reign . . . Reign was ancient. God, the power he must have! The things he must have seen and experienced. And he seemed so . . . regular. The two of them were living proof that vampires were not the monsters fiction and folklore made them out to be.

And soon, George would be just like them. As long as the plan went as it should. Once Reign and Olivia came to the country and blessed them all by sharing their dark gift as thanks for their "rescue" of James, everything would be as he had dreamed. He would be powerful, immortal. And maybe then these blasted headaches and nosebleeds would finally stop.

"Of course, sir." He rose to his feet, grimacing as his nose began to bleed, as though on cue. He pressed the handkerchief to his nostrils to staunch the flow. "I will gather my things and leave for the country immediately."

As he strode from the room, he heard Reggie's low voice, "If you want me to do what you say,

Father, you had better start being kinder to my friends."

Atta boy, Reggie.

Forty minutes later the two of them were in a carriage headed east. Less than an hour after that they were at the country house with James, playing croquet on the back lawn and carrying on like boys. George's nose had stopped bleeding and Reggie was the chipper chum he always was when his father wasn't around.

And, as they always did when they were together, they talked about what they were going to do once they became vampires and never had to worry about anything ever again.

It hadn't been a dream.

When Reign awoke that evening, to the velvet darkness that enveloped his room, Olivia's naked body was curled into his, warm and silky and smelling of amber and sex.

He smiled, trailing his fingers down the soft curve of her spine, feeling her shiver under his touch. They had spent the remainder of the night and into the dawn talking and making love.

Talk consisted of sharing stories—some humorous and some sad—about their lives, which they had never shared before. They avoided subjects that might renew any sense of discomfort between them or ruin the bliss the night had wrought.

Their lovemaking included becoming reacquainted with each other's bodies in the slow and leisurely manner they hadn't bothered to attempt until now. Sharing blood had made them both as content as lazy house cats, and Reign took full advantage of the opportunity to explore every inch of his wife's delectable body, reveling in every sigh and moan.

A voice in his head warned him not to become too comfortable or too content with this development, but he was tired of being suspicious and doubtful. For now, he'd allow himself this little happiness, because he knew just how short-lived it might be.

Carefully, he eased himself away from his wife's slumbering form. She stirred and sighed before drifting back into a gentle snore.

God, how he had missed her.

She had given him the gift of her blood. She had taken his, and he was humbled by it—humbled by her sweetly offered forgiveness. It made the truth of what he had done to her all the more raw, but they could heal that in time. Now that he had her back, there was no way he was ever going to let her go again.

He tucked the blankets around her before shrugging into the brocade robe he kept draped across the foot of the bed. He was on his way to the adjoining bath to fill the tub for the two of them when a soft knock came upon the door.

He cast a quick glance at the woman on the bed before answering. She continued to sleep. Once more he smiled.

It was Watson on the other side of the threshold. "Beg your pardon, sir, but Mr. Clarke has just arrived."

"Clarke?" Reign kept his voice low, but couldn't hide his surprise. Clarke would have only gotten his latest telegram that morning, so if his man of affairs was there, it had to be important. Very important. Had something happened in London—another murder? This was not the time for speculation. He knew better than to allow those thoughts. Seemed he'd been having a lot of them lately.

Hearing Olivia's reassuring snores, Reign stepped out into the corridor and closed the bedroom door behind him with a faint click. "Where is he?"

"Your study, sir."

"Thank you. If Mrs. Gavin should wake and inquire after me, send her to my study as well."

"Of course, sir."

In his robe and bare feet, Reign hurried down the winding staircase. One of the house maids gaped at him as he walked by, undoubtedly shocked to see her employer in such a state of undress. Reign hadn't thought to dress first. He didn't care, and Clarke wouldn't either. Any other opinions hadn't occurred to him.

When he entered his office, he found Clarke standing at the window, waiting for him. His friend's face was strained—an expression Reign had come to recognize as a harbinger of doom.

He shut the door. "What? Is it Maison Rouge? Has there been another murder?" His blood ran cold as he gave in to the very thoughts he'd fought just minutes berfore. "Madeline?"

Clarke shook his graying head. "Madeline is as well as can be expected. Saint is there."

"Saint? At Maison Rouge?" It seemed almost too perfect to be true—another fantastic coincidence? It hardly mattered if it were. Relief, swift and cool washed over him. "He'll take care of Maddie and the girls." His old friend was many things, including a thief and sometimes a liar, but he would never turn his back on people who needed him, especially the ladies of Maison Rouge.

"Yes," Clarke agreed brusquely. "That is not why I'm here."

"You got my telegram?"

"This morning as I was on my way to the train station. I decided to come in person rather than forward my discovery. To be honest, I was afraid of it falling into the wrong hands."

Reign raised his brows. "That's being overly suspicious isn't it? Even for you." He forced some lightness into his tone, but everything in his friend's countenance set the hair on the back of his neck on end.

"Perhaps, but I wasn't willing to take the risk." Clarke cracked his knuckles, a nervous habit that did nothing to ease Reign's mind. "William Dashbrooke belongs to the Order of the Silver Palm."

Where had he heard of that before? "Weren't they part of the Templars once?"

"Yes. It was they who used the Blood Grail found by the Templars for their dark rituals."

The Blood Grail. The mere mention of it caused an odd tug in Reign's soul. The cup that held the essence of Lilith, mother of all vampires. The cup that had made him and his friends immortal with one drink.

The Templars had expelled the Order and hid the cup from them. It had remained hidden until Reign and the others had found it while ransacking the Templar base for treasure at the behest of King Philip.

"The grail is hidden," Reign reminded his friend. "The Order will never find it." He didn't mention where the cup was, because not even he knew that. The only one who knew was Temple, wherever in the name of God he was.

Clarke nodded. "I know. The Order has been looking for it in earnest for the past twenty years. Over the last ten their efforts have doubled."

"What has this to do with Dashbrooke, or James Burnley, or me?" Obviously it had to involve one or all three if Clarke thought it important enough to travel all the way to Scotland.

"It's unclear why the Order wants the cup, although I think it's safe to assume they want the power it contains. What disturbs me is that they have gone from being a society comprised mainly of drunken, bored aristos to a legion of men of means and power. A society does not grow like that unless its members are being promised something—something great."

Reign nodded. "But you don't know what that is?"

"I know that the Order has been popping up in cities all over Europe, particularly in England and France. And I know that as of late, there have been quite a few 'scholars' inquiring into the history surrounding five mercenaries who stole the Unholy Grail during a Templar raid over six hundred years ago."

A chill ran down Reign's spine. "How the hell could anyone research us? Everyone believed us to be dead." That wasn't quite true. Dreux—poor Dreux who had killed himself rather than face eternity—had tried to return to his wife. Chapel's fiancée had killed herself rather than become a vampire. Even Reign himself had returned home, only to find his father regarding him with a strange, bright gaze. He had been afraid of his son, and Reign had enjoyed that. And now his father and Dashbrooke were linked by similar rings, worn centuries apart. What had his father's ring represented? It was so long ago, and his father never talked to him except to berate him.

There might have been enough stories, enough rumors to base a history on Reign and his companions. They had been careless in those early years, prancing about, flaunting their abilities. Of course people took notice.

"Reign." Clarke gave his head a shake, as if to clear it. "Your father was a member of the Silver Palm. He wrote about you in his journal after you turned, and before he died. Apparently he left his journals to the Order."

Reign closed his eyes. The ring. The signet of the Silver Palm. *Christ.* No wonder his father had looked at him that way.

Rubbing a hand over his jaw, he turned his gaze to Clarke. "You think these people took James to get to me?"

Clarke shrugged. "I'm not sure what their end goal is, but there are close to a dozen known members in Edinburgh right now."

"Fuck." Clarke might not know, but Reign did. He felt it in his gut with a certainty that grew with each passing second. Dashbrooke and his cronies were using James to get to him, for whatever reason. He'd go to Dashbrooke's now and yank his teeth out one by one if he thought it would get the bastard to talk, but men like Dashbrooke would rather die than betray their brothers. If they didn't, they would meet a far worse fate than death.

Olivia was going to hate him for this. Just when he thought they had a chance, something threatened to tear them apart. Again, that something was his fault.

"Reign, there's something else I need to talk to you about."

Of course there was. There always fucking was. "What?"

Clarke's gaze was full of pity and cold anger. "Your wife."

Chapter 14

"Is Clarke coming with us?" Olivia asked her husband as they lay in bed on the evening they were to attend the Wolf, Ram and Hart at the kidnappers' demand. They had just woken up and had several hours before they were to depart. Strangely enough, Olivia was much calmer than she thought she would be.

She hadn't felt this complete since the first time she and Reign had made love. Only now that feeling was intensified by the sharing of their blood. They were connected now. One.

Reign held her hand in his, his thumb making small circular strokes around her knuckles. "Yes. He'll follow at a distance, and go to the Bucket of Blood for help if we need it."

"He doesn't like me," she remarked, not sure why that should bother her, but it did. He had been pleasant enough in London, but ever since his arrival the night before he had looked at her like she was the serpent that corrupted Eve.

"He doesn't know you," Reign replied, planting a small kiss on her forehead.

"Ah, but you don't deny it."

His only response was to smile and kiss her again—this time on the mouth.

Reign was acting strangely too. He was more relaxed, more openly affectionate. She didn't understand it, but she liked it. It seemed as though all the bitterness between them had suddenly disappeared. Was this sudden change owed to the new intimacy between them, or something else? And was this connected to Clarke's dislike of her? Was he jealous of her on some level?

Olivia couldn't deny that she might deserve the man's animosity on several levels, but if Reign didn't care then neither would she.

She hadn't seen much of Reign after Clarke's arrival. He and his employee spent most of the night in Reign's study talking. They had let her in eventually and Reign had told her what Clarke had discovered about a group called the Order of the Silver Palm, which sounded to her like a more dangerous version of the Friends of the Glorious Unseen. He seemed to think that this "Order" was behind James's kidnapping.

Suddenly, it was all starting to make sense as to why these people knew about Reign, why they wanted Reign.

And she knew then that she couldn't let them have him.

The realization came to her with sudden sharpness and clarity. She didn't know how in the name of God James had gotten tangled up with such a group, but she suspected that he was safer with them than Reign would be.

And she didn't care if it made her evil, but at that moment, protecting Reign meant more to her than the boy she had raised as her own. God help her.

There had to be a way to save them both.

And now, she was just hours away from attempting to do just that.

"I'm sorry." It was so very difficult to say those words, meaning them as she did.

He lifted her hand to his lips and pressed a kiss to her fingers. "For what?"

"Everything." It was so much easier than admitting to particulars. "For involving you in this."

"You didn't." His gaze was clear and sharp as it locked with hers. "If Clarke is correct, the kidnappers involved you because of me."

Yes, and they asked me to bring you to them.

"In fact," he continued, kissing the tip of each finger in a way that sent little shivers down her arm. "I owe both you and James an apology."

Olivia swallowed. Guilt formed a hard lump in her throat. "No, you do not."

He moved then, sliding over her and covering her body with his own. "I'll make it up to you in another way, then." He kissed her and she welcomed the pressure of his lips, opened her thighs and let him take away her thoughts with his body's slick intrusion of hers. Her internal muscles stretched and tightened around the thick length of him as he began to thrust inside her.

Arching her back, Olivia wrapped her hands around Reign's biceps, giving herself up to the sensations stirring within her, the emotions his touch brought to a simmer under the surface of her skin.

"Look at me," he murmured.

Olivia opened her eyes. Reign's forearms were braced beside her head, leveraging him so that he could stare down at her. She didn't respond with words. She tightened her thighs around his hips and moved with him, staring into the smoky depths of his eyes, trying to tell him everything she was afraid to say with her gaze.

"Come for me," he whispered, increasing the depth and speed of his thrusts.

And she did. She came in a great shove of pleasure that blurred the edges of her mind and had her crying out at its ruthless onslaught. It left her trembling and boneless as Reign stiffened above her, growling his own release.

Only he had ever made her climax so quickly, so easily. It was as though their bodies were attuned to one another, instinctively knowing just what the other needed, wanted.

Olivia clung to him for as long as she could, reluctant to let him go until she had to. He caressed her face with light, feathery kisses, each one tightening the invisible band around her chest, bringing her one step closer to bursting into tears.

"I'll go fill the tub," he said softly. "I want to bathe with you."

Despite being sated, Olivia's body shivered in anticipation. "And when we're clean and smelling pretty?"

He grinned. "I'm going to make you come with my tongue."

Oh God. She would have liked that. But it wasn't going to happen. Before she climbed into the tub, Olivia went to her room to gather some clothing. While she was there, she pulled her valise out of the armoire and withdrew a small metal syringe from the inside pocket.

The syringe contained enough laudanum to kill a man. That same amount would render Reign unconscious for twenty, maybe thirty minutes if she was lucky. She didn't want him injured or dead, she just wanted a head start. Originally she had planned to use it to make handing him over to the kidnappers easier. Now, she was going to use it to save him.

Still wrapped in a towel, she hid the syringe in her bundle of clothes and carried them into Reign's room. He was in his trousers but nothing else and the sight of his naked back was enough to make her want to confess all and finally relieve herself of this weight on her shoulders.

"You look decidedly glum for a well-pleasured woman," he joked. "Are you nervous about to-night? Don't be. James will be fine."

"I know." She wished she could believe that. Then, when he went to the armoire to select a shirt, Olivia followed him. She dropped her own clothes on the bed and whirled around, syringe in hand.

She plunged it into his hip, injecting the full barrel of laudanum into him.

He turned around, his face a mask of surprise. "Liv, what the f . . ." And then his knees began to buckle.

Surprise turned to shock, then anger. "Liv, no."

Olivia moved back so he couldn't grab her, and watched as he slowly crumpled to the carpet. "I'm sorry, Reign. I truly am."

"No." He fell forward onto his hands. "Don't do . . . this."

"I have to. You'll understand later." Then, she rushed forward, heedless of the fact that he might still have the strength to subdue her, and fell to her knees beside him. Cradling his head in her hands, she kissed his cheek. "You'll always be my hus-band, no matter what."

He looked at her with glazed eyes and then slumped into her arms. The drug had him in its hold.

Olivia slipped her arms around his ribs and stood. He wasn't any heavier than a human man his size, so she was easily able to get him to the bed. Then, she hurriedly dressed in a demi-corset, split skirt, and loose blouse. Her clothing wouldn't be shocking enough to draw a lot of attention, but she would have freedom of movement, something much more important.

Once she was dressed, she ran up to the attic and through to the door to the roof. From there she vaulted into the night, turning her body toward Old Town and the Wolf, Ram and Hart tavern.

She landed on a nearby roof, and jumped to the ground in an alley, landing in a soft crouch. The knife that she had brought *just in case* was tucked into her right boot. The hilt dug into her calf as she straightened.

Could she really do this? Her actions tonight could cost James his life, but she didn't think it would come to that. For all she knew there could be nothing but another invitation waiting for her inside. Or, they could be there with James. Either way she was going to send a message. If it was just another letter, they would no doubt be watching her as she received it, and she would let it be known that she had no intention of giving in to their demands.

And if James was by chance with them, she was going to free him by any means necessary, even if it meant her own life. Even if it meant the lives of the men holding him. She had never willingly killed someone, but tonight could change all of that.

Holding her head high and her shoulders back, she entered the tavern. There wasn't a large crowd inside, maybe twenty or thirty people that she could see. The same barkeep was in attendance as had been the last time she and Reign had been there. He looked up and met her gaze. And then he nodded to a table in the back where it was darker and more shadowed.

Olivia glanced around her, noting three men who were watching her from different locations in the tavern—one on a balcony above, and one on either side of the room below. Knowing what she was they wouldn't be foolish enough to have three alone, not if they planned a meeting, which this appeared to be. They especially wouldn't be so foolish if they thought she would have Reign with her, so there had to be more scattered throughout the tavern.

She moved into the back section. No one seemed to find it odd that a lone woman would enter this area. No one seemed to find her out of place at all, which struck her as odd.

She was not surprised to see Dashbrooke sitting alone at one of the few tables in the darkened alcove. Surely he realized he was at a disadvantage with her in such dim surroundings?

He looked decidedly cocky for a man whose neck she could snap like a dry branch. Of course, he believed himself to have power over her. He had James.

If she ripped his heart out of his chest, would he live long enough for her to choke him with it?

"Mrs. Gavin," he said in that oily tone of his. "Are you alone?"

Olivia pulled a chair out from the battered, rickety table and sat down, positioning herself so she could see Dashbrooke's meaty hands as they rested on his heavy thighs. "Do I need a chaperone, Mr. Dashbrooke?"

"Of course not, but I am surprised your husband isn't with you."

"Oh? I'm not surprised to see that James isn't with you." *Duplicitous pig.* "Where is he?"

"He's safe."

"If you didn't plan this meeting to give him back to me, why are we here?"

A humorless smile curved his cruel lips. He enjoyed thinking he had power over her. "I thought it might be nice to meet face-to-face while we discuss particulars of the exchange."

"There's not going to be an exchange."

She had the pleasure of seeing confusion flicker in his eyes. "I beg your pardon?"

Now it was her turn to smile. Her turn to be in charge. "I'm not giving you Reign."

A thundercloud of expression rolled over his broad face. "We had an arrangement."

"No, you gave me an ultimatum." Her gaze locked with his. "I don't like being threatened, Mr. Dashbrooke."

He leaned across the table, his face florid. "Either you deliver Reign to the address I'm about to give you by sunrise on Tuesday or I'm going to put a bullet in young Mr. Burnley's skull."

Olivia lashed out, her fingers grabbing his throat like a hawk snatching up a mouse. Sweet, unsettling rage the likes of which she had never known coursed through her veins. "You harm my nephew and I will have your boy Reggie for breakfast." When that didn't seem to have the desired effect, she added, "and that darling little daughter of yours for dinner. And then, I'll suck the marrow from your bones while you're still alive."

Dashbrooke paled and made a gurgling sound in his throat. Olivia squeezed harder. It was coldly satisfying to see his eyes bulge. "Give me my nephew, Dashbrooke, and I just might let your family live." It was an empty threat, of course, she would never hurt an innocent, but she would tear Dashbrooke's throat out with her teeth.

Dashbrooke couldn't speak, but he didn't try to. He held up his hand in what Olivia thought was a gesture of surrender, until she heard a gunshot and felt the sting of a bullet tear into her shoulder.

She rose with a roar, knocking over the chair as she lifted Dashbrooke from his seat and threw him in the direction of the shot. Then she whipped the blade from her boot. Diving to the floor, she sliced neatly through the backs of the boots of a man coming at her with what looked like silver manacles. He screamed as her blade severed both of his Achilles tendons, and fell to the floor on top of the restraints.

Another shot rang out and Olivia rolled behind a pillar, gasping for breath. She realized three things at once. One, the bullet in her shoulder was made of silver and was burning her from the inside out. Second, that at least three quarters of the people in the tavern were on Dashbrooke's side. She was outnumbered, even for a vampire.

And third—that she had had to be the stupidest creature in all the world for believing she could do this alone.

She had hurt Dashbrooke. Even better, she had scared him. Now she had to get the hell out of there and go find Reggie or George Haversham—someone impressed enough with what she was to lead her to James.

It was the plan she should have thought of to begin with, but she had been a little too slow in realizing that while Dashbrooke was their enemy, James's friends were simply his pawns.

Several men were closing in on her. Over the din of people yelling, and innocent bystanders scrambling for cover, Olivia could hear someone shouting for help for Dashbrooke. Maybe she had broken the bastard's neck.

She was going to have to fight her way out, and no one there was going to come to her aid. She peered around the side of the pillar and saw the barkeep with a rifle raised to his shoulder. He spotted her and fired. She ducked. The bullet tore into the wood by her arm.

They weren't trying to kill her. They just wanted to bring her down. Capture her.

Jesus Christ, how stupid was she? She cursed herself as she leapt up to the exposed beams in the ceiling. She kept herself low, tucking into herself as two more shots narrowly missed her. Crouching, she shuffled farther into the darkness, the burning in her shoulder like a hot poker in her flesh.

Dashbrooke had come prepared to capture her. Maybe he planned to use her to lure Reign in, or maybe capturing her had been his plan all along. Maybe he'd had his sights on both she and Reign. But what the hell for?

A window downstairs exploded inward, sending shards of glass flying across the tavern. A dark shape hit the floor and then rolled to his feet.

Reign. Olivia could have wept at the sight of him were it not for the murderous expression on his face. He was followed by Watson and Clarke and several other armed men whom she recognized from the Bucket of Blood. He must have planned for them to be there because there was no way he could have gathered them so quickly.

The barkeep lifted his rifle, and before Olivia could cry out, Reign leaped over the bar, seized the rifle and smashed the man in the face with it.

Then all hell broke loose.

Glass shattered. Guns fired. Shouts rang out. And Olivia crawled along the wide beams, toward the center of the tavern, just above Reign. She could drop down to the bar without jarring her shoulder too badly. She would fight beside him if he would have her.

He barely glanced at her as she landed beside him. He was too busy beating three men who had attacked him. There was no rhyme or reason to this fight now. Everyone in the tavern was involved, whether they were part of Dashbrooke's group or not.

Olivia punched a man in the face and knocked him several feet backward, sending him crashing into a table. Her opposite shoulder was going numb and her arm hung uselessly at her side.

A shout caught her attention and she turned in time to see a woman advancing on Clarke, who was already engaged in battle, with a knife in her hand. Olivia dove at the woman and knocked her to the floor. The wild-eyed female didn't let go of her weapon, however, and she slashed Olivia across the face. It wasn't silver, but it stung all the same. Enraged, Olivia broke the woman's wrist and then cracked her forehead with her own, rendering her opponent unconscious.

Clarke didn't even notice how close he had come to being stabbed in the back.

Olivia pressed her sleeve to the gash in her face as she staggered to her feet. It would stop bleeding soon and start to heal, but for now blood was running down her cheek and neck.

She turned toward the door. Two men were helping Dashbrooke outside, and the others were slowly making their way in the same direction—those who were still conscious, that was.

Olivia bolted for the door. The heaviness bleeding down from her injured shoulder slowed her somewhat, made her awkward. One of the men flanking Dashbrooke had a pistol and he turned it on her just as she grabbed the fat bastard's coat.

He fired.

Pain blossomed in her chest and knocked her backward. She stumbled and fell to her knees. Dazed, she looked down and saw rich, bright crimson seeping through her shirt on the left side of her chest.

"Olivia!" It was Reign, shouting her name. She tried to turn toward him, but she fell face first onto the rough, dirty floor. She tried to breathe but it hurt, and when she opened her mouth to tell Reign she was hurt, all that came out was blood.

So much for immortality, she thought as blackness swept over her mind, blinding her.

She was going to die.

Chapter 15

The last thing on Reign's mind when he left the Wolf, Ram and Hart with Olivia bleeding in his arms, was whether or not anyone sober saw him leap into the sky and fly.

He didn't care that Dashbrooke had escaped. The man who shot Olivia hadn't. Reign had twisted his neck like a rag doll. There'd been no thought to it—he simply grabbed the man and killed him. He would have gone after Dashbrooke as well, had all his focus not been on Olivia—where it should be. Watson and some of the others would track Dashbrooke. Clarke took the carriage and would meet Reign back at the house. He wasn't going to risk jostling Olivia in the cumbersome vehicle, not when he could get her home in a faster, more comfortable manner.

He was terrified. He knew this because he felt nothing. He was totally numb inside, pushed beyond his mind's comprehension of fear and how to face it.

He had seen vampires survive worse wounds,

although none so young as Olivia. The bullet in her chest had missed her heart or she'd be dead by now. But it was still bad—very bad. The silver shot would have to be removed, and if that one in her chest was as close to her heart as it appeared . . .

I will not lose you.

He pushed himself faster, hurtling toward his house so fast that the wind tore at his clothes and stung his eyes. Olivia didn't stir in his arms, and the numbness inside him fractured slightly under a wave of panic.

He arrived at the house ahead of Clarke, and took Olivia to his room. He put her on the bed and removed the blouse and demi-corset she wore. The wound on her back was awful and purple, the puckered edges already trying to close themselves. The wound in her chest was worse, the entirety of her breast bloodied and bruised-looking. Her flesh was trying to heal itself despite the burning silver tucked inside it. The shot had to be removed before it did irrevocable damage.

He couldn't wait for Clarke.

"Liv," he murmured, stroking a few strands of silky brown hair back from her face. Her skin was hot, as though she had a fever. "Liv, can you hear me?"

She moaned and her eyelashes fluttered, but she did not speak. Still, it gave Reign hope. "I'm going to take the bullets out, Luv. It's going to hurt. I need you to be as still as you can."

No response. He could only hope that she had understood him, and that she would be able to keep herself quiet as he worked.

He would never be able to live with himself if he killed her. He would walk out into the dawn and fry. He had almost done just that thirty years ago when she left him. The only thing that had kept him alive was the hope that she might one day come back. If she died all his hope died with her.

"You're not leaving me again," he informed her, his voice hoarse and thick in his own ears. "No fucking way am I letting you go."

He had to leave her side long enough to collect a small knife and tweezers that he kept for just such occasions. A bottle of whiskey would clean the wound. She would have scars—the degree of which would depend on the purity of the silver used. The better the quality of the metal, the worse the scarring would be.

As carefully as he could, Reign climbed onto the bed to straddle Olivia's prone form. He pinned her arms with his knees and locked her upper legs together with his feet. His weight wouldn't do much to keep her still, but his strength would.

He rolled up his sleeves and soaked a handkerchief in some whiskey, which he then used to clean as much of the area as he could. The sight of her battered and torn flesh brought the sting of tears to his eyes.

He lowered the knife and cut a small incision on

two sides of the wound in her chest—just enough to widen it a bit. Then, he took the tweezers in his hand, and gritting his teeth in an effort to keep his fingers steady, he began probing for the bullet.

When he found it, Olivia bucked beneath him. Her eyes flew open as a scream that shook the walls tore from her throat. Reign flattened his other palm on her chest, holding her down as he gripped the bullet with the tweezers and pulled. It did not want to let go of her, but his strength won out and he pulled it free.

Olivia screamed again—with so much pain that Reign could no longer contain his tears and they slid down his cheeks in scalding tracks. The first bullet was out and the hole was gushing fresh blood. He poured more whiskey over it and pressed the damp handkerchief against it. If he had done the job properly, it would stop bleeding in a matter of moments. If not . . .

Olivia lay still beneath him. A light sheen of perspiration gleamed on her brow and cheeks. He couldn't feel the rise of her chest beneath his hand. And she was pale. So terribly pale.

"Please, God," he whispered as tears slipped between his lips. He wiped them away with his sleeve. "Let her live. I'll never question or doubt you again if you let her live."

"Never thought . . . I'd hear that from you," came a hoarse reply.

Reign looked down. Olivia was looking up at

him through narrow lids, her gaze unfocused, her dry lips parted by shallow breath.

She was the most beautiful thing he had ever seen.

"I don't plan to make a habit of it," he replied with forced lightness. "So don't expect to ever hear it again."

Her smile was barely a curve at the corners of her lips, but it warmed his heart regardless. He peeled back the crimson-soaked linen at her breast—the wound had stopped bleeding and was healing.

She was going to live. Now, he just had to get the piece out of her shoulder before it did any permanent damage.

"Reign," she rasped. "I have to tell you something."

"It can wait. Right now I have to turn you over and dig more silver out of your back."

She either hadn't heard him or was ignoring him. He'd put money on the latter. "It's about tonight. And why I drugged you."

"Later." He would be more than willing to listen to a full confession once she made a full recovery, but none of it mattered at this moment.

He lifted himself off of her and slipped his arm beneath her to roll her over. He had just begun to lift her when she caught at his arm with weak, but insistent fingers, halting his progress.

"I'm sorry," she whispered, licking her lips. "For everything."

Reign's expression turned grim as he rolled her onto her stomach. He applied the little knife to her flesh once more. "So am I."

"Dashbrooke's hiding out in a house in Haddington," Watson reported almost four hours later, as he and Reign and Clarke sat together in Reign's study, having a glass of bourbon and discussing what to do next.

His men had followed the injured Dashbrooke to the country. Clarke, meanwhile had done a little reconnaissance of his own and discovered that Dashbrooke had closed his Edinburgh address, so his move to the country had been planned.

"We watched the house for some time," Watson continued. "The men with Dashbrooke didn't leave except to fetch a doctor."

Reign's smile held no humor, but a large amount of satisfaction. "So the fat bastard's hurt."

Watson nodded. "Your missus dealt him a fair bit of damage, aye."

A perverse pride filled him—now that he knew Olivia was going to recover, he could see her actions as brave as well as foolish. "That's my girl."

Clarke eyed him warily as he lifted his glass to his lips. "Speaking of your girl, what do you intend to do about her?"

Reign met his old friend's brutal gaze with an honest one of his own. "Beg her to plague me for all eternity and hope that she'll say yes."

"So that's the way of it, then."

"Yes."

Clarke looked away, wisely silent. Reign appreciated his friend's concern, but he couldn't change what was in his heart anymore than he could change Olivia—and he didn't want to change either.

Watson glanced between the two of them, as though trying to ascertain what exactly was going on, but he was too smart to ask. "What do you want to do about Dashbrooke?"

"Kill him," Reign replied honestly. "But first I need to know if James Burnley is being held in that house as well."

"You still believe the boy to be an innocent in all of this?" Clarke's tone was incredulous at best. "After all that's happened?"

"I don't care if he's innocent or not." Reign reached for the bourbon and poured a liberal amount into his glass. "What I care about is Olivia, and she believes the boy is in danger."

Again, Watson's expression was one of acute interest, and again he did not ask. Smart man. "I left a small company of men to watch the place from a discreet distance. They'll report any activity."

Reign rubbed his jaw. "Once my wife has regained her strength, she and I will venture out to Haddington and examine the situation for ourselves."

"Do you think that wise?" Watson asked, his

brogue making the question lyrical. "I mean, won't they be expectin' you?"

"Never mind that," Clarke bit out. "Do you think it wise to take *your wife* there at all?"

Reign found himself caught somewhere between amusement and annoyance. "I could leave her here with you."

Clarke's mouth thinned and Reign allowed himself a smile. "That's what I thought." Then to Watson, "They very well might be expecting us, but I'm not going to give them the satisfaction of an attack unless it's absolutely necessary. When we do move against Dashbrooke, I want to be as prepared as I can."

Watson nodded, and then gave voice to what Reign was already thinking, "They knew to use silver shot."

"And now they'll have time to prepare for our retaliation," Clarke added.

Reign swirled the bourbon in his glass. The lamplight caught the facets of the crystal, making it shimmer and glow. "Gentlemen, I need you to do something for me."

"What?" they asked in unison, and then shared a brief chuckle.

"Spread the word that Mrs. Gavin is gravely ill and expected to die." He smiled at their startled expressions. "I want to see how Dashbrooke and his minions react to hearing that they just may lose their bargaining power."

For the first time that evening, Clarke actually smiled. "James Burnley is nothing to you."

Reign inclined his head. "I certainly wouldn't walk into a trap to free the boy, but Dashbrooke will start to wonder just what I'll do to some of his loved ones to avenge my wife."

"We'll make the bastard fidget like a whore in a chastity belt," Watson quipped almost gleefully. "He'll be bound to make a misstep."

"At the very least," Reign said, "he'll concentrate solely on me, rather than me and Olivia. We'll have an element of surprise when we do make our move."

"Do you think Olivia will go along with it?" Clarke asked, his smile fading.

Reign flashed him a bright grin. "That bloodthirsty little wench? To destroy Dashbrooke, she'd dig her own grave."

And didn't he adore her for it.

"Where the hell do you think you're going?"

Halfway out of his bed, her limbs infuriatingly weak, Olivia froze at the sound of Reign's gruff—angry—voice.

Closing her eyes, she slumped back against the pillows. She couldn't meet his gaze. Not just yet. "I wanted to get up."

"It's not even dusk yet. Where did you think you were going to go?"

The suspicion in his voice gave her strength. She

could face his anger, even buoy herself with it. She opened her eyes and looked at him.

He looked like hell—that wasn't so easy to face. "I'm covered in blood. I thought I might get a bath."

He gave a sharp nod. "I'll draw one for you."

She watched him cross the floor in his rumpled and bloodstained clothes. Some of that blood was hers—she could smell it. Her wounds had closed over, and while still very tender, were healing well, so it wasn't as if he had tended to her recently. Why hadn't he changed?

When he walked out of the bath, stripped from the waist up, the rush of water filling the tub a gentle rumble behind him, Olivia knew the answer. He had been waiting for her to wake up—waiting for this moment.

Her heart cracked. Why was he doing this to her? Why didn't he say anything about her going off on her own? About her drugging him?

He came to the bed, flung back the covers, and scooped her up into his arms as though she was a child. "What are you doing?" she demanded.

"Carrying you to the bath."

"I can walk."

He made a scoffing noise. "Right."

She regarded him closely as he carried her. This close she could see the wariness etched in the lines around his eyes, the tightness of the muscle in his jaw. The arms that held her were like unyielding iron, his spine and shoulders rigid. Yet, he kept his anger in. Was he trying to lull her into a false sense of security before he unleashed his fury on her?

Or was he more angry with himself for trusting her, and wanting her trust in return?

She was already naked, so Reign took her straight to the tub and gently lowered her into the hot, fragrant water. Olivia sighed and shivered as the heat enveloped her, warmed her and soothed her. Then she shivered again as she watched Reign remove what was left of his clothing.

Nude, he was a magnificent sight. Golden skin, lightly dusted with dark hair, pulled smoothly over long, defined muscles. His was a body that came from a mortal lifetime of riding horses, wielding swords, and hard training. He had been a warrior in his prime when he became a vampire—a year younger than she had been in mortal years. His rugged features hid his age. He could easily pass for any age between nine and twenty and forty, simply because his face was perfect in its masculinity. There was nothing youthful about it, nor was there anything that would have him look old.

He was lovely—beautiful even. When she first met him, her sister Rosemary had thought him frightening, his appearance and personality overwhelming. Olivia had taken one look and decided she had to have him. Never in her life had she been as bold as she had with him. He asked her to dance and that same night she took him to her bed, with every intention of keeping him there.

"What did you ever see in me?" she asked as he turned off the taps and climbed into the bath with her. The tub was so full that some water sloshed over the edge onto the floor.

His arms hanging loosely over the sides, he regarded her through heavy-lidded eyes. "I ask myself that very same question almost daily."

If there had been anything but humor and a touch of gentle reproach in his voice she might not have flushed with pleasure as she did. He spoke as though the answer should be obvious, with an intimacy that made her foolish heart kick against her ribs.

"You were unlike any woman I had ever known," he amended, his tone more serious. "For the first time in my life I knew I had found someone who could make eternity fascinating every damn day."

She blinked, her eyes inexplicably hot. "I couldn't possibly live up to such an expectation."

"You haven't failed yet."

"You haven't seen me for thirty years," she replied dryly.

He smiled sadly. "Not a day went by that I didn't think about you."

Olivia stared at him, helpless and so humbled she felt crushed by it. "You haven't even asked me why I did what I did last night."

Reign's smile faded. "You wanted to meet the kidnappers—Dashbrooke—on your own."

Her throat tight, Olivia dipped her head. "Yes."

"Did he say anything about James?"

She closed her eyes against the anguish that washed over her. Dear James. Whatever would become of him now? Had her threats, her bravado, to Dashbrooke worked? Was her nephew even alive?

"Not much, no."

"Don't fret, Liv. I'm sure James is safe."

She opened her eyes and found him leaning toward her, so close she could see the striations of gray and silver in his eyes. "There's something I need to tell you. And after I do, you might decide to reevaluate whether or not I've failed your expectations."

His head tilted slightly. Her gaze fell upon the strong column of his throat, her gums itching. She was hungry and he smelled so good. She was needy and he was so strong. She was guilty and he was her only salvation.

"What is it?"

"It's about James," she rasped. "About the ransom Dashbrooke wanted."

He watched her patiently, as he took a cloth and a bar of soap from the side of the tub and dipped both in the water, rubbing them together to form a thick lather. "Go on."

Olivia drew a deep breath. Now was not the time for fear. She had gotten herself into this situation and now she had to own it. Regardless of what happened next, she could go on with her soul relatively clean. Unless, of course, Dashbrooke killed James, in which case she might as well be dead herself.

"He wanted you." It all tumbled out after that first confession. "I didn't know it was him at the time, but he told me to go to you. I didn't want to, but I didn't know what they'd do to James, and I would have done anything to save him. I was supposed to bring you to Scotland and exchange you for him."

He set the soap aside and swung his calm gaze to hers. "I know."

It was as though the water had suddenly turned to ice, so great was her shock. "You know?"

Reign took one of her hands in his and lifted her arm so he could run the soapy cloth along the length of it, scrubbing away the blood and dirt of the night before. "Clarke told me when he arrived. Seems he took a little trip to Clovelly and found the original note in your room. You should always burn things like that, Liv."

Her mouth opened, and hung like that for a moment. So many things she could say, so many questions she could ask. "You never said a word."

He moved on to her other arm. "I wanted to see if you would tell me yourself."

And now that she had, it was too late. "I drugged you."

He nodded. "Put me out for a good twenty minutes. I tried to tell you that I knew, but then my tongue turned as heavy as a brick. That was a lot of laudanum you gave me."

"Why aren't you angry?"

The slick cloth ran over her chest. She winced as it brushed the bruised flesh near her heart. His touch wasn't the least bit sensual, but her nipples tightened all the same.

His gaze flickered to her face before falling on the task of washing her. "You despised me enough that you would never come to me without good reason."

He was right, but that didn't stop her from wallowing a little in her shame. Her thoughts of him had changed so much, so very quickly. "You don't hate me?"

He must have heard the catch in her voice, because he stopped what he was doing and looked at her—really looked at her—with an expression so sweet it robbed her of breath. "No. I understand you too well to ever hate you. You did what you thought you had to do. There is something I want to know, though."

"What?" Anything. She'd tell him whatever he wanted to know, give him anything he wanted.

"Why didn't you do it?" He paused in his gentle scrubbing of her skin. "James could be safe right now."

He didn't sound like he particularly believed that. To be honest, Olivia wasn't certain she did either. "Because . . ." She could not bring herself to tell him she loved him. It was foolish she knew, but she just couldn't say the words. Not yet. Nor would she be trite and go on about how he had been so good to her. "Because I couldn't betray you."

From the way his lips parted, his breath hitching ever so slightly, she knew she might as well have made a declaration of love.

"So you chose me over the boy you consider your own son."

When he put it like that . . . God, she should feel horrible, shouldn't she? "I only knew I couldn't betray you." It was a whisper, but he heard it. How could he not?

There was a great upheaval of water as he came up on his knees. He captured her face in his hands and kissed her, with such desperate longing that Olivia's fingers tingled with it. She clutched at his shoulders as she opened her mouth to his, rejoicing as his tongue slid inside. And when he moved backward, she went with him, allowing him to stretch out his legs so that she could straddle his lap. He was iron-hard as the silky head of his erection pressed against her, igniting a need that went so far beyond the physical it was damn close to spiritual.

She couldn't do this. Not yet. Not without saying the words that needed to be spoken. Breaking their kiss, she leaned back onto his thighs. "I'm so sorry," she blurted. "Oh, Reign. I tried to tell myself it was the right thing. I tried not to care. I even told myself they wouldn't—couldn't—hurt you."

"Shh." Bending forward, he kissed her again, and then trailed feathery kisses over her damp eyelids and cheeks. "It's all right. Don't torture yourself anymore. I'd go willingly to Dashbrooke if you asked me to."

Trembling with need and emotion, Olivia reached down beneath the water, shivering as wet heat lapped against her. She wrapped her fingers around the thick length of his cock and lowered herself onto it, sighing as it slowly filled her.

Reign was perfectly still as she settled onto his lap. He was buried to the hilt inside her, and when she moved, friction danced along that eager little ridge of flesh between the lips of her sex. She teased them both by being as still as possible.

Then he wrapped his arms around her and pressed his lips to the spot where the bullet had entered her chest. It didn't hurt, but rather filled her with a strange, tight heat that seemed to push outward, too much for her body to contain.

"I thought I was going to lose you," he murmured, his breath hot against her damp flesh. "I've never been that scared, not even when you left."

Olivia churned her hips downward, engulfing the length of him with her body. She shivered in his embrace. "It's all right," she soothed. "I'm still here."

Reign raised his face to hers, a vulnerability in his gaze that humbled her. "I prayed, Liv. I prayed to God to keep you with me."

That heat that had filled her rushed upward and spilled out of her eyes, sending a river of scalding tears down both of her cheeks.

"Don't ever put me through that again." The harshness of his demand was lessened by a hoarse tone. This time it was she who took his face in her hands. She kissed him with everything she felt as she moved her body up and down on his. Her movements were jerky and frantic, splashing water over the sides of the tub as she rode him, bringing them both to a swift and intense climax that had them both crying out into each other's mouths.

Afterward, Reign finished bathing her now exhausted body and then lifted her out of the tub. He dried her with soft towels and carried her to her bed in the adjoining room where soft, clean sheets engulfed them. He held her against him and offered her his throat in a gesture that was so simple and trusting that it brought fresh tears to her eyes once more.

She'd cried more since being reunited with him than she had in the last thirty years.

She pierced his flesh with her fangs, taking his strength into her, making it her own. He shuddered against her, slid into her once more and made love to her tenderly, patiently, until she begged him to let her come. He didn't have to ask for her to look at him. She held his gaze easily, letting everything she felt shine in her eyes since she couldn't yet bring herself to say the words that would strip her so bare she might never recover.

Then, sated in so many ways, Olivia snuggled against her husband's chest and sighed in contentment. Without looking she knew the bruise on her chest had faded noticeably. She could feel Reign's blood coursing through her veins, healing her.

"Sleep for a bit," he told her, wrapping a warm, heavy arm around her shoulders. "When you wake up I'll tell you how we're going to rescue James."

She glanced up at him, dangerously close to tears again, damn it. "You're still going to help him?"

He looked surprised that she'd asked. "Of course. Regardless of what he might have gotten himself into, you don't think I'd leave our nephew in Dashbrooke's hands, do you?"

Our nephew. If she hadn't realized she'd loved him every day for the last thirty years, she did now. "Thank you."

He gave her a squeeze. "Thank me by letting me give you a proper honeymoon once this is all over."

Olivia was becoming accustomed to this tightening in her throat and chest. "Why, Mr. Gavin. Are you asking me to be your wife?"

"Fuck, yes."

Laughing, Olivia wrapped her arms around him and squeezed. "Yes."

He kissed her then and for the first time in so many, many years, Olivia knew what it was to believe that everything was going to be all right. That there was such a thing as a happily ever after.

She drifted off to sleep holding on to that thought as tightly as she could.

Chapter 16

"Obviously we overestimated your aunt's attachment to you, James."

Reggie Dashbrooke watched as his friend stiffened under Reggie's father's icy regard. Even bedridden from injuries, the old man was an intimidating bastard.

It felt good to call his father a bastard, even if only in his head.

"She'll come for me," James said, his voice strained, but full of conviction. "She won't risk anything happening to me."

The lot of them were gathered in his father's bedchamber, clustered at the foot of the bed like a group of naughty schoolboys brought before the headmaster's desk. Even Fitzy was there, recently returned from London.

George Haversham sneered at James. "She chose her husband over you—a bloke who she hasn't seen since before you were born."

James's expression weighed heavily on Reggie's heart. He knew his father was up to no good. He knew he planned to hurt his friends. Before last night Reggie thought he didn't have a choice but to play along, but now, seeing his father battered and bruised, he wondered if there wasn't a way out of this.

"They'll come." Reggie surprised himself by speaking clearly and forcefully. His gaze fell on George, who actually flushed under it. "Reign will want blood for what happened to James's aunt."

George's eyes widened. That terrified gaze shot to Fitzy. "What in the name of God will he do to us?"

"Make you gods," Reggie reminded him. "Once we have the vampires in captivity, we'll be able to take their blood and become immortal ourselves." He turned his head to the man on the bed. "Isn't that right, Father?"

Surprise flickered in the older Dashbrooke's eyes before a pleased smile curved his thin lips. He looked like a big fat lizard sunning himself against the pillows. "Quite right, my boy. Quite right."

Liar. At that moment, all the bitterness and inadequacy Reggie had ever felt under his father's icy stare came rushing to the surface, congealing into a hatred so strong, Reggie's heart pounded with it.

"But what about the news that she's dying?" Fitzy demanded. "Sorry, James, but if she dies, there's nothing to stop Reign from slaughtering us all—and to hell with making us vampires."

"She's not going to die," Reggie insisted and hoped to God it was true, not for his own sake, but for James's, and for George, who didn't seem to realize that his headaches and nosebleeds were symptoms of something that would cut his life short if he didn't become immortal.

James shot him a thankful glance and Reggie smiled at his friend. James might be a bit spoiled and self-serving, but he had always been good to Reggie. Had always been there to insist that Reggie was good enough, even though his father insisted that he was a disappointment.

Reggie wasn't about to sacrifice that for his father's approval. His father's approval didn't matter anymore. She didn't know it, but Olivia Gavin had become an inspiration to him. She had chosen to protect the man she loved rather than betray him.

Reggie wasn't going to betray his friend, and he didn't care if James blamed him for ruining his plans.

"We need to prepare," he announced, ignoring how the others were watching him, their expressions ranging from curiosity to outright surprise at this new side of him. "They will spy upon us first, look for our weaknesses." He glanced out the window at the slowly sinking sun. "They'll spy tonight. Attack tomorrow evening."

"How do you know?" It was Fitz who asked, breaking his normal silence.

Reggie looked at him. "Because James's aunt will be even more worried about him now. And because they'll want to attack while Father is still weak."

They were all watching him, but there was only one with whom Reggie concerned himself. He turned to his father, saw the tiny flicker of fear in the older man's gaze. He was playing with his ring, the symbol of the Order, that had always meant more to him than his own son.

Reggie almost laughed, but he contained it. "Don't worry, Father. I will take care of you."

When Olivia woke for the second time that day, the sun had set and the wounds in her chest and shoulder had faded to yellowish green bruises. The spots were tender, the muscles stiff, but not so much that she was in pain. Her own exceptional healing, mixed with Reign's blood, had her almost completely healed.

Her husband was nowhere to be seen. She listened for the sound of his voice and heard him downstairs talking to Watson and Clarke. They were waiting on her.

She slipped out of bed and rang for Janet. As fast as she was, there were some things a woman could do faster with help—such as fasten buttons up the back of a gown, or fix her hair.

The maid arrived in a few minutes, carrying a bundle of clothes.

"Mr. Gavin thought you might want to wear these tonight, Missus." She kept her expression neutral even though curiosity shone in her eyes.

The clothes Reign sent for her were a pair of loose black trousers with a matching shirt and a pair of sturdy boots.

"Thank you, Janet. I'll wear a demi-corset as well." Her other corsets were simply too long to wear with the trousers. It was strange to not feel the snug pressure of the stays around her abdomen and hips—free, but strange. Thankfully she had two, because her other one—the one she wore to confront Dashbrooke—was ruined.

After she was dressed, Olivia sat before the mirror and let Janet brush the tangles from her hair. Then the young woman plaited and coiled the heavy mass until it was neatly secured high on the back of her head.

The whole process took longer than it had the night before without the maid's help, but Olivia felt better prepared this night—stronger and more at ease. Perhaps that sense of security came from within herself, or perhaps it came from knowing that whatever happened this night, Reign would be with her.

Dressed and ready for battle, she went downstairs to join her husband and his friends in Reign's study. They looked up as she walked in: Watson with an expression of curiosity, Clarke with barely veiled distrust, and Reign with such pleasure at the sight of her that Olivia's knees trembled. He had given her that very same look the night they first met, when she threw propriety to the wind and took him to her home and into her bed. She hadn't regretted any of it. In fact, now that she knew all that she did, the only thing she regretted was running away from him.

He rose to his feet, towering over her and clad in head-to-toe-black as she was.

"Watson has given me the location of the house where we believe James is being kept. Shall we go?"

Just like that? God, he was *such* an amazing man. She looked between Watson and Clarke. "Just the two of us?"

Clarke looked away. He didn't like her and Olivia knew why. His loyalty to Reign was admirable, and she deserved his coldness. That didn't mean she intended to suffer under it for long.

"Tonight we're spying," Reign replied as he came toward her. "Unless we're forced to act tonight, we'll return to the house tomorrow evening to rescue James."

Of course. They would investigate the house, check for guards and weak points and then make their move. It made perfect sense, but the impulsive side of her nature—the side that was so afraid for James—chafed at it all the same.

Regardless of the turmoil inside her, she nodded in acquiescence. "I'm ready."

Reign addressed his men. "You know what to do if the house is besieged."

Watson nodded. "Aye." Clarke bobbed his head as well, his cool gaze locked on Olivia. Yes, she was going to tire of that very quickly.

"Good." Reign held out his hand to Olivia, but his attention was still on the other two. "If we're not back by dawn, send word to the Bucket of Blood and move on Dashbrooke immediately." The men agreed and Reign guided her from the room.

"What are they supposed to do if the house is attacked?" she asked as they climbed the stairs to the attic. Better to think of that than what might become of them if they didn't return by dawn.

"Burn it," Reign replied as they crossed to the exit to the roof. "Preferably with the invaders inside."

"Oh." Part of her was horrified, but another, more bloodthirsty part agreed with the plan. Hopefully it wouldn't come to that. "Do you think there's much chance of that happening?"

"No. They want us to come to them. It would be easier for them that way."

"Aren't we giving them exactly what they want?" She wasn't afraid. She wasn't afraid of anything with Reign beside her—except perhaps of losing him.

He flashed a grin in the darkness as they walked out into the night. "Only if they catch us."

Olivia returned the grin. "Which they won't."

It was easy to share his bravado and draw strength from it.

They vaulted off the roof together, letting the night give them wings. The first time she had flown had been by accident when she had tried to kill herself by jumping off the top of the clock tower at Westminster, the one that housed the bell called Big Ben. It had been the same night she'd accidentally killed a person while feeding. She had drifted through the night sky sobbing, feeling as though all of her choices had been taken from her.

They hadn't been, of course. But she had certainly made some bad ones over the years. She glanced at the man beside her. He was not one of them.

They flew east out of Edinburgh, past the outskirts of the city and its lights and smells, to a small, rural area slightly southwest of Haddington township.

The house stood by itself, fenced in by trees and other foliage planted for privacy as well as decoration. It was a pretty, modest country home that didn't look at all like the lair of a villain.

"Do you see any guards?" Reign asked as they drew closer.

"In the drive," she replied, spotting a shadow moving across the front of the house. "You?"

"I think the back is clear. They're probably patrolling." He reached out for her hand, and when she took it, led her down toward the dark garden behind the house.

"I don't smell any dogs," she whispered when they touched down on the well-manicured lawn. They were partially hidden by a hedge—not that anyone other than another vampire or perhaps a cat might see them.

"Dashbrooke doesn't strike me as the type to have pets," Reign replied, his gaze fastened on the guard now circling the house. "He's too much of an animal himself."

Once the guard continued on his tour, she and Reign raced across the grass to the dense, black shadows cast by the manor. They crouched below a window—one of the few that glowed from light within.

"Look in," Reign whispered near her ear, his hot breath on her skin making her shiver. "Is James in there?"

Slowly, Olivia straightened as much as she dared and peered inside the window. There were three young men sitting at a table drinking ale and sharing a loaf of bread with cheese. One of the boys she recognized as George Haversham, who was laughing at something one of his companions said.

And the companion who had spoken with such wit was James.

"He's there," she whispered, jerking away from the window and pressing her back against the smooth stone of the outside wall. Relief, coupled with confusion coursed through her veins.

"Why is he sitting there laughing with his friends when he's supposed to be a prisoner?" She wondered aloud. She forced herself to meet Reign's bright gaze. "George Haversham isn't being kept against his will, we know that. And if Haversham is one of James's captors, why is he sitting there laughing with him?"

Reign glanced through the window, then back at her. His expression was sympathetic, but not pitying. "Because he's not a prisoner, Liv."

Which meant that James played a willing part in all of this. That he had helped stage his own kidnapping—put her through all that worry and terror.

"No," she murmured, feeling strangely calm. "It can't be."

"Maybe he's been kept here under false pretenses," Reign suggested, but she could tell he didn't believe that. "There's no knowing what lies Dashbrooke might have told him."

Yes, that had to be it. James might be a foolish boy, but he would never betray her. Would he? He just might, if he thought the reward great enough. If Dashbrooke had somehow toyed with his mind.

Reign's fingers closed around her arm, the warmth of them snapping her out of her thoughts and back to the moment. "Save your questions for after we save him. Right now, I need your mind clear."

She nodded. "Of course."

He released her arm, but not before giving her a hard, fast kiss on the mouth. "That's my girl."

Before the guard circled around again, they made the leap to the gabled roof. One look inside one of the dormer windows confirmed that the attic was used for storage and not a bedroom. It would be easy to break the latch on one of them—or simply break the glass if necessary—and slip inside.

"Why not the cellar?" Olivia asked. "Wouldn't that be easier?" They could go in through the kitchen.

"Too much chance of running into a servant," Reign whispered. "Or several. I'd rather as few innocents are hurt as possible."

She hadn't thought of that. "I'm not much for strategy, am I?"

He smiled. "You do well enough. You managed to best me on several occasions."

Olivia grinned as well. "But you're easy."

Reign shot her a look that told her she'd pay for that remark later—in all kinds of deliciously sensual ways.

This was what she had walked out on thirty years ago. If only she let him explain, but she'd been so scared she ran away—scared of what she was. Scared of forever.

She wasn't scared anymore.

After another survey of the grounds and peeking in a few more windows, they had a good idea of how best to approach the house the next night, where to enter and how many guards they would likely have to face.

They also saw Dashbrooke in his bed, bandaged and bruised and looking as foul-tempered as a whore trying to work a poorhouse. It gave Olivia more pleasure than it ought to see Dashbrooke that way, knowing that she had caused it.

She stole one more glimpse of James through that downstairs window before they departed. He was still there with his friends, acting as though he hadn't a care in the world, looking like a boy his age should.

He never looked that happy when he was with her.

Olivia and Reign flew back to Edinburgh in silence and entered the town house the same way they left. When they entered the study, however, they were surprised to discover that Watson and Clarke had company.

Reggie Dashbrooke—the one boy they hadn't seen while in Haddington—looking much older than his years, his reddish hair mussed and his eyes tired, rose from the sofa as they entered. The sight of him brought a low growl to Olivia's throat. She advanced toward the boy, but Reign stopped her with a gentle hand. She shook off the restraint, but she didn't move.

Reggie's gaze was locked on her, and there was no fear in it, even though she detected a faint whiff of the emotion on his skin, heard the racing of his heart that tugged at her fangs and tempted the demon inside her.

"Don't kill me," he said softly, but firmly. "I'm on your side."

"Why in the hell should we trust you?" Reign asked the younger Dashbrooke as he shoved a glass of bourbon into the boy's hand.

Reggie took a deep swallow of the liquor. So far the young one had held his composure, a fact that earned him a degree of Reign's respect. The boy knew he had no friends in that room, and yet there he was.

"I have no way to prove myself to you except by the sheer fact that I am here."

Across the room—Reign had thought it wise to put as much distance as possible between Reggie and his wife—Olivia snorted. "Your father could have sent you."

The young man didn't try to deny it. "True, but he didn't. In fact, I think he'd kill me if he knew I came to you."

Reign's brow puckered at Reggie's choice of words. They didn't sound like youthful exaggeration at all. In fact, young Mr. Dashbrooke sounded painfully honest.

"Why are you here, Mr. Dashbrooke?" Reign asked, leaning his hip against the edge of his desk.

Reggie chuckled bitterly. "An attack of conscience? Or a moment of weakness, as my father would put it. I've come to offer myself as leverage."

"Leverage?" Clarke frowned. "You want to align yourself with us as a bargaining tool against your father?"

The young man shook his head, his blue gaze never leaving Reign's. For some reason, he had made Reign his focal point in all of this. It was as though he thought Reign the most likely to be sympathetic, which was so absurd Reign might have laughed if the foolish little bastard didn't appeal to some softer side of his nature.

"My father won't exchange James for me. He'll say he will, but he won't."

The resignation in the boy's tone irritated a rawness deep inside Reign. A rawness that had no business still existing after hundreds of years. "You have a very low opinion of your father."

"He has a very low opinion of me," Reggie countered with a shrug. "But that doesn't matter, he'll place what the Order wants above his son, and it won't be a difficult choice for him." He glanced at Olivia. "Not like I imagine it was for you."

Olivia paled at his choice of words and Reign was annoyed with Reggie for being so crass. At least Olivia knew that Dashbrooke wouldn't be quick to kill James, not while the boy was still useful.

"What do you know of the Order, Reggie?" he asked.

"The Order of the Silver Palm. They're like the Friends of the Glorious Unseen, only worse. They don't want to merely venerate vampires. They have agendas and they see vampires as a way to achieve those goals."

Clarke scoffed. "Idiots. Do they really think they stand a chance against a vampire as old as Reign?"

Reggie stared at him for a moment, looking the older of the two, before returning his attention to Reign. "I've heard Father discussing one called Temple with his friends. The Order claims to have captured him."

Icy heat blossomed in the pit of Reign's stomach, rushing outward to his extremities. *Temple captured?* It was impossible. Temple was the best of them all, the strongest and the fastest, certainly the fiercest. How could mere men ever take him?

Reign couldn't even conceive it. But after this was over, he would look into it, and find his old friend just to be sure. In the meantime, he had to listen to the same advice he had given Olivia earlier and keep his mind focused on the here and now.

"If your father won't bargain, what good are you to us?"

Reggie easily accepted the change of subject. "Because the lads will want to make the exchange, and when my father refuses, they'll begin to realize what he has planned, and maybe they'll forgive me for ever going along with him."

Olivia sat down beside him and patted the boy on the shoulder. Such a mother hen. "What does your father have planned, Reggie?"

"George, Fitz, and James, they think you'll make them vampires. My father has convinced them that we'll all become immortal, but he wants the two of you as his prisoners. The Order wants you. I don't know why, but I know that my friends are expendable to my father, and even if they do manage to become vampires, he's going to do to them the same as he does to you."

"How do you know we don't deserve whatever the Order has in mind?" Reign asked. "What makes you so sure betraying your father is the right thing to do?"

Reggie didn't look at him, he was gazing at Olivia with adoringly large blue eyes. And she was staring back at him with a mixture of surprise and anger. "I've always thought that James was fortunate to have you. He can be an arse sometimes, but he's always been good to me—and that's because of how you raised him. Vampire or not, I'd rather have your respect than my father's any day." He turned his gaze to Reign. "Both of you."

Damn if Reign didn't feel for the boy. He knew what it was like to yearn for a father's respect and never quite achieve it.

But Reggie wasn't acting merely out of spite, Reign believed that the boy was truly doing what he believed to be the right thing.

"I don't want to see my friends get hurt," Reggie added. "They've given him blind trust and he's going to repay them with deceit."

Reign glanced at Olivia, who answered with a look that told him the boy had succeeded in winning her over, if only a little. He could also tell that she was thinking about her nephew and wondering just what Dashbrooke had promised James, what lies he had told to win the boy over. He had to admit, it was good to think of the boy as a victim—even a stupid one—rather than the enemy.

"What do you hope to get in return for aiding us, Reggie? Surely your father will never understand your betrayal." Or maybe he would. God knew Reign understood why Olivia had set out to do him as she had.

"No," the boy agreed, "he won't. But at least I can live the rest of my life knowing that I'm nothing like him."

Fair enough.

Reign smiled grimly. "Then Reggie, my boy, consider yourself our prisoner."

Chapter 17

They sent the "ransom" note to George Haver-sham at Reggie's suggestion. It was necessary to send it to one of the younger men so that the others would find out as well.

"My father won't tell them," he'd explained to Olivia and Reign. "I don't want them to think I've abandoned them and fall deeper under Father's sway."

Olivia found it sad, the way Reggie accepted his insignificance in his father's life.

"Perhaps you're wrong about him," she suggested. They were sitting at a small table in the front parlor just before dawn. "He planned to bring you into the Order, didn't he?" And she had seen the ring.

Reggie looked at her with a slow blink, as though he couldn't quite believe his ears. Olivia couldn't quite believe she had actually tried to make Dash-brooke sympathetic either.

"Only if I prove myself," he replied. "Which I haven't. And do you really believe I could be wrong about a man who could have a priest killed without an ounce of regret?"

"You know about the priest?" Perhaps Reggie wasn't as innocent in all of this as she thought.

The boy looked away. "I overheard one of his friends inform him about it. He shrugged and said that sometimes loss of human life was necessary to benefit the greater good."

"Lovely piece of work, your father," Reign remarked from where he sat across the room. He and Olivia were sitting with Reggie for a few hours while Watson and Clarke slept.

Reggie actually smiled, although slightly. "Did you like your father?"

Olivia watched Reign closely. His only reaction to the question had been a slight tightening of his lips. She waited for his response as eagerly, if not more so, than Reggie.

"My father was a prick," Reign answered, his tone brisk with conviction. "The only thing I ever did that came close to pleasing him was become a vampire."

Reggie straightened, grasping the chance to talk to someone who understood. "You told him?"

Reign shrugged, a movement that spoke volumes to Olivia. After six hundred years, it bothered him to speak of his father. That was too much power for a dead man to have.

"I felt it was the right thing to do. If he couldn't respect me, maybe he might fear me instead."

She'd hug him if Reggie wasn't there. Her poor Reign.

"Was he afraid of you?" Reggie's questions weren't insistent or callous, but held a bittersweet curiosity that obviously loosened Reign's tongue.

"No."

The two men, one impossibly ancient, the other heartbreakingly young, shared a smile.

"Your father sounds like mine," Reggie remarked, taking a sip of the tea Olivia had brewed for him.

"They had much in common," Reign informed him. "They belonged to the same Order." He watched the boy carefully as he spoke.

Olivia turned her attention in the same direction, waiting for Reggie's reaction. Blue eyes widened as his smooth, boyish jaw gaped. "Your father belonged to the Silver Palm?"

Reign nodded, his lips taking a faint, sardonic curve. "Ironic, isn't it?"

Disbelief rang in the young man's laughter. It wasn't a malicious sound, and Olivia found herself smiling at it. "A little, yes. Did your father ever talk about bringing you into the Order?"

Reign shook his head. "No." He didn't have to say anything else for Olivia to know that he believed his father was too embarrassed of him to suggest it.

"You're right," Reggie said. "Your father was a prick."

The three of them shared a chuckle before the conversation turned dark once more.

"Is that why they want you?" Reggie asked. "Because your father was part of the Order?"

"I don't think so." Reign lifted a glass of bourbon from the low table beside his chair and took a long swallow. "Their interest isn't limited to me if what you say about Temple is true."

Reggie's gaze narrowed shrewdly. "He's a friend of yours?"

"He was." The now empty glass thudded gently on the tabletop. "Now he's more like family."

"If you're so close, how come you don't know what's happened to him?"

"I said that he was family, not that we were close."

The men shared another grin and Olivia shook her head in mock disgust. "Ugh. If the two of you continue on like this much longer you're going to need matching outfits."

Reggie blushed, but Reign shot her an amused glance. He didn't mind her poking fun at him, but then he never had seemed to take himself as seriously as other men she'd known. She supposed six centuries could give a man a good sense of self-awareness.

She smiled at him. *I love you.* The words sprang to her tongue, but she managed to keep them silent, their echo ringing only in her head. That was not something she wanted young Reggie to witness.

Interest flickered in Reign's gray eyes. He had seen the change in her expression but didn't know what it meant. Thank God.

Reggie checked his watch. "It's almost dawn. Shouldn't the two of you . . . I don't know, hide for the day?"

Olivia plucked a biscuit from the plate in the center of the table. Reggie hadn't touched them and it would be a sin to let them go to waste. "We're fine." She didn't mention that as long as the sunlight didn't touch them they were safe. Reggie might be on their side against his father, but that didn't mean she trusted him with her life.

"Do you want to sleep?" Reign asked him. "I can show you to a guest room."

The young man shook his head, his coppery hair falling over his pale brow. "No, thank you. I want to be awake when my father sends his reply."

Olivia understood, and apparently so did Reign, though he didn't give voice to his opinion. Instead, he engaged Reggie in small talk, keeping him occupied until finally, just a few minutes after Clarke joined them, a knock sounded at the door.

Thankfully, neither Reign nor Olivia had to brave the breaking dawn to answer it.

"It's from Dashbrooke," Clarke informed them, handing the envelope to Reign as he rejoined them. In his anticipation he forgot to glare at her, a fact Olivia wasn't to point out to him.

Poor Reggie sat up so straight he was poised on the edge of his chair. "What does it say?"

The seal of the letter tore as Reign whipped his finger through it. He withdrew a small piece of stationery that he opened and read aloud. "My dear Mr. and Mrs. Gavin, you win. I will do whatever you wish provided you return my dear son to me safe and unharmed. Bring him to me this evening and I will hand Mr. Burnley over into your custody. Sincerely, William Dashbrooke, Esquire."

Anger made Reggie's face even more pale and his cheeks flushed. He turned to Olivia, his expression stiff as he tried hard to hide his pain. "It's a trap."

Olivia nodded, her heart breaking for him. "I know."

"Because he called me his 'dear son'?"

Reaching across the table, she covered his tightly clenched fist with her hand and gave him a soft pat. "Because he said he'd give us James in return." Dashbrooke wasn't stupid enough to hand over the one person keeping him alive.

"What are you going to do?" For the first time since coming to them, real fear—real uncertainty—shone in his eyes. It made him look younger than he was.

"We're going to give your father what he wants," Reign informed him as he stood.

"Me?"

"No, you silly boy." He flashed Reggie a roguish smile. "Us. Now go the hell to bed. You need your rest for tonight. Clarke, show Reggie upstairs will you? Give him the room at the end of the hall."

Olivia could practically taste Reggie's relief. What had he thought they'd do to him, eat him? Still, it was obvious that Reign wasn't taking any chances either. He was putting Reggie far enough away from them that they'd hear him coming if he tried to attack them, but close enough that they'd hear if he tried to sneak out.

Reggie bid them a good morning and followed after Clarke. Olivia waited until they were both gone before turning to Reign.

"Do you think it's wise, doing what Dashbrooke asks?" She was thinking not only of James's safety, but Reign's and Reggie's as well.

He crossed the room to her, took her hand and pulled her to her feet so that he could slip his arm around her shoulders. "I think letting Dashbrooke think he's in control is the best way to throw the bastard off his guard."

She leaned into him as they walked toward the door. "We can't let him hurt any of those boys."

His arm, strong and warm slid around her. "I think you'd better worry about what those boys will do to Dashbrooke once they figure out that he meant to double cross them. Young Haversham's not going to like being denied his immortality."

"It's not his immortality I'm worried about,"

Olivia responded as they started up the stairs toward their room. "It's yours. Mine too."

Reign squeezed her shoulders. "Dashbrooke's no match for you or me. Don't you worry."

But Olivia was worried, and she could tell from the tenseness around his mouth that Reign was as well. Did he doubt her?

"You trust me, don't you?" she asked, stopping in the middle of the stairs so she could twist her body to look up at him. "You don't think I'm going to betray you, do you?"

He smiled tenderly at her. "No. I trust you. You haven't let me down yet, have you? Now, come. You need to rest."

Olivia allowed him to guide her the rest of the way up the stairs in silence. After all she had done, he didn't think she had let him down? Good lord, what would she have to do to actually disappoint him? Whatever it was, she hoped she never did it.

Especially not tonight.

Many hours later, after a long nap and dinner, Olivia walked into Reign's bedroom—or rather *their* bedroom—to talk to her husband before the assault on Dashbrooke's house to find the room shrouded in darkness, save for a single candle on the bedside table.

And Reign lying naked on the bed, his beautiful body, more than six feet of glorious shadows and light.

"You're a little underdressed," she joked, her mouth dry at the sight of him.

He sat up in one swift motion, swinging his long legs over the side of the bed. He stood, and walked toward her, not the least bit self-conscious of his nudity, but with the determined stride of a man well aware of how little he was wearing—and just what he intended to do about it.

Who was she to fight him? "Do we have time?" They had to leave soon, didn't they?

"We're going to make time," he informed her, pulling her into the warm circle of his arms. One hand pressed against her back as the other tilted her head to the side.

Olivia heard what he left unsaid. They were about to walk into a volatile and decidedly dangerous situation. There would be nothing left undone or unsaid between them before they went—just in case.

Reign kissed her neck, the warm hollow of her throat where her pulse fluttered helplessly. His teeth grazed her skin, sending a shiver down her spine. She wasn't going to think about what might happen that night. There were too many awful things—too many wonderful things—that could transpire that there was no use in entertaining any of them.

There was nothing she needed to think about other than the man with her now.

Her hands caressed the smooth flesh of his back

and shoulders, feeling the satiny swells and contours of his muscles beneath her fingers. The only thing that marred the perfection that was Reign was a scar on his right shoulder. She had seen it the first night they had spent together—a cross branded into his back. He had told her some story as to how he came to have it, now she knew that had to be a lie.

"Where did this come from?"

He raised his head only enough to speak, his breath a gentle whisper against her throat. "Zealots who thought they could drive the devil out of me."

"Thank God they didn't succeed," Olivia murmured as his fangs nipped at her, flooding her with heat and buckling her knees.

He chuckled, tormenting her sensitive flesh once more. "You are so damn perfect."

The words struck her and for one brief moment Olivia feared she might cry, but then his fangs pierced her neck and she shuddered with pleasure, clinging to his shoulders like a vine latched onto a wall.

He drank briefly—enough to have her throbbing in places she didn't know she could throb. Enough that she was dizzy with longing and sensual pleasure, and eager to touch him, taste him.

When his tongue had closed the punctures in her skin, and her legs had regained some of their strength, Olivia sank to her knees on the carpet, trailing her hands down Reign's back and buttocks. His hips were level with her face as she caressed the hair-dusted, ropey expanse of his abdomen. She opened her mouth and ran the flat of her tongue over the silky head of his erection.

"Jesus." His hands cupped her head—not pushing, but holding her so she couldn't move just yet. She didn't want to move.

She licked him, kissed him, opened her mouth and took him inside, savoring the feel, the musky salt of his skin. His fingers tightened, digging into her skull as she laved him with her tongue, caressed him with her lips. Her hands clutched at his flanks, as she engulfed the heavy length of him.

Reign's low groans and sighs were the only sound in the room and Olivia responded to them on so many levels. Her body thrummed with sexual power, delighting in knowing she could make him shiver. Her heart swelled with gratefulness that she had been given the gift of his body, ached with love for him.

Tension built in his thighs. She could feel him tremble with it. His hips moved, thrusting as he held her still. Olivia gazed up at him, met the silvered brightness of his gaze as release struck him. He tossed back his head, a deep moan tearing from his throat. She clung to him, unwilling to let him go until the last tremor shook him.

When she finally released him, Reign pulled her to her feet and kissed her, heedless of the taste of himself on her lips. He tugged the pins from her hair with deft fingers, bringing the heavy mass tumbling loose around her shoulders.

"Turn around," he ordered. She did, and he set those fingers to work on the fastenings of her gown. Within seconds the bodice sagged around her arms. Olivia turned around so that he could shove the offending fabric to the floor as she tore at the hooks of her corset. He helped her with those as well as the gown pooled around her feet. He tossed the corset across the room as she struggled out of her combination, shredding the delicate linen in her desperation to be naked against him.

Finally, she stood before him in nothing but her stockings and garters. He pulled her against him and she gasped as her flesh met his. Rough yet smooth, hard yet supple, he was the most delicious thing she had ever felt.

"The first night I met you I wanted to feel your skin against mine," he whispered against her ear. "You ruined me for any other woman."

Smiling, Olivia rubbed against him, delighting in the velvety texture of his body hair on her flesh. "Good, because I would so hate to have to kill any other woman who dared touch you."

Reign laughed. She shivered as his warm breath caressed the side of her face and neck. Closing her eyes, she sighed as his lips followed the same path.

His fingers combed through her hair, massaging her scalp and neck with firm, gentle strokes. The winding heat inside her increased with every touch of his fingers, every brush of his lips. Her cunny was hot and wet, aching with the need to be filled by him.

"I want you," she whispered softly, rubbing her cheek against his temple. "So badly."

His response was to turn her toward the bed and lower her onto the mattress. Propping himself above her, he smoothed the hair back from her face, while the lone light in the room cast him in a golden light.

Reign smiled tenderly. "Thank you."

Her gaze locked with his, as a slight frown wrinkled her brow. "For what?"

His hand slid up her thigh. The muscle there quivered at his touch and she lifted herself into his palm. She wanted him to touch her, stroke her. He brushed his lips across one of her nipples, sending a sharp thrill racing through her. "For coming back to me, no matter what the original motivation was."

"Oh," was all she could say, robbed of speech as he traced the tip of his tongue around her nipple, causing the already puckered flesh to tighten and ache for more.

"You incredible man," she murmured, as his hot, moist mouth drove her to distraction. "I don't deserve you."

"No," he agreed, moving his head to the other breast. "You deserve better."

Hot tears leaked from the corners of her eyes, leaving a scalding trail as they trickled into her hair. *You're wrong.* But she didn't say the words aloud, knowing she would start sobbing if she did, and she would rather die than ruin this moment. She arched against his mouth instead, and gave herself over fully to the sensations he aroused within her.

Reign knew he had struck a chord emotionally with Olivia. Her silence spoke louder than any words ever could. He didn't have to be a mind reader to know that she thought he was wrong to think so highly of her. When this night was over, and they had nothing but the rest of their lives to concern themselves with, he would endeavor to make her see herself as he did.

Olivia moaned and arched her hips against him as his fingers trailed down her belly to the humid apex of her smooth thighs. Her thighs parted readily for him, requiring no coaxing—not that he'd thought she would.

Her body jerked when he slid a finger into her tight wetness. Her hot, greedy flesh gripped him so tightly, so sweetly, his cock swelled to full erection in anticipation. Her fingernails dug into his shoulders as she undulated beneath him.

Christ, he loved the feel of her tight little nipple in his mouth, her juices on his fingers. Loved the taste of her skin, the sounds she made when he nipped lightly with his teeth.

He suckled her flesh until her fingers tangled in his hair, tugging at his scalp. Her hips churned now, pressing her mound against the heel of his hand as he thrust two fingers inside her. He knew what she wanted, even if she didn't say it.

His mouth left her breast as he inched down her strong, soft body. He kissed the soft flesh of her rib cage, traced the edge of her navel with his tongue. He pressed his lips to the soft curve of her belly, rasping the soft flesh there with the stubble of his jaw. Olivia gasped softly in response.

Poised between her legs, braced on one elbow as he continued to stroke her, Reign nuzzled the damp thatch of sable curls, breathing the salty scent of her deep into his lungs. Her hips jerked, bringing a satisfied smile to his lips.

He had never felt this with any other woman. She was the other half of his soul. At first he had thought her a simple obsession, a sensual fascination. It had taken exactly two days to realize that this incredible woman was meant for him. He would never cease to worship her, never fail to be amazed and humbled by her. He didn't just want her; he needed her. For the past thirty years he had been dead inside, and for centuries before that as well. He only truly felt alive when he was with her.

He brushed his lips against those curls, feeling the dampness there. He slipped his fingers out of her, lifted them to his mouth and licked the wetness from him. Salt and honey and musk flooded his tongue.

"Do you want me to eat you?" he asked softly, trailing his gaze over her luscious body to finally meet her heavy lidded stare.

"Yes."

He dragged one finger down the plump cleft of those drenched lips. "Do you want to come on my tongue?"

She shivered. "Yes."

A low groan broke free of Reign's throat as he lowered his head. His fingers parted her slick flesh for the invasion of his tongue. He wanted to hear her pants of pleasure, wanted her to grind her body against his mouth as orgasm ripped through her.

He worked her into a frenzy with his tongue, licking and sucking, even nibbling ever so gently, concentrating on the rigid nub of her clit. She quaked every time his distended fangs brushed her sensitive walls, clutched at him with her fingers and her thighs.

When she came, it was with her hands pushing his face into her, bathing him with her juices. She cried out, her moans a symphony to his ears. He lapped at her greedily, drunk on the taste of her. It wasn't until she went limp that he lifted himself from between her thighs. Rock hard, his cock ached to finish what his tongue had started.

Olivia lifted herself on her elbows, her strong

features flushed with the rosy glow of satisfaction. "I want you inside me. *Now*."

"Roll over," he told her, his voice low and rough in his own ears.

She went eagerly, rolling onto her stomach to reveal the long line of her spine and full curve of her buttocks to his appreciative gaze.

He nudged one of her knees up to the side, opening her thighs and angling her so that she leaned partially on the opposite hip. The position opened her body to his, and as he guided the head of his cock into her awaiting wet heat, he closed his eyes with a sigh. Olivia replied in kind.

The angle of her hips made the friction between them acute. Her sweet round buttocks cushioned his hips as he thrust into her. Her back was warm against his chest as he curved his knee into hers. The tight grip of her sex around his and the soft encouraging moans slipping breathlessly from between her lips heightened the hunger in his blood.

Tossing back her hair, Olivia glanced over her shoulder at him, her expression so arousing he almost came right then. Instead, Reign gritted his teeth and reached under her lifted hip. His fingers parted the soaked curls between her thighs to caress the sensitive crest his tongue had savored moments earlier. He stroked it ruthlessly, drawing a sharp gasp from the woman beneath him.

The rhythm of his body matched that of his busy fingers, thrusting in as his fingers stroked up.

Olivia rocked against him, lifting her buttocks to his pelvis before pressing down on his hand.

"Do you love me?" he asked, purposefully easing the pressure of his fingers, denying her what she wanted.

He could feel her body tensing, could feel the tremble of her thighs as she tried to bear down on his fingers. She was close to climax.

"Yes." She gasped as he thrust hard, plunging deep within her. Then he pulled almost all of the way out, torturing them both by keeping only the head of his cock inside her. "I love you. I've never stopped loving you."

Satisfaction more potent than sexual release washed over him, filling him with a peace he had never felt before.

And then she pressed back against him, taking the entire length of him into her once more in one swift motion. "Do you love me?"

Buried inside her so swiftly, coupled with her admission of love, broke what was left of Reign's control. Ruthlessly, he rubbed her with his fingers as he thrust deep inside her.

"Yes," he growled against her ear as her fingers closed over the hand between her legs. "Liv. Beautiful, Liv. I love you." She rode his cock and fingers with abandon, sending them both over the edge and into the swirling oblivion of orgasm.

Afterward, they lay together, sweaty and sated on tangled sheets. They talked about insignificant things, shared humorous memories and laughed together in the darkness.

Reign held Olivia against his chest, stroking her hair as she related an incident from her youth in which she and two friends tried to help the game-keeper on a local estate try to capture an escaped piglet. He laughed as she talked about how slippery the animal had been to hold on to. At that moment, when amusement softened her voice, and it felt as though they were the only people in the world, Reign was certain that there had to be a God and that He was good.

Because this was surely heaven.

Chapter 18

"What in the name of God is that?" Olivia demanded when she saw what Reign had attached to her corset. They were in her room and he was helping her dress for the evening's intrigue. "Is that metal of some kind?"

"Yes." Holding the formerly delicate corset in both hands, he came toward her, his fingers dark against the pale fabric. "Put it on."

Dubious, Olivia took the undergarment from him. He had ruined her only demi-corset, the other having been destroyed when she was shot. "It's not going to be very comfortable now."

"Shag comfort." He pointed at the thin plate of metal that would cover her left breast and part of her chest. "Where are you vulnerable?"

She batted her eyelashes. "Everywhere you touch me, sweetheart."

His expression didn't lose much of its gravity when he grinned at her, but it lost enough. "Arse. Where are you vulnerable as far as someone who would want to kill you is concerned?"

"Heart and head."

He nodded at the corset. "That will help protect your heart. I expect you to take care of your head."

She would never have thought of such a novel device. "What about your heart, is it protected?"

"Were I the poetic sort I could say that you alone wield the power to wound my heart, but you know I'm rot at such pretty talk."

"I don't know," she said, her throat tight. "You did a fair job of it just now."

Reign leaned forward and kissed her forehead. When he straightened, he patted the left breast of his waistcoat. "I have a similar plate right here."

And she had foolishly wondered why he was dressing up to confront Dashbrooke.

"Are you worried?" she asked as she slipped out of her robe and reached for the drawers laid out on her bed.

His hot gaze raked over her nakedness with frank appreciation. "No, but neither am I stupid."

Olivia said nothing as she fastened the drawers around her waist, but her fingers trembled enough that he noticed.

"We'll get him, Liv." He helped her into the corset. "We'll rescue James."

It wasn't James she had been thinking of. "Why did you forgive me?" she demanded. "You knew what I had done and you weren't angry."

Hands on her shoulders, he turned her to face him. His face was grave, his gaze tender. "I was mad as hell that you took off on your own. Livid that you didn't trust me enough to tell me the truth, but there was never a choice of forgiveness. You did exactly what I would have done."

"But you trusted me."

He laughed at that—not cruelly, but with great gusto. "Sweetheart, I told you that I knew from the beginning you were up to something. I was waiting for you to stick the knife in my back the whole time."

How the hell should she feel about that? "But you slept with me."

"You slept with me."

"You initiated it!"

He laughed again, and she hit him—right in the metal plate over his chest. It stung, damn him.

Reign pulled her to him in a fierce hug. "I do love you, Liv. You know that?"

"Yes."

"I knew if you betrayed me that it was my own fault, but I was hoping you'd have a change of heart." He released her. "You did. Now, get dressed and let's go kick Dashbrooke's arse."

Olivia did as he asked, and quickly. Sometimes a woman just had to stop questioning and be grateful for what she had been given. This was one of those times. She was going to stop fretting about herself and Reign and turn her attention to something far more grievous—getting James away from Dashbrooke, and whatever evil he had in mind.

Five minutes later she had laced up her boots and was jogging down stairs to meet Reign and the other men. The servants had been released from the day's duties early and there was no one outside of their little band of warriors left. Reign didn't want anyone in the house tonight, just in case the Order had a few surprises in mind.

She was the last of their group to enter the study. Reign, Reggie, and Watson were pleasant enough, but Clarke watched her like he might a viper.

"Can I depend on you?" Olivia asked him. At his puzzled look, she continued, "If I need someone to watch my back tonight, can I depend on you, or should I look elsewhere?"

The gray-haired man looked at Reign before he responded, an action that rubbed every last nerve she had raw. "You can depend on me. Tonight."

"That's all I need." She met his gaze with a challenging one of her own. He was right to dislike her for what she had almost done to Reign, but if he thought to cow or intimidate her, he was a fool.

Reign had regard for her pride. Some men found bold women abrasive and unattractive, obviously her husband was not one of them. "Clarke and Watson will follow us on horseback. They'll clear the grounds and sneak in while we divert Dashbrooke and his followers."

Olivia turned to Reggie with a faint smile. "I hope you are not bothered by heights, Reggie."

The freckle-faced young man shrugged. "I

cannot tell you. I've never been any farther from the ground than the third-floor balcony at my grandmother's house in London."

Reign clapped him on the shoulder. "Might want to keep your eyes closed then, boy."

They wasted no more time on small talk after that. After reviewing what plans they had, Clarke and Watson left, leaving the rest of them to make final preparations. The five of them were all agreed on their goal—free James and capture Dashbrooke.

And keep Reggie safe, of course. Olivia didn't want to believe that Dashbrooke might harm his own son, but Reggie and Reign had no problem entertaining the idea at all.

Reggie wanted to fly with her instead of Reign—not because he trusted Olivia more, but because he suffered from the common male malady of thinking that touching another man for longer than a brief, manly hug, might somehow make him a pederast.

Reign winked at the boy. "Don't blame you at all, Reggie I'd take her over me any day." Then, with an evil grin, "Just watch where you put your hands. It's a long way to the ground."

The young man didn't seem to know whether to take him seriously or not. Olivia rolled her eyes. "Just put your arms around my neck, Reggie, and hold on." He did as she instructed and once she was certain he was ready, she wrapped her own arms around his waist and lifted them both into the sky.

Flying with a passenger wasn't new to Olivia, as she had flown with James many times, but it was odd to hold a veritable stranger so close and share such an amazing aspect of what she was. Fortunately, Reggie proved to not be afraid of being so high in the sky. In fact, he gawked around so much that Olivia was certain he was going to smash his skull against hers. Fortunately, he didn't.

It wasn't until they arrived at the house in Haddington that the gravity of the night's intrigue fully sank in. James's life, and Reggie's as well, might end tonight if she—they—weren't careful.

Reign must have seen some of the terror in her eyes as they stood on the step awaiting entry, because he pressed a hard kiss to her forehead and gave her cold hand a gentle squeeze. "It will be all right, Liv. I promise."

Reggie, who stood behind them, placed a tentative hand on her shoulder. "My father knows James is the only thing keeping you from ripping his throat out. He won't hurt James if it can be helped at all."

Oddly enough, the young man's words helped a little. Olivia smiled her thanks.

The door opened to reveal George Haversham. The moment his gaze fell on Reggie, his face lit up in relief. He didn't speak, however, merely stepped aside so that they might enter.

They followed Haversham through the foyer. As they walked, Reggie stepped in front of them, making it look as though he truly was their prisoner, and also providing a bit of shield against whatever weapons his father might have.

Brave boy.

Olivia's gaze swept their surroundings, searching for anyone or anything that might be concealed and waiting to strike. She saw nothing, heard nothing. She didn't even smell anything, other than the boys in front of her. All other sounds and scents were fainter, coming from deeper within the house, and from the sound of it, one room.

Turning her head, she met her husband's gaze. He smiled at her—the smile of a man not accustomed to losing, who intended to win. Without words he told her not to be afraid, that they were the ones with the power here, not Dashbrooke. She had to believe in that.

Haversham led them down a wide hallway, lined with portraits and landscapes of various size and age. The wedgewood-blue paint needed a fresh coat and wooden planks beneath their feet were rubbed smooth with wear. It was a quaint little house, if not a tad shabby. Hardly a villainous lair at all.

"Reign, Olivia," Dashbrooke cooed as they walked in. "Thank you for coming."

The bastard was sitting on a divan like a bloated pasha, looking far too smug for Olivia's liking. He was flanked by at least a dozen men, all of whom were big and muscular; warriors dressed in black and ready to protect their master.

"And you've brought m'boy back as well." Dashbrooke's gaze narrowed on his son. "You don't seem any worse for wear."

Reggie lifted his chin, and Olivia felt a swell of pride for the boy. "They didn't hurt me, Father."

Dashbrooke sneered. "They wouldn't have nabbed you at all if you had half a brain!"

"Where's James?" Olivia demanded, stifling a wince on Reggie's behalf. Hopefully Watson and Clarke would be here soon as well and they could get these boys out of here.

"Right here," came a low, familiar voice.

Olivia's eyes closed. Just for a second she allowed herself to bask in the overwhelming relief of hearing her boy's voice once more, knowing that he was safe.

She faced him as he entered the room. There was another boy with him—Fitzhugh Binchley, she believed. They joined Haversham at the back of the room. The three of them didn't move toward Reggie, no doubt because of his proximity to herself and Reign.

Her husband was surprisingly closemouthed during all of this, but nothing escaped him, of that she was certain.

Olivia didn't care if it was risky or not, she went to James and drew him into her embrace. "I'm so happy to see you!"

He didn't hug her back, just stood there, wooden in her arms.

"Why didn't you exchange him for me like you were supposed to?" he demanded. No greeting, no expression of relief to see her as well. That wasn't right—not for a boy who should have been at least a little afraid.

She held him at arm's length so she could look into his big brown eyes. The accusation there might have been more cutting if it hadn't been mixed with obvious petulance. "Because I couldn't hand Reign over knowing what might happen to him."

"What about me?" He struggled against her hold but she didn't release him right away. "Didn't you think about what might happen to me?"

"Of course I did."

"He means more to you than I do."

"That's not true, but Reign's my husband."

"And a vampire. I'm just a human." He sneered. "Just goddamn Food."

She slapped him—not hard, but enough to leave a slight mark on his fresh cheek. "Don't you make me the villain, James! I don't know how they managed to trick you into going along with this scheme, but I know you weren't really abducted. You've been lazing around here with your friends drinking and playing cards while I've worried myself sick!"

He had the sense to at least look abashed, but not enough. And when he cast a glance at

Dashbrooke—an approval-seeking glance—Olivia knew the truth.

"You've been involved in this all along, haven't you?" Somehow, she kept her voice calm, even though her heart was breaking and she wanted to scream. "You knew Dashbrooke wanted Reign and why, and you didn't care. You knew I'd do anything, even crawl to Reign, to bring you home. Why? What promise did he make you?"

"The one you wouldn't," her son—nephew—replied hotly. "He promised me immortality. He said I could finally be like you."

The tone of his voice said much more than mere words. That he wanted to be like her—and in the same token be with her always—tugged at Olivia's heart. But not quite enough.

"And how did he plan to give you eternal life? Did he explain that? Did he think Reign or I would give it willingly? Or at all?"

James looked confused now, and cast another glance at Dashbrooke, who had lost his smug smile, but not the gleam in his piggish eyes.

"I'm not going to make you a vampire, James." Olivia kept her voice low and controlled. "Don't you understand? He never intended to fulfill his promise to you, or your friends. All he wanted was me and Reign."

"And now I have you" came Dashbrooke's triumphant cackle.

Olivia turned in time to see the other men in

the room pull pistols and knives from their clothing. More men came in from a side door; several carried swords and two carried what appeared to be nets, the threads of which glittered in the lamplight. Silver. She'd wager that all the blades were edged with the toxic metal, the pistols loaded with it. Reign stiffened, his body as tense as coiled wire, but he didn't pounce. He was waiting for them to attack first.

Her shoulders sagged, but just for a moment as she glanced at James. "You see?"

Defiance colored his cheeks and brightened his eyes. He did not want to accept any blame for this. He still did not understand. "None of this would have happened if you had turned me like I asked! I begged you!"

Was this anger she felt? Or pity? "And like a child, you schemed to get your way. Bravo, James. Obviously, I did an excellent job in raising you." Then, wary and oddly calm, Olivia straightened her spine. She reached into the back of her trousers and removed a small blade from the sheath strapped there. Then, she whipped her hand around, flinging the blade through the top of a boot belonging to one of the men with the nets. There was a scream and a solid thud as the blade nailed his foot to the floor.

One of the men with a sword rushed at her as a bullet whizzed past her head. Dashbrooke was screaming for his men not to kill her or Reign. He needed them alive.

Olivia ducked the slash of a broadsword and came up to land a blow to her attacker's jaw that shattered his face and dropped him like a doll. Whirling around, she caught a glimpse of James and the other boys, diving behind a sofa for cover. Good, they were safe for now.

And then she turned her back on them and leaped onto a man sneaking up behind Reign with a dagger in his hand.

Reign whirled around to confront his attacker, only to watch the man be knocked unconscious by one swift blow of his wife's delicate fist.

"Nice shot," he quipped. "Behind you."

And then she pivoted to disarm a man with a particularly nasty sword. A pistol fired as Reign moved. The bullet struck the metal plate concealed in his waistcoat. It hurt like hell and he'd have a brief bruise, but that was better than silver shot in the heart.

"I said don't kill them!" Dashbrooke shouted above the din.

Men rushed from both sides as Reign and Olivia fought, practically shoulder to shoulder. Olivia took pains not to kill her attackers, but Reign wasn't quite so careful. The most important thing to him was survival—his, Olivia's, and the four boys almost pissing themselves in fear behind the sofa.

Something sailed through the air and landed on his head and shoulder. It was a net made of silver.

Shit. He threw it off, but not before the fine strands of metal singed his face and hand.

Now he was mad. He turned and grabbed the man who had tossed the net by the head and twisted. The body fell to the floor with a remorseless thud.

He turned for the next attack and saw Olivia pin a man to the wall with his own blade through the shoulder. She might not be a killer, but she was a bloodthirsty wench to be sure and he loved her for it. There was nothing more perfect than a woman willing to fight for the survival of those she loved.

There had only been perhaps a dozen or so men in the room to begin with, and perhaps that amount again had joined them. That made for twelve opponents each. Twelve men armed with silver weapons—one of which had just sliced his arm. And his back.

There were two of them, trying to flank him and take him down that way. Reign grinned and ducked as the first swung his sword, then he came up under the man, grabbed the blade from his hand, and ran him through. He jerked the sword out and whipped around to impale the other as well.

It had been too long since he'd been in battle, but the skills were still there, the undeniable will to survive and triumph.

By the time it was over, not a member of the Silver Palm was on his feet. The majority of them were merely wounded, but several were dead.

Reign and Olivia were wounded, but not badly, a fact that surprised Reign given the amount of weapons and opponents they'd faced.

"You good?" he asked Olivia as he moved toward where she stood in the center of the room, her eyes wide and her mouth slightly open as she gazed straight ahead.

Reign followed her gaze.

Oh, Christ.

Dashbrooke had one meaty arm wrapped around James's shoulder and chest. In the other hand, he held a pistol.

That was aimed at James's temple.

Olivia cried out. Despite all that James had done, she still loved him as though he were her own son. She was mad as hell, but that didn't stop her from caring.

"Ah, that's better," Dashbrooke gloated. "I knew it was just a matter of time before I regained control. You vampires might be superior in strength and speed, but you really aren't the smartest of creatures."

"Yes," Reign agreed. "The thought of manipulating young boys to get what we want would never occur to stupid sods such as us."

Dashbrooke cast a suggestive glance at Olivia. "But your wife likes young men, doesn't she? One could say she has quite the *appetite* for them."

Reign only laughed, even as Olivia bared her fangs at the fat bastard. "Sorry, mate. Insecurity is not a failing of mine."

The smugness drained from Dashbrooke's face. "The two of you are going to do exactly what I tell you, or this little bastard is going to have a very large hole in his skull. Am I understood?"

"If I say yes, will you shut the fuck up?"

"Am I *understood*?" The barrel of the pistol dug into the side of James's head so hard the young man winced. Beside him, Reign felt Olivia stiffen, smelled the wave of fear that rolled off her.

"Yes," he growled, despising having to say it.

So intent was Reign's focus on Dashbrooke and vice versa, that neither of them noticed Reggie's approach until he was standing at Reign's right shoulder.

He had blood smeared on one pale cheek, and a gun in his hand. It was pointed at Dashbrooke.

"Let him go, Father."

Dashbrooke spared a brief glance for his son. "You are just like you mother, Reginald—such a disappointment."

Reggie's expression didn't change. "To you perhaps, but I'm feeling rather pleased with myself at the moment."

So was Reign. "That's a good lad."

"If you are done living vicariously through my son," Dashbrooke interjected, "perhaps we can get on with Mr. Burnley keeping his brain and the two of you doing what I want?"

Reign started to turn his attention back to Dashbrooke, but then Reggie snagged it again. "I'm not joking, Father. Put down the gun and let James go."

"Or what?" his father demanded. "You'll shoot me?"

The arm holding the pistol never wavered as Reggie stared him down. "Yes."

It was at that exact moment that Dashbrooke lost control. Reign could see it. The bastard knew he was beat, that his chances of survival had just dropped, and it was making him desperate.

"You want him?" Dashbrooke roared. "Take him!"

It happened in a flash. Dashbrooke pushed James forward and lowered his pistol. A loud bang reverberated throughout the room as the shot discharged. James's knees buckled. Olivia screamed. And a blossom of crimson appeared on the back of James's shirt.

Reign dove for the boy just as a second shot rang out. This time it was Dashbrooke who fell to his knees, but there was no crimson on his shirt—it ran down his forehead instead. Reggie had kept his word.

Somehow, Reign managed to catch James before the boy hit the floor. Olivia fell to her knees beside him, followed by James's friends. Reign didn't care about them. He cared about his wife, who was pale and weeping, her hand pressed to her mouth.

"He's going to be all right, Liv." He made the

futile promise once again, but James wasn't all right, that was obvious from the wet, rattling sound he made as he gasped for air. Blood leaked from between the boy's lips.

James shook, his young body fighting to live as Reign held him. His eyes, so much like Olivia's, were round and slightly unfocused as they searched the faces of those gathered around him. Finally, his gaze settled on his aunt.

"I'm sorry," he whispered, the words taking on a watery sound as blood spewed from his mouth.

"Don't," Olivia croaked. "There's nothing to be forgiven for."

Reign disagreed, but now was not the time. If Olivia wanted to forgive her nephew, that was her choice.

Would she forgive Reign for not being able to keep the boy safe as he had promised?

"He wanted to be immortal," Reggie remarked, his tone disembodied as the shock of killing his father began to take hold. "More than any of the rest of us, he wanted to live forever."

The boys shared a meaningful look that tightened Reign's jaw. And when Olivia fell forward, wrapping her arms around James's narrow trunk as she sobbed with great, shuddering breaths, he knew what he had to do.

And he had to do it fast. James's heart was already dangerously slow.

He took one of the boy's arms in his hand and lifted it to his mouth. He bit and drank quickly, not even taking the time to enjoy it. Olivia looked up at her nephew's gasp, and her tears trickled to a stop as she saw what Reign was doing.

"No," she whispered, but she didn't mean it, he could tell.

Reign held her stare for a second as he let go of James's wrist. Then, he raised his own arm and bit himself in the same spot. He held the open wound to James's mouth. "Drink it."

Feeble hands caught at his arm, holding on as though afraid he might try to take the gift of life away. James's mouth fastened onto the punctures and pulled. Reign winced, but didn't move. This was not the pleasant experience he had when Olivia fed from him, in fact, it turned his stomach. He wasn't doing it for his own benefit, he was doing it for his wife.

It was a simple process, requiring only a blood exchange. The tricky part was whether or not the demonic essence would take hold. In Reign's experience, the likelihood of success increased with the age of the vampire. In his youth he had tried to change others and failed. He hadn't known it could be done until he witnessed Temple do it two centuries into their immortality.

There was a very good chance that James's body would accept the change, but there was still the chance that the change would kill him, or worse, make him insane. It didn't always work, as he had discovered that night with Temple.

Finally, when James had taken more of his blood than necessary, Reign pulled his arm away. The boy tried to fight him, but was as ineffectual as a kitten.

Olivia took his hand and pressed her mouth to his wrist, closing the wounds with her tongue so he wouldn't have to. It was a strangely intimate gesture that tugged at his heart.

The three boys clustered around them gaped in open wonder. "Is James going to become a vampire?"

Reign's lips tightened. "We'll have to wait and see. Come, let's get him home."

Watson and Clarke stayed behind to interrogate the surviving Silver Palm members. Fitzhugh Binchley volunteered to ride into Edinburgh and rally some of the Bucket of Blood folk to come help them. Before dawn they would burn the house to the ground, letting the fire deal with the dead inside.

Reggie and George Haversham took horses from the stables and agreed to meet them back at the town house. Then Reign and Olivia flew home, Reign carrying James in his arms.

They would deal with the boys and the ramifications of this evening later. Right now all that mattered was getting James back to the house, and getting that awful look of terror out of Olivia's eyes.

So on the way back to Edinburgh, as the wind stung his eyes and dried his lips, Reign indulged in something that seemed to be becoming a habit as of late, even though in this case he knew it wasn't going to be of any help.

He prayed.

Chapter 19

There was nothing she could do for him.

Two nights after the horrific events at Dashbrooke's country house, Olivia watched from across the room they'd "borrowed" at the Bucket of Blood, as Reign taught her nephew how to properly feed from humans without hurting them.

James listened intently to Reign's every word, gazing at her husband as though he were some kind of god, and not the man he had so obviously resented just a few short days ago. And when the time came for James to assuage his hunger, he did exactly as he had been told, taking enough to sustain himself, but not enough to harm his victim.

"There," Reign said encouragingly as James lifted his head from the unconscious woman's throat. "Well done."

James licked his lips and smiled at his mentor. "May we fly back to the house?"

Reign lifted his gaze to Olivia's. She could tell from the subtle change in his expression that he guessed at the turmoil in her thoughts.

"May we?" he asked.

Olivia nodded. "You two go ahead. I'll take the carriage back." She had some thinking to do, and she wished to be alone to do it.

James flashed a brief grin and was out of the room in a flash. Reign took a more leisurely exit, stopping to kiss Olivia before he left, James calling for him down the hall. The boy was eager to stretch his wings, as it were.

Olivia left as well, after making sure that the woman on the bed was indeed fine. She went downstairs and out into the street where the carriage sat waiting. She climbed inside and settled against the squabs, allowing her mind to drift back to those awful moments when she'd seen Reign give his blood to James, and the equally awful ones that followed as they waited to see if the process was successful. She needn't have worried.

The change had taken to James, and James to it with frightening ease.

He loved his new senses and abilities, reveled in the changes in his body. He was a newborn vampire infatuated with all the world had to offer, and his friends listened to the stories of all his changes with rapture.

All except for Reggie, who seemed to have soured on the idea of immortality, at least for the present. He made George Haversham agree to see a doctor in London about his headaches. His concern touched Olivia, but she turned away before someone asked Reign to turn Haversham as well. An eternity of youth was not what the boy needed.

How long would James's enthusiasm last? Thirty years from now, how would he feel about his youthful countenance? When everyone treated him like a boy instead of a man, would the frustration become too much? Or would he live out eternity as a boy, never growing up and never learning responsibility?

If he stayed with Olivia and Reign that was exactly how he would end up. Olivia would allow it, as well. She knew herself well enough to see that. She would look after him and coddle him as long as he wanted it. She didn't want to coddle him. She wanted him to stand on his own two feet and take responsibility for who and what he was. He needed to be away from her—somewhere she couldn't run to if it looked as though he might be in trouble.

Closing her eyes, she leaned her head back and tried to keep her mind quiet for the rest of the drive. Finally, the carriage rolled to a stop in front of the town house. When she stepped out onto the walk, it was with the perfect clarity of knowing exactly what she had to do.

The hard part was going to be doing it.

She didn't waste any more time fretting. The boys and Reign were in the parlor when she arrived and she joined them. After greeting them all, she made her announcement—the one she and Reign had discussed earlier that evening.

"Reign and I will be leaving tomorrow night."

"Where are we going?" James demanded, his brow knitting like a child who had just been told he couldn't have a sweet.

Olivia drew a breath, but Reign replied before she could. "Olivia and I are going north for a bit before returning to London. You're going to New York."

Four mouths dropped open, and James flushed angrily. "You can't just leave me now that you've turned me!"

"You got what you wanted," Olivia reminded him softly. "I'm glad you are still alive, James and I want to keep it that way. The Silver Palm may be looking for us and the only way I can be sure you're safe is if you're in another country."

"I'll be safer with you."

Guilt stabbed at her heart. "But you can't be with us, darling. You have to make it on your own."

"But—"

"We've decided," Reign interjected, his deep tone brooking no refusal. "Olivia was shot once because someone thought to use you against her and I won't have that happen again."

The flush rushed from James's cheeks. He hadn't known about her being shot, obviously.

"One of Dashbrooke's men," Olivia told him. "It happened a few nights before we came after you. It's not safe for us to be together, James. Please, go to America where I know you can be safe."

"No." He shook his head adamantly. "I won't."

"Your obituary has already been sent to the papers." Reign locked gazes with the younger vampire. "Everyone in London thinks you're dead. You cannot go back."

For a moment Olivia thought James might cry and she reached for him, but he jerked away. Angry. He'd been angry with her for so long and she never saw it.

"You wanted to be a vampire," she reminded him. "And now you are. This is the life you chose, James. Every choice you've made has led you to this place. Now you have to live with the consequences."

A mulish expression darkened his features. "I only wanted to know what your life was like. I only wanted to share that with you."

Olivia understood, and her heart was heavy with it. "You're my boy," she whispered. "You'll always be part of my life."

George Haversham and Fitzhugh Binchley exchanged uncomfortable glances. "Can we go home?" Fitzhugh asked.

Reign nodded. "Clarke has tickets for you on an afternoon train to London." He turned to Reggie. "There's one for you if you want it."

Fitzhugh and George looked down at their feet. Reggie shook his head, his own gaze fastened on James. "I'll go to New York with James. It's not safe here for me either. My father's friends will look for me—either to recruit me, or to avenge his death."

That took some of the sadness out of James's expression. "Thank you, Reggie." He turned his attention back to Olivia, straightening his shoulders and looking so grown up that her throat tightened at the sight. "Will I see you again?"

Reaching out, she placed her hand on his arm. "After a while, when we're certain it's safe, Reign and I will come visit you."

James's jaw was tight as he nodded. A hint of moisture glistened in his eyes, but he managed to hold it at bay. Olivia hoped she'd be as strong, but when he turned and wrapped his arms around her, a hot tear slipped down her cheek.

"I'm sorry, Aunt Liv."

"I know." Damn, her voice was already strained and hoarse.

"I love you."

The tears were flowing like a stream now, unstoppable and quick. "I love you too."

Reign offered her a handkerchief and she took it to dry her eyes while he said good-bye to James and the other boys. Then her husband put his arm around her and held her tight against his side, giving her his strength and support as the second most important man in her life walked out of it.

"Do you think he'll be all right?"

It wasn't the first time Olivia had asked him that

question, but it was the first time she'd voiced her concerns since James and the other boys left earlier that day. It had been four days since the incident at Dashbrooke's, and Reign and Olivia had moved from his Edinburgh home to a small rented cottage in the Highlands.

Olivia thought they were hiding out, and that was partially true, but Reign also just wanted to be alone with his wife, with no intrigue to get between them.

He called it a belated honeymoon. And just to drive that point home, he kept her in bed as much as he could. They were there now, having just woken up. Outside their snug abode the night was settling in, bringing a fresh breeze and the scent of darkness.

"He'll be fine," he assured her in the same soothing tone he used every time she asked. Actually he had no idea what would happen to James. If he could survive the centuries looking like a boy, being treated like a boy, then he'd be all right. If he couldn't . . . Memories of his friend Dreux's suicide came flooding to the surface. "I'm sure he'll be fine." He said a little prayer—a new habit for him—for added hope.

"Do you think he hates me?" Her voice was muffled by his chest, where her cheek rested, but he heard the sadness in it.

"Liv, he almost got you killed and would have cheerfully handed both of us over to Dashbrooke to achieve his own goals. Little fucker's lucky you don't hate him."

She lifted her head to look at him, her thick hair tumbling over her naked shoulder in a tousled mass that appealed to his baser natures. "If you despise him so, why did you change him? Why not let him die?"

Now he just wanted to shake her. Surely she didn't need him to answer that? "Because it would have hurt you if he died—more than making him a vampire ever would." If it was anyone but James, he'd even go so far as to remind her that no one would be able to use or take advantage of him now, but he couldn't say that and mean it.

Smiling softly, she leaned down and kissed him. "Thank you."

He wrapped his arms around her and held her naked body tight against his own. "Thank me in other ways."

She snuggled against him with a chuckle. "Reggie will take care of him, won't he?"

Christ. He loved her, but he was so sick and bloody tired of hearing about James. He'd heard enough about the boy over the last couple of weeks to last a lifetime. "Yes. Stop worrying. You have to let him go and be his own man."

And then, just to make certain she didn't take the conversation any further, he kissed her, exploring her mouth with his tongue as his hands roamed every warm, soft inch of her.

When he rolled her onto her back and positioned himself between her splayed thighs, he found her hot and wet and ready for him. He gazed down into her strong, beautiful face and was so bloody thankful for the second chance he had been given he couldn't begin to describe it.

"Thank you," he said thickly. "For forgiving me."

Smiling seductively, she arched her hips so that his cock slid fully into her. Her gasp mingled with his groan. "I will always forgive you. I love you."

His throat was too tight to speak, so Reign didn't even bother to try. He lowered his head to warm, fragrant skin in the hollow of her neck and pierced that fragile skin with his fangs, taking her inside him as his body thrust into hers.

She bit his shoulder, heightening the already spiraling sensations firing between them. Everything was sharper, clearer, more intense. Reign kept it going as long as he could, slowly churning his hips against hers, shivering as the slick walls of her squeezed his cock. Trying to prolong it was no good, not when Olivia gripped him like that, her mound rubbing against him, her little gasps of pleasure vibrating along his skin where her mouth was fastened.

He came as soon as he felt Olivia begin to orgasm, unable and unwilling to hold back any longer. Squeezing his eyes shut, Reign let the pleasure engulf him, letting it make him forget that there was real evil in the world and the fear that the Order of the Silver Palm wasn't finished with them, not in the least.

By the time Reign and Olivia returned to London, several weeks had passed since their original departure.

Since the Silver Palm knew Reign's address in Belgrave Square, they agreed to stay there only as long as it took Reign to right his affairs and pack what belongings he needed to take with him. From there they would travel to Olivia's home in Clovelly to do the same, before boarding a ship to France. Once settled Reign hoped they could find out just what the hell the Silver Palm wanted with them.

He was in his study, sitting at his desk going over his correspondence with Olivia sitting on the sofa with a pad and pen making arrangements of her own, when Clarke came into the room.

"You have visitors," he informed them. He was still cool to Olivia, but at least he looked at her now. Reign didn't give him a hard time for it. Olivia would win him over eventually.

"Who?" he asked. Olivia looked up, little lines of worry appearing between her brows.

"An old friend," came a voice from the door.

Reign's head snapped around. He'd know that voice anywhere.

"I'll be buggered." Rising from the desk, he crossed the room in several quick strides to meet the dark-haired man standing just inside the door-frame. "Saint!"

His old friend smiled, though there was a terse-ness to it that gave Reign pause. The displeasure wasn't directed at him, though, of that he was certain.

"The murders," Reign murmured. He had been so preoccupied with his own situation that he had arrogantly forgotten about the horror here in London. A quick look at the papers had filled him in and brought a sick feeling to his stomach. "I planned to call on Maddie tonight. How is she fairing?"

"My mother is fine, thank you." It was then that Reign noticed the woman who had come to stand beside Saint.

"Ivy?" It was Madeline's daughter. Reign shot a glare at Saint. The bastard. "You didn't."

When Saint turned his dark gaze to the honey-haired woman beside him, it was with such love that Reign was embarrassed to witness it. "I did."

"Congratulations." Honestly he couldn't think of anything else to say. Then, his brain snapped back into place. "May I introduce my wife, Olivia, to you both?"

After introductions were made, Olivia and Ivy did that thing that all women seemed to do when meeting someone in similar circumstances—they became instant friends—and then Saint wasted no time in explaining why they were there.

"Did you get a package from Temple?" he asked.

Reign shook his head. "No, but I haven't opened all my mail yet." He rubbed a hand over his jaw as he glanced toward the pile of packages and envelopes on his desk. "You know, I heard the damnedest rumor about him."

"He's been abducted," Saint said bluntly.

Olivia grabbed his arm and Reign lifted his face to the ceiling. "The Order of the Silver Palm?"

Saint had one dark brow arched when Reign lowered his chin. "I take it you've heard of them?"

Briefly, Reign filled him in on what had happened in Scotland, leaving out of course, that Olivia had originally planned to hand him over to the Order.

"They're behind the murders as well." Saint pushed his thick hair back from his face, revealing a faint mass of delicate scarring. There was a similar pattern on the back of his hands. "They tried to nab me as well."

Reign touched his face where the silver net had brushed his skin, knowing that the pattern burned into his flesh matched the one Saint wore. "What the hell do they want?"

"I don't know, but Temple wants us to go to Italy. Go look for a box from him."

His three companions followed him to the desk where Reign brusquely rifled through the packages there. He found the box within seconds and tore open the paper wrapping. Inside was a silver amulet and a note telling him to go to an address in Rome.

Saint nodded at the amulet. "Pick it up."

Dubious, Reign nevertheless did as his friend instructed. "It doesn't burn." Wonder turned to revelation. "It's part of the Blood Grail!"

"The cup that turned the five of you?" Olivia asked.

Saint nodded. "For some reason Temple melted it down and sent us pieces. I'd wager that Bishop and Chapel received similar packages."

Reign's jaw tightened as his fingers closed around the silver. Energy tingled through his arm. "Temple knew the Order was up to something."

"Or it could be a trap," Olivia suggested, ever suspicious.

Reign shook his head. "The Order would want the cup intact, I think. No, Temple did this."

"Then we have to do what he asks." Olivia nodded sharply. "We have to go to Rome and save him."

Reign turned to her. She wasn't tired of saving people? "You are the most amazing woman."

She grinned. "Yes."

Saint and Ivy watched both of them with sly grins, as though they understood this strange magic Reign felt whenever Olivia was near.

"We planned to leave tomorrow night," Saint said.

Reign tore his gaze away from his wife. "If you can wait an extra two days, you can come with us. I've a ship booked to take us to Calais. We can travel by private train car from there to Venice."

Saint grinned. "You always were a useful sort."

Reign returned the smile, a rush of excitement coursing through his veins. Obviously he hadn't had enough adventure in Scotland. They would go to Clovelly and close Olivia's house and ship her belongings to the new place in Paris. They could settle into their new home after the Order was defeated.

Saint and Ivy stayed for an hour longer. After making quick plans to reunite two nights hence they spent the rest of the time sharing their experiences and knowledge of the Silver Palm.

The Order knew too much about them, and that wasn't good.

After Saint and Ivy took their leave, Reign and Olivia sat on the sofa in his study. "Are you sure you want to do this?" he asked her. As much as he wanted to pound the Silver Palm into the ground, as much as he wanted to help Temple, he wanted Olivia happy more. Perhaps more danger was exactly the diversion she needed to stop flaying herself over James.

"I am—not just for your friend, but for us and for James. I want to see those manipulating bastards pay for what they've done."

"That's my bloodthirsty wife." Laughing, he

cupped her cheek with his palm. "Do you know how much I love you?"

Big brown eyes sparkled with unshed tears. "Yes," she replied with absolute conviction. "I do, and someday I hope to show you the depths of my love for you."

"You already have." The night she risked her life rather than betray him.

Perhaps Reign's choices hadn't always been the right ones, but they had all contributed to bringing him where he was right now—with the woman he loved. With that thought in mind, Reign took Olivia in his arms and kissed her, knowing that regardless of where future choices took them, they would make the journey together.

Dear Readers:

I've always been fascinated with dreams and the idea of immortal beings pulling the strings in the human subconscious. The Nightmare Chronicles, my brand new series, marries the idea of a world beyond our own with romance and a taste of horror.

Please turn the page for a sneak peek into BEFORE I WAKE, the first book in this series, set in present-day New York City. Dawn Riley is the daughter of the god of dreams. She walks in two worlds but belongs in neither.

Welcome to her nightmare.

Kathryn

"**Y**ou're a Nightmare."

Diet Dr Pepper halfway to my lips I paused, staring at the old man standing beside me at the Duane Reade checkout. My heart nudged hard against my ribs. "Excuse me?"

His face was the color and texture of a worn piece of leather and his hair was a mass of tight, frizzy gray curls. But his eyes were as sharp as a child's. "You're a Nightmare, girl. What're you doin' here?"

I glanced around to see if anyone else in the drugstore had heard the old fella's surprising—and very *vocal*—accusations. If anyone had, they were pretending they hadn't.

He was just a crazy old man. No need to panic. No need to do anything. "Sir, I don't know what you're talking about."

"You are not of this *plane*," he insisted, doing this weird little stomp with his foot that made me wonder if he had to pee. "You shouldn't be here."

I took a step away just in case his bladder gave

out. It was instinct, driven by pure self-preservation. One thing living in a city the size of New York teaches you is that some people just don't have the same boundaries as the rest of us.

Also, he creeped me out.

"Uh, okay. I shouldn't be here." I twisted the cap back on to my Dr Pepper as the cashier started scanning my items. Just a few more moments and I'd be out of there. I should have gone straight home after work, but I needed tampons.

"You do know, don't you?"

I had hoped that agreeing with him would end the conversation. Apparently, I was wrong. "Know what?"

"What you are." He was staring at me now with a look of wonder. "Shee—oot. I bet you don't even know how you got here."

"I walked." I would not, however, be walking home. God, I hoped I'd be able to hail a cab pronto once I left the pharmacy. I never wanted to be somewhere else quite so badly in all my life.

He did that foot thing again, only this time his face twisted in annoyance. I took another step away. "I don't mean here. I mean *here*. On this earth."

I swallowed. My throat felt like I'd just swallowed a piece of carpet. "Sir, I was born here. Same as you." Maybe it was all the years of psychology classes, or maybe it was a little fear, but I needed to bring him back to the real world. *This* one.

He peered at me—a little too closely for my liking. "You may have been born here, girlie, but you don't belong. I wonder how you managed to slip through."

I wanted to get the heck out of there. What the hell was he talking about? "Just luck, I guess."

He stared at me with eyes that were slightly rheumy, but keen. "Luck, nothing. How old are you?"

"Sir, I'm not going to tell you that." Next he was going to ask my weight and I'd have to kill him.

"Twenty-eight."

His voice rang in my head like a gong. He was right. If I was creeped out before, I was ten times that now. It could have been a lucky guess, but I doubted it.

"You're mature," he informed me. "At your full potential. No tellin' what havoc you might wreak."

That was *it*. I threw some money at the clerk. I hadn't heard the total, so I could only hope it was enough. I grabbed my bag and started for the door, grateful for once that most of my five feet ten inches was leg. The clerk didn't yell after me, so I assumed I had given her enough to cover my bill.

I miraculously hailed a cab right outside and jumped in. As we drove off, I looked out the window to see the old man standing on the sidewalk near the door, watching me. He was drinking a bottle of Brisk—bought with my change I bet.

He waved as the cab pulled away, and he yelled something. I couldn't quite hear the words, but to my paranoid ears it sounded as though he yelled, "YOU. DON'T. BELONG."

I knew I didn't. The question was, how the hell did he?

I was six years old the first time my mother told me I was a Nightmare. I cried, because I thought she was mad at me. But then she took me up onto her lap and told me I was special because no other child on earth had the King of Dreams for a father. She told me I could dream whatever I wanted, that in my dreams I could *do* whatever I wanted and I believed her.

I asked my father what it was like to be the Lord of Dreams. He didn't know what I was talking about. It was shortly after that I realized he wasn't my father. My real father was the man who played with me in my dreams, who put a sweet smile on my mother's face. The man I called dad looked at me like he didn't recognize me, and at my mother as though he knew he was losing her to a man with whom he couldn't compete.

Was it any wonder that I soon found myself preferring the Dream Realm to the real world? Of course there were parts of the Dream Realm—The Dreaming—that my father told me to stay away from. Apparently my uncle Icelus had let some of his "creations" wander free. Since Icelus's domain was all things disturbing and frightening, I listened to my father and never ventured outside of his castle, terrified of these monsters and what they might do to me. I already knew to be careful of the eerie mist that surrounded the land.

My childhood seemed normal to me. I was in grade 9 before I realized that something wasn't right. That *I* wasn't right. It never occurred to me that I was different, even though my mother told me in so many words. Other people didn't think of their dreams as being real. Didn't talk about them as though they were significant.

Jackey Jenkins picked on me mercilessly. She was petite and thin and blonde, with a great tan and a perfect wardrobe. I was tall and curvy and so white I looked like Casper. She always raised her hand and I only spoke when spoken to, and yet in the classes we shared, I made better grades. Looking back I could say she was jealous. That she resented the fact that she worked so hard for what came easy to me. Despite being her polar opposite, I had good friends and people tended to like me once they got to know me—especially teachers. Jackey reacted in the only way she could—she made my life hell.

One day I got my period at school. I wasn't prepared and spent the rest of the morning with a coat tied around my waist. As I was leaving school to go home to change, Jackey yanked up the jacket and showed everyone outside (and you know there had to be a crowd) the back of my jeans. People laughed. Not a lot of them, but some.

I was so mad, so humiliated, tears filled my eyes, which pleased Jackey to no end. I remember telling her that I was going to get her for what she did.

And I did. It was the great "Carrie" moment of my life. That night I went into Jackey Jenkins' dreams and I tortured her as only one teenage girl can another. It didn't make her nice to me. It just made her afraid, and I think that made her hate me even more. I didn't have quite the feeling of satisfaction that I thought I should, not when every time I looked at her I could see in Jackey's expression just what a freak I was.

Shortly after that I heard she was seeing a shrink because she was afraid to go to sleep at night—and she became less and less pretty as the circles beneath her eyes darkened. Eventually I think she recovered, but I didn't.

Normal people didn't go into other people's dreams. Normal people *couldn't*. And if they could, they didn't go about trying to terrify young girls.

I had become one of the monsters my father warned me about.

After that I stopped playing with dreams. I built my own little world that I could go into and I didn't let my mother or Morpheus or anyone else inside. I was going to make myself normal if it killed me.

To say my mother was disappointed was an understatement.

After that, I managed to finish high school without any more Freddy Kruger-esque behavior, and I went on to university in Toronto and got my Ph.D in Neuropsychology. My grades were well above average, but it was my research on dreams that brought me to the attention of Dr. Phillip Canning—an associate of my mentor's. Dr. Canning was at the top of his field in sleep research. I had read all of his papers and his books on treating Parasomnias and Post Traumatic Nightmares. You can take the girl out of the Dream Realm, but you can't take the Dream Realm out of the girl, and all that. I didn't need all my textbooks to realize that there was a part of me that *needed* to work in that field.

I needed to help people have a normal night's sleep—to help them protect themselves from the dangers of a world they thought harmless and "all in their head." Weirdly enough, at the same time I needed to deny that world for all I was worth.

Now, here I am a genuine doctor of psychology and a full-time (albeit still plebian) member of Dr. Canning's team at the MacCallum Sleep and Dream Research Center in New York City. My two years of proving myself are almost up and soon I'll be able to practice on my own. I do a little bit of everything as low man on the totem pole—clinical and research—but mostly I work in dream analysis and therapy, with heavy emphasis on nightmares.

So much for denial.

At Avon Books, we know your passion for romance—once you finish one of our novels, you find yourself wanting more.

May we tempt you with . . .

- **Excerpts** from our upcoming releases.

- Entertaining **extras**, including authors' personal photo albums and book lists.

- Behind-the-scenes **scoop** on your favorite characters and series.

- **Sweepstakes** for the chance to win free books, romantic getaways, and other fun prizes.

- Writing **tips** from our authors and editors.

- **Blog** with our authors and find out why they love to write romance.

- **Exclusive content** that's not contained within the pages of our novels.

Join us at
www.avonbooks.com

An Imprint of HarperCollins*Publishers*
www.avonromance.com